Material Girl

Material Girl

Keisha Ervin

www.urbanbooks.net

Urban Books, LLC
78 East Industry Court
Deer Park, NY 11729

ISBN 13: 978-1-60162-280-8
ISBN 10: 1-60162-280-5

First Printing September 2010
Printed in the United States of America

10 9 8 7 6 5 4 3 2 1

Distributed by Kensington Publishing Corp.
Submit Wholesale Orders to:
Kensington Publishing Corp.
C/O Penguin Group (USA) Inc.
Attention: Order Processing
405 Murray Hill Parkway
East Rutherford, NJ 07073-2316
Phone: 1-800-526-0275
Fax: 1-800-227-9604

Material Girl

A Novel By

Keisha Ervin

Dedication

I dedicate this book to you, the readers. It has been six years since *Me and My Boyfriend* hit bookshelves around the world, and you all have been ridin' wit' me ever since. If it wasn't for your commitment and love toward my work, I would not be here. I thank you all from the bottom of my heart, and I pray that we continue on this journey for many more years to come.

Acknowledgments

Lord, I feel more connected to you than ever. I have finally learned to be patient and to not let things worry me as much, and that is through your Word and my undying faith. Please continue to shower me with your love, mercy, and grace.

Kyrese, OMG, how I raised such a funny, smart, charismatic, and charming young man, I don't know. You are the epitome of everything I prayed you would be. I love you with every fiber of my being.

Words can't express how much I love, appreciate, adore, admire, and respect my family and friends. You all have been my sounding board, backbone, comfort, and support. I love you all from the bottom of my heart.

Keisha Ervin contact info: keisha_ervin2002@yahoo.com
www.myspace.com/keishaervin www.facebook.com/keishaervin
www.twitter.com/keishaervin

"I used to write about finding love. Now I want to write about what happens after you've found it."
—Carrie Bradshaw

"This may come, this may come as some surprise, but I miss you."
—Sade, "Is It a Crime"

Chapter 1

Dylan Monroe was the type of chick most females loved to hate. Her ego was as wide as the equator and as long as the Mississippi. Everything from her vintage Dior shades to her YSL nail polish screamed diva, but she had every reason to feel like she was that bitch. Since the age of fifteen, she'd been rockin' Louboutin red bottoms. Taking trips to Paris and St. Tropez was like going to the mall for her.

She'd dated all types of men: white, Latino, Arabic, doctors, lawyers, and politicians. A-List celebrity men, such as the uber famous star of a pirate movie franchise, and even the notorious dread-head rapper from Louisiana had spent sex-crazed, alcohol-induced nights in her bed. For a while she was even one of the many mistresses of a certain famous golf player. Dylan thought about leaking the affair to the media, but she was too embarrassed to come forward. Chicks often hated her and called her a slut, but what people didn't understand was that Dylan didn't sleep with random guys just for the pleasure of it. She did it because she thought that maybe, just maybe, one of them could be "the one."

Yep, Dylan had slept with them all, but none matched the swagger of the one she couldn't have. His name stayed tattooed on her brain. He was the persistent hunger pang in the pit of her stomach that wouldn't go away.

For months Dylan had tried her best to put him out of

her mind. She'd prayed to God on a nightly basis to help her get over him. She'd torn up all of his pictures, took his number out of her phone, and told her friends to never utter his name, but there he was.

Dylan's heart thumped loudly in her chest as the palms of her hands moistened with sweat, almost causing her to drop the glass of Chardonnay she held. She could smell the sweet scent of his Clive Christian cologne all the way from across the room. It was strong, intimidating, and overpowering, just like he was.

Sure, other men donned the scent, but none wore it quite like him. She wondered, if she kissed his skin, would it still taste the same on her tongue? Dylan turned around slowly and braced her rapidly beating heart for the sight of his face. Through the crowd of concertgoers she spotted him. He looked even better than he had six months before.

State was the epitome of what a man was supposed to be. He possessed heart-palpitation, dry-mouth, can't-even-speak good looks. Women across the country pined to be with him. Hailing from Hackney, London, he was six feet, 190 pounds; a Sierra Leonean and Ghanaian god with skin the color of dark chocolate. He owned a thriving record label, a clothing company, two restaurants, and was the co-owner of a professional basketball team.

That night he wore a black L.A. cap, which covered his low cut with waves, but enhanced his piercing brown eyes, defined nose, come-kiss-me lips, and goatee. He rocked your typical hoodboy attire, but with finesse. Dylan swore she never saw a man make a black leather jacket, white V-neck tee, Artful Dodger jeans, and tan suede Tims look so good. He donned a simple yet stunning gold rosary and a Nixon watch.

Not only was he rich and successful, State was her first in

every significant moment in her life. He was the first man to ever say no to her, the first to make her want to settle down, the first she'd ever said I love you to, picked out rings with, and made wedding plans with. He was the first man she'd ever become pregnant by, and the first she'd ever had an abortion for. But most importantly, he was the first man to ever break her heart.

In the beginning, what they shared was only supposed to be a casual fling. Dylan never saw herself getting her feelings into it, but soon she found herself out in the streets, calling him her baby. An on-again, off-again three-year relationship filled with mind-numbing sex, shopping sprees, weekend getaways, an unexpected pregnancy, and the promise of them one day getting married had her stuck for a minute.

For a while, Dylan was content with their chaotic relationship, but she didn't realize that the side effects of dating him may include:

A) Nausea

B) Insomnia

C) Loss of appetite

D) Headache

E) Weight loss

F) Depression

G) Not answering her phone calls at night

H) Non-stop crying until he answered the phone

I) Never wanting to socialize with her friends

J) Random chicks mean-muggin' her in the club

K) Magnum condoms found in the glove compartment of his car when they went raw

L) Bacterial infection

Tyrannical outbursts when confronted about side effects G, H, I, J, K

***

Dylan thought things would change, but as soon as State took the proposal of marriage off the table and gave her $500 to have an abortion, she knew she couldn't play the role of a kept woman anymore. Fed up, she hit State with a text message calling it quits, and decided to keep it moving—until now.

Dylan stood paralyzed. Loud music echoed in her ear. Men scrambled for drinks, while lines of women awaited their time in the mirror before Wale came out on stage to perform. But Dylan was in her own world. How well Wale could rhyme and how much he could get it didn't mean a thing to her anymore. She was stuck on a tightrope between her heart and common sense. To her, State was the one thing she couldn't have. His love and commitment was something so unattainable, yet she would give her right rib to retain it.

Dylan was so caught up in his presence that when he noticed her watching him, she had no time to look away. Before she knew it, he was coming her way. Dylan quickly swallowed the huge lump in her throat and gathered her emotions, but the closer State neared, the more she felt faint. None of this was supposed to be happening.

When she left her house, it had been just another typical Saturday night. She'd spent two hours getting her hair and makeup done only to be an hour late to the Grey Goose Presents: Rising Icons concert featuring Wale, who she planned on taking home with her that night. Unwilling to look completely lame, Dylan quickly grabbed the arm of a random cutie and acted as if they knew one another.

"Long time no see," she said with a smile.

"Excuse me?" The guy looked at her, confused.

"Shhh. Play along." She spoke out of the side of her mouth.

"Dylan?" State said, standing before her.

Dylan turned her attention from the guy and eyed State as if she didn't recognize him.

"Really, Dylan?" He looked at her like she was being ridiculous.

"Ohhhhh, State, my bad." She slapped her hand against her forehead. "How are you?" She hugged him.

"Good. Wassup wit' you?" He smiled, wrapping his strong arms around her slim waist.

"Nothing," she gushed nervously, hugging him back tight. *Please don't smell him. Please don't smell him,* she thought as her nose met with the side of his neck. *Fuck!* She closed her eyes, cherishing the scent.

"Damn." He stepped back, still holding her hands. "You look incredible."

"This old thing?" Dylan looked down at her brand new fuchsia double breasted blazer, black tank top, Fiona Paxton two-toned beaded necklace, black ripped leggings, and Alexander McQueen booties.

"Old or new you, look good as a muthafucka," State confessed, massaging the sides of her waist while giving her body a once-over glance.

Dylan's entire body blushed.

To State, she was stunningly beautiful, but in her own unique way. She had a hard but chic edge to her. She rocked her hair in an asymmetrical bob like Rihanna. The two even looked alike. Her skin was a sweet shade of butterscotch, while her eyes were hazel with flecks of green. An array of small tattoos adorned her body, and State wanted nothing more than to take the time with his tongue to find them all.

Okay, Dylan, say something witty and clever, she thought.

"You look . . ." She pointed at his broad chest. "Umm . . ." She looked toward the guy she had been standing with and tried to change the subject. "You know I went to school with—" She realized she didn't know his name. "Oh my God . . . yeah, so . . ." She laughed.

Okay, dummy, pull it together and don't ask who he's here with. You don't care, she told herself.

"So, you here by yourself?" she asked anyway.

"Yeah, I just swung through for a quick minute. You mind introducing me to your man?"

"Honey, please. *This is not my man,*" she stressed. "State, this is my friend . . . Timmmm—"

"Corey." The guy spoke up and reached out his hand for a shake.

"Yeah, Corey and I were just catching up on old times. You know . . . gettin' jiggy wit' it." Dylan twisted her butt, doing the old school dance.

Oh my God! Did that just happen?

"You mind if I speak to you in private?" State gestured toward the other side of the room.

"Sure. I'll talk to you later, Corey!" she said over her shoulder.

He put his hands up to his mouth and yelled back, "But I don't even know you, lady!"

"That Corey is such a mess." Dylan laughed, waving him off.

"Sure he is." State replied, knowing good and well that Dylan didn't know Corey from a can of paint. "But anyway, if I knew you were gonna be here, I would've got here a lot sooner."

"Is that right?" Dylan tilted her head to the side, not believing him.

"Fuck yeah. I miss the hell outta you," he answered honestly.

"I can't tell. I haven't heard from you in months," she countered.

"I mean, what was I supposed to do? You just sent me a text like, that's it, I'm done."

"And your reply was okay."

"You made it seem like you had your mind made up, so I had no choice but to go along with what you were sayin'."

"Mm-hmm." Dylan twisted her lips to the side as if to say she didn't believe him.

"But anyway, how you doing? How you been?"

"Good."

"You know, it's crazy how I'm running into you like this 'cause I just told C.I. the other day that I wanted to speak to you." C.I. was State's cousin and his lawyer.

"Is that right?"

"Yeah, it's been so much shit I wanted to say."

"Like what?"

"First, let me apologize for anything I did that made you cry. And I know you might be thinkin' *niggah*, *please*, but that's real talk. I wish that we could go back to the first time we fucked around and do things right, 'cause honestly, my life ain't been nothing without you."

Dylan wanted to take his words with a grain of salt, but State always knew the right words to get inside her head. She wished she could say that love didn't live in her heart anymore for him, but it did, and no matter how hard she tried, she couldn't get him out of her system.

"I missed you too," Dylan opened up and confessed.

"C'mon." He extended his hand.

"Where we going? The concert is about to start."

"Man, fuck that. Let's go back to the crib."

Dylan couldn't even front and act like she didn't want to.

"I was thinking the exact same thing." She placed down her drink and took his hand.

The next thing Dylan knew, she and State were no longer discussing what they'd been up to or how much they'd missed seeing each other. Instead, moans of gratification filled her bedroom as he rocked inside her slowly. The ten inches of hard, pulsating dick inside her was thick and delicious.

"Shhhhhhhit," she groaned as she bounced up and down on his cock.

Sure, it was wrong, sleeping with a man she'd sworn off months earlier, but the sensation of him penetrating her and his lips and tongue gliding across her throat was spellbinding. Dylan wrapped her arms around his back and held on tight.

A swell of muscles encompassed his upper half. State lifted them both off of the bed and placed her body against the wall. The rough surface heightened her pleasure. His warm mouth placed a trail of caramel kisses from her lips down to her erect nipples with velvet ease.

Dylan gasped for air as her thighs rested on his strong shoulders. State had a champagne tongue, full of hunger and lust. Shamelessly, he sucked the wine from her grape until he was satisfied and she could no longer scream shouts of ecstasy.

State gripped the curves of her hips with a look of lust in his eyes. The freakiness they were creating was sinfully decadent. It was as if they were space ships in the night, searching for new heights of erotic bliss.

Thoughts of how easily he had let her go entered Dylan's mind, but she'd deal with that later. State was hitting her with the death stroke. She could feel his dick all the way up in her rib cage. Fervently, she kissed his soft lips. Each touch of his mouth caused her to fall further down the rabbit hole of denial.

State wrapped his arms around Dylan's small waist and carried her back over to the bed. Her plump ass now faced him. He eagerly entered her from behind.

"Mmmm, yesssssss!" She clutched the sheets tight.

"That's how you want it?" he asked, grinding his hips in a circular motion.

"Yes! Oh my God, I missed this dick!" Dylan screamed, as her first orgasm approached.

A surge of energy took over her body, causing her to shake while warm cream slid down her inner thigh. She could hear his cell phone ringing in the distance, but State ignored the call.

State couldn't take it anymore. Ready to explode, he pulled out and placed hot lava onto her back.

As the seconds turned to minutes and the minutes turned to hours, Dylan and State became one. In between the faint murmur of fading heartbeats, they explored the hidden areas of each other's bodies that no one else had dared to find.

The next morning, Dylan awoke expecting to see his sleeping face, but in its place was a hand-tied bouquet of ivory calla lilies and yellow-throated green cymbidium orchids. They were the prettiest flowers she'd ever seen. Dylan sat up and placed them up to her nose. The scent was magical. To her surprise, tucked inside the bouquet was a small note. It simply said:

> You're never far away from my mind.
> State

A huge smile graced the corners of Dylan's lips. A part of her felt whole again. Even though she'd tried to change her environment and her mindset, the feelings she had for State still lingered underneath the surface.

Dylan was determined, though, not to fall head over heels for him. State hadn't lived up to his word before, and there was no way in hell she would allow him to play her for a fool once more.

No matter how hard they tried to stay away from one another, State always knew he and Dylan would end up back together again. What they shared was special. Homegirl was fly in every sense of the word. She had a swagger like no other. She was beautiful, vibrant, quirky, and fun to be around. She was his backbone. But three years into their relationship, his feelings changed, and he found himself having to be high just to be around her.

At that point, things were never cool between them. Every five seconds they were arguing and fighting over dumb shit. If Dylan looked at him the wrong way or breathed too loud, he got an attitude. And although he cared deeply for her, State found Dylan to be lazy, undetermined, and a little dingy at times. Plus, every five seconds she was pushing the idea of marriage down his throat. She just wouldn't let the shit come natural. State couldn't even take a dump without seeing a bridal magazine somewhere. The only thing Dylan wanted to watch was *Bridezillas* and a bunch of other WE-TV nonsense. It got to the point that he began to feel claustrophobic.

To him, things were going outside of moving too fast. State had always been a playboy, and was very happy to be one. He loved his Hugh Hefner lifestyle, and was admired around the world for it.

Dylan had other things in mind, though. She had their entire life planned out, and although State loved her, at the time he wasn't ready for a wife and baby. So, while she walked around dreaming of the perfect house with a white picket fence, State did the only thing he knew how to do and pulled back. He made it perfectly clear to Dylan that none of the things she needed from him were going to happen. And yeah, he knew she would be disappointed, but never in a million years did he think she'd get tired and leave.

Unfortunately, State persisted to reminisce about the way she kissed his lips. The way she loved him too much. Everything about her stayed in the forefront of his mind; but despite his feelings for her, State still found solace in someone new.

Back at home, he unlocked his door and entered his multi-million-dollar apartment. Pure pandemonium was going on inside. Stylists and personal assistants were moving at lightning speed, making calls on their BlackBerry smartphones, sending e-mails, picking out clothes, and packing luggage. State wasn't at all fazed by the madness. This was his life.

"Yo', Ash, where you at?" he called out, placing down his keys.

"I'm in here," she yelled from upstairs.

State took the steps two at a time and walked into his bedroom. Clothes, shoes, and bags were sprawled everywhere, and in the midst of it all was his wife, Ashton. She was heading out on the first leg of her European tour.

Even without any makeup she was strikingly beautiful. Ashton was a five foot three, 110-pound, African American, Filipino, West Indian and Mexican R&B diva. They'd had a whirlwind love affair that so far had only spanned three months. State never thought that he would like someone as much as he did Dylan, but Ashton captured his heart with just one wink of the eye. Plus, she was good for his career. State never thought it would happen, but on a drunken night in Vegas, he and Ashton decided to go the Little White Chapel and get married.

"Hey, baby. I missed you." She smiled, jumping over stuff to get to him.

"I miss you too." He squeezed her tight and kissed her lips.

"I've been callin' you all night. I didn't think you were going to make it home before I left. Did y'all get the track finished?"

"Yeah," State lied.

During one of his and Dylan's sex breaks, he'd sneaked off into the bathroom and texted Ashton to let her know he'd be in the studio all night.

"Good. It sucks that I won't be able to take my ring with me while I'm gone." She held up her left hand and admired her Harry Winston emerald-cut 21.16 carat diamond ring.

"You'll get to wear it all you want once the tour is over. Then we'll go public and have the wedding you always dreamed of."

"Sounds like a plan. I'm just happy that I get to have you all to myself before I fly out tonight." She unbuttoned his pants.

"What you lookin' for?" State kissed her neck and massaged her butt.

"This." Ashton bit her bottom lip. Horny as hell, she unzipped his jeans and pulled out his hard dick.

Gazing up into his brown eyes, she eased her way down. State prayed that she wouldn't smell the scent of another woman on him. Once her pink, pouty lips hit the tip of his dick and she took him in inch by inch, State knew he was in the clear. Holding his head back, he closed his eyes and anticipated what was sure to be an explosive orgasm.

"I'm a Barbie girl in a Barbie world."
—Aqua, "Barbie Girl"

Chapter 2

Dylan was an hour late for breakfast with the girls. That morning, they were all meeting at Crepes: Etc., which was only a few blocks away from her crib. After showering and getting dressed, Dylan hailed a cab and rushed inside the restaurant. To her surprise, neither one of her friends were there. Perturbed and relieved at the same time, Dylan found a seat near the window and waited.

Where are these hoes at? She wondered after twenty minutes had passed.

Dylan looked out the window to see if she could spot them anywhere. Suddenly, she saw Billie, her best friend, and her cousin Teyona (a.k.a. Tee-Tee, a.k.a. Dick 'em Down Diva) walking toward the restaurant.

Billie, the most conservative of the bunch, was newly separated from her husband of eleven years, St. Louis Rams superstar Cain Townsend. She was a mother of three and the "HBIC" of St. Louis. Billie was not only the president of the Rams Wives' Club, but she also served on the board of the St. Louis Art Museum, was the president of her building's board, and the president of the PTA. Most industry wives feared her. Billie was known for being cold and aloof, but to Dylan she was nothing but supportive and loving.

Tee-Tee, on the other hand, was everything Billie wasn't. He was overly eccentric, loud, opinionated, and never took anything too seriously. He enjoyed the company of a different man almost every night of the week, and there wasn't a pair of high heels in the world he didn't love.

"Hey, girl!" He waved as he and Billie passed the window.

Instead of speaking, Dylan hit him with the middle finger and smiled.

"Took y'all long enough. Y'all ass can't never get nowhere on time," she griped as they sat down.

"Don't blame me. Blame drunk-ass." Billie pointed with her head toward Tee-Tee.

"Heffa, don't start," Tee-Tee warned as he secured his all-black Chanel shades over his eyes. The bright lights and the loud chatter inside the restaurant were killing him softly.

"Um, you do realize that you're not outside anymore?" Dylan looked at him like he was crazy.

"Hoooooooooooney." He popped his lips. "If you had a night like I did, you would have on shades too."

"Wow." Dylan shook her head, knowing he had a hangover.

"Did you order yet?" Billie asked.

"No, I'm not inconsiderate like you two skanks," Dylan quipped.

"Oh, bitch, get over it." Billie scrunched up her face.

"I hope you choke on your food." Dylan joked, yawning.

"Speaking of choking . . ." Tee-Tee perked up. "Why, last night I was wit' this guy, right, so we gettin' it poppin'. He kissin' me in all the right places, sayin' all the right things, so I'm ready for the dick. Now, y'all know I'm a bad bitch. There ain't a dick out here my mouth can't handle. Well, honey, this niggah pulled down his paaaaaants, and his dick was so big, I thought I was gon' get lockjaw just by lookin' at it!"

"And what you say his name was again?" Dylan teased, pulling out her cell phone.

"I didn't, ho." He squinted his eyes.

"Quit being stingy wit' the beef."

"Chile, please. That Jimmy Dean sausage is all mines. Now, it wouldn't fit all the way in, but baby, the ten inches that did rocked my ass to sleep!"

"TMI, TMI, niggah! TMI!" Dylan quickly erased the visual.

"Uh, don't hate, and don't think I haven't noticed you over there yawning all over the place. Why you so tired? It ain't like you got a job. Don't tell me you got a new boo?"

"I wish." Dylan rolled her eyes, hoping they wouldn't realize she was lying.

Tee-Tee didn't mind her relationship with State. Billie, on the other hand, couldn't stand him, and constantly questioned what Dylan even saw in him. Besides that, Dylan just didn't feel like explaining why she decided to mess with him again. Billie would never comprehend it. And no, Billie didn't run her life, but for now Dylan would rather keep her and State's relationship between the two of them.

"Remember I was going to that Rising Icons concert."

"That's right." Tee-Tee snapped his fingers. "You did say that. So, how was it? Did Wale pull his dick out?"

"No, coon, he didn't."

"Did you sleep with him at least?"

"No."

"Well, what was the point of you going? Sounds to me like you had a dull night."

"Anyhow you're mighty quiet over there." Dylan quickly changed the subject. "What's eating you, Gilbert Grape?" she asked Billie.

"Don't even get me started." Billie rolled her eyes to the ceiling.

"What's wrong, honey?" Tee-Tee scooted closer. "Tell Mama."

"Where do I start? Let me see." She paused for dramatic effect. "Remember the dude Jerrod I met at EXO that night we went together?"

"Yeah, he was kinda cute."

"Fuck cute. That niggah almost killed me."

"What?" Dylan eyed her seriously.

"Girl, it was the worst date of my life."

"Hold up." Tee-Tee closed his eyes and shook his head. "Did you say Jerrod?"

"Yeah." Billie nodded.

"About five feet eleven, dark skin wit' a low cut?"

"Yeah."

"Gurrrrrrl, that ain't nothing but Musty Nuts, a.k.a. Heidi's ex-boyfriend."

"I knew I smelt his ass from somewhere!" Billie clapped her hands together.

"You know I got Delicious and them on speed dial." He held up his phone.

"His broke ass ain't even worth it." Billie rolled her eyes.

"Where did y'all go?"

"Café DePaul."

"Is that new?" Dylan asked. "I ain't never heard of it."

"Me either, so why I go and put on my nine hundred dollar orange Costello Tagliapietra dress and my Jill Sander heels? This muthafucka picks me up, and we in the car, and I'm smelling something. So, before I start passing judgment, I'm like, is it me? So, on the sly, I smell underneath my arms— nothing. I'm straight, but the smell is just funkin' up the car."

"What it smell like?" Tee-Tee questioned.

"Badussy!"

"Are you serious?" Dylan said with skepticism.

"No, I'm dead serious. So, he talkin' about his ex-girlfriend and how she did him so wrong and played him to the left after he bought her a three-hundred dollar dog. And, y'all, I was tryin' my best to stay focused on the conversation, but I swear to God I kept on blacking in and out."

Tee-Tee and Dylan cracked up laughing.

"Thankfully, after a thirty-minute ride we pull up to the place, but it's a hospital. So, before I flipped the fuck out, I'm thinkin' maybe he needed to check on somebody or something. But this niggah tells me to come on and get out, like it's nothing. So, we go inside, and we walkin', and guess what?"

"What?" Tee-Tee's eyes grew wide with anticipation.

"This dumb muthafucka takes me to the hospital cafeteria called Café DePaul."

Dylan had to wipe tears from her eyes because she was laughing so hard.

"Girl, he pissed me off." Billie couldn't help but giggle. "I couldn't believe he had the nerve to take me to a hospital cafeteria for our first date."

"So, what did you do? Did y'all sit down and eat?" Tee-Tee asked.

"Hell naw! What I look like, one of the *Real Chance of Love* girls? I cussed his stankin' ass out, called me a cab, and got my ass up outta there."

"That shit is crazy as hell." Dylan finally calmed down.

"Who you tellin'? I had to take three baths just to get the smell up off me."

"You stupid." Dylan looked down at her menu.

"No, what I need to do is date someone closer to my age." Billie drank her coffee.

"And what age would that be this week?" Tee-Tee joked.

"Yo' mama," Billie joned.

"Whateva." Tee-Tee flicked his wrist.

"But enough about me. What you got on the agenda today?" Billie turned her attention to Dylan.

"Shopping, of course, and my monthly meeting with Morty." Dylan grimaced in reference to her accountant/trust fund manager.

"Oh it's that time again? It seems like it was just a week ago you got yelled at for spending ten thousand on that Hermès Birkin bag."

"I know, right, but I'm like, it's Hermès, Morty. Victoria Beckham has one. There is no way I'm not gonna have one too."

"You're a mess, but seriously, you do need to slow down. The money your father left isn't gonna last forever."

"Huuuuuuuuh! Not you too. My motto is you only live once. Besides, my finances are straight, and once I go see Morty, he'll confirm it."

"Dylan, your spending is out of control!" Morty yelled from across his desk as he glanced down at her figures.

"Ewwww, you don't have to yell." She drew back. "I'm sitting right here."

"I mean, how many times do I have to tell you? You cannot continue to blow money like this. I mean, look." He held up a piece of paper and placed it in her face. "One thousand dollars at Sephora, six thousand at Splash, twenty-five hundred at Intermix—"

Dylan cut him off. "They were having a fifty percent off sale on gloves."

"Twelve thousand at Target!" Morty screamed.

"Ummmmmm, I needed new towels." Dylan looked at him as if nothing was wrong.

"This is ridiculous, Dylan. You have to stop, and I'm sorry to say that if you don't, you'll be broke in less than a year."

"Now you're just exaggerating." Dylan smiled and waved him off.

She knew that she had financial problems, but they couldn't be as bad as Morty was making it out to be. Then again, Dylan never read any of the letters she got from the collection agencies or credit card companies. When the mail came, she simply threw it on top of the fridge and forgot about it.

"Okay . . . keep thinking it's a joke," Morty cautioned. "Keep living in this li'l make-believe fantasy world of yours if you want to. I've done all I can do. Now it's up to you."

Dylan had gone from having one of the best days of her life to the worst in a matter of hours. After getting her asshole torn out by Morty, now she had to deal with even more unexpected news—but this news was far worse than learning she was almost penniless. Fifteen minutes had gone by, and Dylan hadn't moved an inch. She stood at her kitchen counter, holding her cordless phone in a daze. The one new message left on her voice mail had caught her completely off guard. She hadn't heard from her mother in close to a year, and liked it—no, loved it that way. Candice Channing/ Monroe/Van der Woodson/ Moretti/Briatore, a.k.a. Candy, was a lot of things, but a mother, confidant, and friend she was not.

From as far back as Dylan could remember, she'd been raising herself. All of her life, she'd viewed her relationship with Candy as if she were the mother and Candy was the child. Instead of spending quality time with Dylan, Candy enjoyed picking up men, drinking vodka, scheming, and dishing out insults, mostly to Dylan. Candy was never satisfied with anything in her life. She was always on the search for more. Whether it was a new man, a new car, or purse; whatever Candy wanted, Candy got.

She didn't care if she had to lie, cheat or steal; nothing or no one, including Dylan, was gonna get in her way. Like her daughter, Candy was born with a silver spoon in her mouth. Her mother was screen siren and classically trained singer Dahl Channing. Candy referred to her as Mommie Dearest, due to her emotional and physical abuse. Her mother was cold-hearted, and when she died, she left Candy with nothing. Candy was only eighteen. With only her stunning good looks and a voice like velvet to carry her through, she married young in hopes of keeping the lifestyle she was accustomed to.

Her husband's name was Bill. They'd met and married after dating only a month. To Bill, Candy was the sexiest woman on earth. If he could, he would have kept her bottled up in a glass jar for only his eyes to see, but Candy had other plans. While Bill worked hard at his family's very profitable and well-known brewery company, Candy shopped frivolously and pursued a singing career.

At first Bill didn't mind her pursuit of fame, the constant smoking and heavy drinking, but when Candy became pregnant with Dylan, his feelings quickly changed.

"No married woman with child should be hanging out into the wee hours of the morning, singing for a bunch of drunken fools," he said. In Bill's mind, a mother's place was in the home, not in the streets.

Of course, Candy felt differently. Since childhood, she'd dreamed of being a star just like her mother, and she wasn't going to let her pregnancy or her husband's disapproval stop her. Candy prayed that Bill would eventually come around to seeing things her way, but by the time Dylan was five, the once unsinkable love they shared had become non-existent. Candy's career hadn't taken off as she'd planned, and Bill had found comfort in someone younger and new.

Candy pretended like she didn't see it coming, but deep down inside, she had already felt him slipping away. Plenty of nights had gone by where she left him at home alone. Time and time again, she let him down. She didn't care that she was causing him so much misery and pain. And yes, when he left she was filled with regret, but Candy couldn't concern herself with that.

At the ripe age of twenty-five, she found herself divorced with a five-year-old daughter who looked too much like the man who had betrayed her heart. Determined not to let her unfortunate circumstances take over her life, Candy got even. She knew that Bill loved Dylan more than life itself, so out of spite, she filed for full custody and won. Candy knew it would hurt, but she felt it prudent for him to experience a woman's scorn.

And no, she didn't have any job skills, but she did have a steady alimony and child support check coming in monthly. Five years and two divorces later, Candy and Dylan had moved more than twelve times.

Dylan yearned for her father. It wasn't fair that she only got to see him twice a year, so like most little girls her age, when alone, she shut out the real world and created her own. Dylan was the only little girl she knew who laid out Barbie's clothes for the week.

Furthermore, she didn't want to deal with the fact that she had more uncles and step-dads than she could possibly name. Some were nice, some were funny, and some were ugly. But the one that stood out the most was the one who was a little too touchy.

His name was Chauncey. He was her mother's boyfriend after her third divorce. One night while Dylan was asleep, he came into her room and placed his hand underneath her covers.

Dylan could feel his cold, clammy hands ease up her thigh, but pretended to be asleep, praying he would go away. Each second that went by felt like an eternity as his fingers neared closer to her panties. Before Dylan could come to grips with what was happening, Chauncey began to massage her vagina. Frightened beyond belief, Dylan opened her mouth to scream. She heard the sound of a loud thud echoing throughout the room, and someone fell to the hard wooden floor. Opening her eyes, she found her mother standing over Chauncey's limp body with a metal shovel.

After the police were called, Candy held a shaken Dylan in her arms and promised that from then on, things would be different. But three weeks later, they were on to another city and Candy was under a new man.

For years, Dylan continued to be subjected to her mother's lifestyle; that was, until she turned eighteen and moved in with her father permanently. Having missed his daughter terribly, Bill spoiled her rotten. The family-owned brewery was now his. Dylan didn't have to want for a thing.

Sadly, she and her father only spent a couple of years together before he died of a heart attack. Dylan now lived off of her trust fund.

What the hell could she possibly want? She wondered as she sat on a bar stool. *It better not be money. Hell her ass still owes me five grand from the last time we spoke.*

Already aggravated, Dylan picked up the phone and dialed her mother's number. Three rings later, her mother answered.

"Holla-holla!" Candy said instead of hello.

"Hi, Ma," Dylan responded dryly.

"What's going on wit' you, chunky? I ain't heard from you in a while."

"That's because you haven't called." Dylan's mouth tightened at the mention of her childhood nickname.

"I ain't forgot that I owe you that li'l money." Candy spoke while inhaling the smoke from a cigarette.

"Last time I checked, five grand wasn't li'l money."

"Aw shit, girl, calm down. I'ma give you back your money, but look . . . I'ma be in town, right, for a few weeks. I wanted to know if I can come stay wit' ya."

"What's wrong with the Four Seasons? Normally you stay there."

"Well, you know I'm in between gigs right now."

Gigs meant sugar daddies.

"Huhhhhhhhhh." Dylan sighed, running her hand down her face. "I've been real busy, Ma. I wasn't planning on having any company right now."

"Just spit out whateva you tryin' to say, girl. Don't beat around the muthafuckin' bush. If it's gon' be a problem, then just let me know, 'cause Mama gotta make moves and fast. Huh," she chuckled. "You ain't gotta do me no favors. Candy gon' be all right regardless. You already know how I get down."

"I never said it was problem. You can come. I don't care."

"That's my girl." Candy snapped her fingers, pleased with the outcome. "Well, look, let me get a couple of my affairs together and I'll be there, a'ight?"

"Mm-hmm," Dylan replied with her eyes closed.

"I'll holla."

Dylan didn't even waste her time saying good-bye. She simply hung up the phone and hung her head low. Candy never came into town for just a visit. There was always something more. Dylan just hoped she wasn't in any kind of trouble, but knowing Candy she probably was; and Dylan, being the softie she was, would have to bail her out like always.

"I got a secret it's here in my heart,
and I can't even tell my friends."
—Kelly Price, "Secret Love"

Chapter 3

"They told me round the hooooood, every time they see me I look good." Dylan sang Keri Hilson's version of "Turn My Swag On" as she stood in front of her full-length mirror, posing from side to side. The brand new $500 dress she wore had a vintage romantic sensibility to it, but she wondered if it was too cute and not sexy enough.

As a child, Dylan had come up with a theory that if you possessed the right clothes, cars, and accessories, nothing else in life really mattered—and it didn't. Dylan never had to worry about a thing—not her mother, not Chauncey, not her insecurities, not the loss of her father, nothing. Money made all of it go away. It was like her armor. It made her feel good about herself. Without it she felt insecure, maybe because she knew that without it she had nothing.

In high school, she was expelled for violating the school rules. Due to that, college was no longer an option. Instead of working, at the age of nineteen she traveled the world and began her short-lived career as a model. When Ford dropped her, she returned to the States. Dylan soon developed the reputation of a socialite, being identified as the leading "It Girl."

Dylan hung out with all of the beautiful people, from Diddy to Victoria Beckham. Truth be told, she was the one who encouraged Miss Lara Croft, Tomb Raider herself to ditch the Morticia Adams look and go for a more sultry vixen approach. A certain *American Idol* runner up didn't even know what coming out of the closet was until she told him that nobody was buying his "I love women" act. And the infamous pint-sized Brooklyn rapper, well, she was still a work in progress, but Dylan hadn't given up on her yet.

After her failed attempt at modeling, she was bored with the Hollywood scene, so Dylan turned to acting. After two straight-to-DVD films, she was offered the opportunity to be Paris Hilton's best friend on *The Simple Life*, but turned it down, a decision she regretted even to this day. Now, here she was, almost broke, with nothing to fall back on.

Reluctant to let her choices affect her night, she took another look at herself and examined her outfit once more. The dress she wore was soft pink, with tiered ruffles and a scoop neck. To complete the ensemble, she rocked a pair of Alexandra Neel Cleopatra fringe stiletto sandals and a clutch purse.

"Consuela!" She called out for her fifty-year-old Puerto Rican maid.

"Yeeezzzzzz." Consuela dragged herself into the room. She and Dylan had a love/hate relationship.

"Do you like my dress?" Dylan twirled around so she could get a better view.

"Ju look like an oversized cupcake."

"Ugh! Just get out. I don't know why I asked you in the first place. Go clean something, why don't you."

"Whaaaaa'eva." Consuela shrugged and left the room.

Tired of fretting over her outfit, Dylan took one last look at her makeup and hair and decided to go with it. She and State were going out on a date, but she had no idea where. All week she'd been trying to pry information out of him, but State wouldn't break. The only thing he would tell her was to be fly and on time. Although a little frantic, Dylan couldn't wait to see what he had in store for her.

For the past month, State had been surprising her with cards, flowers, and designer duds. It was nothing for him to spoil her with the finer things in life, but what Dylan cherished the most were the quiet moments they shared.

If it was up to her, they would spend every waking moment wrapped up in each other's arms, as they did each and every night. Dylan loved that she could go to State's place, have a glass of wine and chill. And no, she wasn't officially his girl again, but Dylan had never felt sexier or more alive. Yet, there was still a nagging suspension that his newfound dedication to her would fade and he'd break her heart all over again.

Grabbing her purse, she walked downstairs. Dylan loved her home. She lived at the Chase Park Plaza. It was one of St. Louis's most prestigious hotels. Her luxury private residence was an exact reflection of her personality—lively and eclectic.

The living room was gigantic. The walls were a striking shade of hot pink. One wall was decorated with three Andy Warhol portraits of Marilyn Monroe. Underneath was a built-in fireplace. On the wall beside it were two sets of French doors that led out to the patio. All of the furniture, which was a pale green, white, and brown, was modern with an art deco appeal. Dylan had two sofas across the room from each other, four love seats, and two cocktail tables.

Just as she stood in front of the mirror adjusting her cleavage, her house phone rang.

"*Hola!*" Consuela answered the phone dryly. "Hold on. She's right here fixing her boob."

"I'm gonna kill you," Dylan mouthed, snatching the phone.

"Yeah, yeah." Consuela walked away, unfazed.

"Hello," Dylan said sweetly into the phone.

"You ready?" State asked in a deep tone.

"Yeah, you here?"

"Yeah, I'm outside."

"Dang, you couldn't come upstairs? All I get is curbside service," she halfway joked.

"Stop the nonsense and bring yo' ass."

"Here I come," she said, pressing the end button on her phone. "Consuela, I'm gone!"

"Peace out, homey!" Consuela replied, trying to be hip.

Outside, Dylan spotted State leaning against his silver Nissan GT-R. The sound of Trey Songz's hit song "Invented Sex" bumped softly from the speakers. A smile a mile wide instantly popped onto Dylan's face. She couldn't care less how much paper or how many gifts he showered her with; State could get it how he wanted.

That night, he donned a pair of brown aviator shades, a white V-neck tee, yellow-gray-and-white plaid button-up, dark denim jeans, and a pair of yellow-and-white high top Adidas. State was the truth. The closer she got to him, the more her pussy ached to be tortured and teased with kisses from his lips.

Face to face, he gently took her hand and pulled her close. State would never be able to get over just how beautiful Dylan was. The sight of her alone made his dick hard.

Dylan could feel his manhood growing against her thigh. Every fiber of her being wanted to say fuck the date, go back upstairs to her place, and explore all of the freaky thoughts in her mind.

"I missed you," he confessed, kissing the side of her neck.

"I missed you too," she replied, barely able to breathe. "Now, where are we going?"

"None of yo' business, nosey ass. Now, come on. We gotta go or we gon' be late," he said, walking to his side of the car.

Dylan stood for a second, stunned that he wouldn't even

open her door for her. Deciding that it wasn't even worth it to start a fight, she opened the door herself and got in. Even though she was little perturbed by his lack of chivalry, Dylan couldn't keep her eyes off of State during the entire ride. He possessed an animal magnetism that attracted women to him—especially Dylan. The way he smiled, tasted, and even whispered into her ear turned her on. She wondered if there would ever come a day when she wouldn't feel this way about him. She hoped not.

Minutes later, they pulled up to The Pageant Theater. Dylan looked up at the marquee and saw that Solange Knowles and Raheem Devaughn were performing.

"You ready?"

"Are you serious? I love Raheem Devaughn. His CD *The Love Experience* is my shit," Dylan beamed.

"What, you thought I forgot? Are you surprised?"

"Hell yeah, I'm surprised." She grinned.

He got out and once again neglected to open her door.

After grabbing drinks from the bar and finding their seats, Dylan and State sat side by side, anxious for the show to begin. Once it did, they were both on their feet, clapping and cheering. Solange, being the opening act, performed first. Dylan was pleasantly surprised by how well she did. Her '60s era Supremes-style music was on point. But Raheem DeVaughn was who she really wanted to see. When he finally came out dressed in a bad-ass Gucci tuxedo suit and bow tie singing "Guess Who Loves You More," Dylan lost her mind.

Raheem DeVaughn was the personification of soul music for her generation. His voice was powerful, but smooth like silk and sweet like jazz. His whole entire set was good, but when he began to sing "Mo' Better" from his latest CD, *Love Behind the Melody,* that's when Dylan really had a fairytale moment. She and State had been rocking, doing their thing. When the words, "You pat me on the back and rub away the pain, 'cause you're my baby, my darling; you're priceless" floated into the air, he took her hand gently in his and they began to dance cheek to cheek. She knew that would be a moment she would never forget.

It was as if they were in their own world and no one else existed. She was his and he was hers. He'd never played with her heart, and the abortion was just a figment of her imagination. In his arms, Dylan felt important. She couldn't put her finger on what it was, but there was something about him she just wasn't willing to let go.

Nobody understood the connection they shared. God didn't bring him into her life for nothing. *There has to be a reason why we're together. Maybe we are meant to be,* she pondered.

After two encore performances, the concert was over. Dylan and State walked slowly down the street, stuffing their faces with hotdogs from a corner vendor.

"This is sooooooo good," Dylan declared, taking a huge bite.

"I told you you would like it."

"Okay, you were right. Get over yourself." She rolled her eyes as he wiped mustard from the corner of her mouth.

"I swear if I didn't like you so much . . ." He wrapped his arm around her neck and kissed her cheek.

"You would do what?" she responded.

"Fuck the shit outta you."

"Well, niggah, don't like me then," Dylan joked.

"Be quiet." He chuckled.

"I really had fun tonight," she said seriously. "You really made me happy." She hugged his waist tight.

"I try."

"So, what now? Is the night over?"

"Nah." He pulled out his cell phone and checked to see who was calling. "I got another spot I wanna hit up before we go home."

Dylan hated to be nosey, but she couldn't help but sneak a look at his screen. The only thing she could make out was the first three letters of the name. *Who the fuck is Ash?* she thought as her stomach dropped. Dylan also wondered if State would be bold enough to answer the phone while she was right there. Thankfully for him, he didn't. Instead of answering, he sent her call to voice mail and placed his phone back into his pocket.

"Who was that?" Dylan quizzed, hoping he wouldn't lie.

"This chick."

"Why you ain't answer the phone?"

"What you mean, why I ain't answer?" He turned up his face and looked at her like she was insane. "Why would I?"

"I'm just asking you a question, State. You don't have to get an attitude," she stressed as the State she knew appeared.

"Nah, but that's stupid." He took his arm from around her shoulder. "I'm here wit' you. What I need to talk to somebody else for?" He looked her square in the eye and lied.

"I don't know. You tell me." She gave him the evil eye.

"Like, straight up, Dylan, we having a good time. Don't start with that insecure shit. It turns me off."

Dylan stopped and looked at him as if he'd lost his mind.

"And you can stop lookin' at me like that. I'm here tryin' to show you that I'm on some other shit this time, but you hung up on a fuckin' phone call. I'm tellin' you now I ain't got time for a whole bunch of petty-ass shit. I love you." He placed his right hand on the nape of her neck and looked her square in the eyes. "You the one I wanna be wit', and the sooner you realize that, the better off we'll both be."

Dylan didn't even respond. State had hit her with the same speech so many times it had gotten to the point where all she heard was the Charlie Brown sound: *Wa-wa-wa-wa-wa-wa*. She wanted desperately to believe him when he said he loved her, but deep down, she knew that what they shared wasn't love, but a relationship of convenience. She needed him to give her the illusion of being loved until he got it together and could love her for real, or until she could find someone new. Until then, Dylan settled for a bunch of words she couldn't fully believe in for the sake of feeling wanted.

"Why you think I'm going so hard? I want you to see that I'm for real this time. Ain't no going back."

"So, what does that mean? Are we back together again officially?" She said, dying to see how he would reply.

"If you say so." He shrugged, unsure of what he was getting himself into.

"Seriously, State." She lightly pushed his arm.

"I mean, I don't know. I guess."

"*I guess* is not good enough. I need to know that this time it's gonna be different."

"I already told you I'm on some other shit. I wanna be wit' you; that is, if you'll have me." He pulled her into him.

Dylan couldn't even utter the words she felt because on the inside, she felt like she was repeating the same fucked-up cycle of settling for a man she knew wasn't the one, just so she could say she had somebody. Dylan just prayed that this time would be the time they finally got it right and he'd love her like she'd wanted him to all these years.

For a while they walked in silence, hand in hand, stewing in their own thoughts.

If he could, State would give Dylan the world and everything it had to offer. She was a special woman with a gentle
spirit. He felt good when he was around her. She fed his ego,
but visions of Ashton's face haunted his conscience. If she
found out what was going on, she was sure to leave him for
good.

He shook off the thought and asked, "Anything else on
your mind?"

"Yeah." Dylan met her eyes with his. She desperately wanted to tell him that she was afraid he would never love her, and
that if given the chance, he'd discard her heart like before, but
instead of going into detail, she only said, "I guess I'm just
scared that I'll end up on the losing end of the stick again."

"That ain't gon' happen. You got all of me this time." State
felt like an absolute dick as the words slipped from his mouth
and landed on Dylan's heart.

"So, tell me." She hugged him tight. "While we were apart,
did you miss me?"

"Let's just say I listened to a hell of a lot of Raheem Devaughn."

The Pepper Lounge was a hidden jewel located in the heart
of downtown St. Louis. It was a two-story brick venue with
thirty-foot oak ceilings and a massive speakeasy-style bar. That
night, it was filled to the brim with people kickin' it. Dylan
loved the chaotic atmosphere. To her left were a group of
women table dancing, and to her right was a guy joyfully
accepting a body shot offer from a tall, long-legged blonde
bombshell.

Normally, when she wasn't attending an industry event,
Dylan and her girls would hit up a hip-hop and R&B club,

but this time she wanted to do something different. Dylan wanted to hear some fist-pumping, sweat-your-tracks-out kind of music. She and Tee-Tee were on the dance floor, jumping up and down, dancing like giddy school girls to FeFe Dobson's energetic pop punk hit, "I Want You."

Dylan's inner rock goddess was on full display, even down to her outfit. She sported a totally cute black lace and leather sleeveless jacket with a flower brooch, a sleeveless net shirt, black bra, fitted pants, six-inch black heels, and fingerless gloves.

Billie stood back with a disgusted expression on her face while keeping an eye on everyone's purses. There was no way in hell she was about to act a monkey, and on top of that risk ruining her Guillaume Hinfray chain link pumps. Billie was too old, in her mind, and too prominent a figure to let loose and leave all of her inhibitions behind. Plus, the people at the lounge weren't her type of people. There were way too many skanks and losers in the crowd for her taste.

"Um, excuse me." She signaled the bartender. "Can I have a glass of Moët please?"

"Sure." The cute bartender, who looked like Robin Thicke, smiled as he poured her a glass. "Here you go." He handed her the drink.

"Thanks." Billie gave him a twenty-dollar bill. "Keep the change."

Before taking a sip, Billie grabbed a napkin and wiped the rim of her glass.

"You know you need to stop." Dylan placed her hand on her hip and shot Billie a look.

"What?" She shrugged.

"Don't act like you ain't having fun. I saw you over here bobbing your head to The Ting Tings."

"Why you make up these stories is beyond me." Billie smirked, turning her head.

"Bitch, I see you smiling." Dylan laughed, making Billie face her.

"Whateva, and by the way, do you have a vibrator or something up in your purse? 'Cause it's been buzzing the entire time we've been here."

"Hell no. I must have a message." Dylan unzipped her purse and pulled out her cell phone.

In her inbox was a text message from State. It read:
From: State
Where da fuck u @?
Fri, Feb 27 11:03PM

All Dylan could do was giggle and reply back.
To: State
Out
Sat, Feb 27 12:22AM

Seconds later, he sent her another message that said:
From: State
Don't make me come fuck u up.
Sat, Feb 27 12:22AM

Wanting to mess with him even more, Dylan responded:
To: State
Picture that
Sat, Feb 27 12:23AM

"Who in the world are you textin' wit' a big-ass goofy grin on your face?" Billie leaned over and tried to look at her phone.

"This guy I met," Dylan lied, snatching the phone away from her view.

"Really?" Billie said suspiciously. "I thought you weren't seeing anybody new."

"Damn, Inspector Gadget, we just met." She lied again, feeling horrible. Dylan had never lied to Billie, but she was somewhat embarrassed to admit that she was seeing State again.

"Well, when were you going to tell us about him?"

"When it was serious, Miss All-Up-In-My-Damn-Business."

"Heffa, please," Billie scrunched up her face. "I don't care who you date, as long as it's not State's lousy ass. Excuse me," she yelled, flagging down the bartender once again. "Can I have three more glasses of Moët?"

"Coming right up." He winked.

Is this cutie flirting with me? Billie thought, but quickly pushed the idea out of her mind because he was white.

"What is that supposed to mean?" Dylan asked as she received another message.

But before Billie could answer, Tee-Tee rushed over, visibly lit.

"I heard something about State. Is he here?" He scanned the club.

"No. I was just telling Miss Thang here that I don't care who she dates, as long as it's not State. And what I mean by that"—she turned her attention back to Dylan—"is that Lord knows we don't wanna go through that fiasco again."

"What fiasco?"

"Come on, Dylan," she said. "We know you're supposed to be over him, but let's not forget how you cried and stressed over him constantly because he wouldn't commit to you. And shit, that muthafucka used to play you left and right."

"Well, all of that is in the past." Dylan swallowed her friend's harsh words.

"She is right," Tee-Tee jumped in. "Homeboy did string you along; but, honey, I blame you. You're just too sweet. You've got a heart as big as your feet," he teased.

"Fuck you." Dylan laughed a bit.

"But none of that matters," Billie said. "You've moved on and you're happy, right?"

"Yep." Dylan halfway told the truth.

"Well, let's have a toast." Billie handed Dylan and Tee-Tee their drinks. "To happiness." Billie raised her glass.

"To happiness." Dylan and Tee-Tee clinked glasses with her as the DJ began to spin The Black Eyed Peas hit, "I Gotta Feeling."

"Awwwwwww shit," Tee-Tee shrilled, gulping down his drink. "Meet me on the dance floor!" he told Dylan.

"Hold up, el drunko, I'm coming," Billie announced.

"I thought yo' old frigid ass didn't want to dance."

"Ah, fuck it. You only live once." Billie downed her drink as well.

Dylan watched intently as her friends walked out onto the dance floor to do their thing. She was pleased that Billie was finally coming out of her shell, but her continuous disapproval of State was wearing thin. Billie was making it harder and harder for Dylan to come clean about her renewed relationship with him. Yes, he'd led her on and done some fucked up things in the past, but people can change, right? All Dylan could do at this point was trust in his word and pray that this time around he would prove not only her, but her friends wrong.

Remembering the unopened text message she had waiting, Dylan checked her phone.

From: State
U miss me?

Sat, Feb 27 12:25AM

To: State
Of course
Sat, Feb 27 12:40AM

From: State
What u doing later?
Sat, Feb 27 12:41AM

To: State
U
Sat, Feb 27 12:41AM

"This time I want it all."
—John Legend, "This Time"

Chapter 4

An hour later, Dylan, Billie, and Tee-Tee exited the club buzzed off champagne and Nuvo. A slight drizzle of rain was falling from the sky.

"Oh my God, my feet are hurting so bad," Billie complained.

"You ain't said nothin' but a word." Tee-Tee dug inside his over-sized purse and pulled out a pair of flats and a pair of tennis shoes. "Which one you want, girl? Take your pick," he proudly offered.

"Tee-Tee, what are you doing carrying around shoes in your purse?"

"Girl, a bitch like me is always prepared. You never know when it's about to be a Code Ten, Man Down sitchiation."

"Yo' ass always wanna fight somebody." Dylan laughed. "One day somebody gon' whoop yo' ass."

"Screw you, Satan. I'll be damn if a bitch run up on me," Tee-Tee shot back.

"I swear to God yo' ass is crazy."

"Do you want me to take you home or not, hater?" he asked.

"Nah, I'm good. I'm just gonna catch a cab."

"You sure?"

"Yeah," Dylan assured. "Go ahead. I'll be fine."

"I don't know why you think you so slick." Billie chuckled,

shaking her head. "We all know you're going to get you some from this mystery man of yours."

"I love that you know me so well." Dylan placed her hand on her chest and cheesed.

"Well, just do me a favor and have a orgasm for me, 'cause Lord knows I ain't had a piece of dick since 1864."

"You are a fuckin' idiot." Dylan giggled, giving her and Tee-Tee hugs good-bye.

"Call me tomorrow," he said.

"I will. As a matter of fact, let's have a late lunch."

"Sounds like a plan."

Once Billie and Tee-Tee retrieved their cars from the valet and left, Dylan stood along the sidewalk and flagged down a cab. After letting the driver know where she was heading, she sat quietly gazing out of the backseat window. The world was still. All she could hear was the sound of water from the pavement splashing against the tires. For the first time, she realized just how bright the lights from the city skyline were. She wondered if State was watching the sky too.

"How *you* doing?" Tee-Tee did his best Wendy Williams impression into his phone as he drove along the highway heading home.

"Eww, you sound so stank," Billie replied. "Like you got a mouthful of nuts—and I ain't talkin' about no Planters, either."

"Honey, I had nuts for dinner last night. But anyway, what you doing?"

"Driving." She chuckled.

"Tonight was fun."

"It was." Billie yawned. "But I'm tired as hell. I gotta get up early, though. The twins are having a bake sale at school and I'm participating."

"Go 'head on, Mommie Dearest," Tee-Tee teased. "Do yo' thang."

"You got the wrong mama. Now, yo' auntie, on the other hand, is a whole 'nother story."

"Right. Did Dylan tell you she was coming to stay with her for a while?"

"Yeah, she did."

"Girl, as soon she gets here, I'm coming over. Hell, I might spend the night too."

"You and Candy together are a mess."

"That's my girl. But speaking of Miss Dylan, I think she and State are back to messing around."

"Nuh-uh. Dylan ain't that stupid." Billie quickly dismissed the idea.

"We both know she's not dumb, but when has Dylan ever been so secretive about dating somebody? Normally, as soon as she meets a dude, she got us on three-way making wedding arrangements."

"I feel you, but after how he never got her ring and made her have the abortion, I don't think she would be silly enough to go back to him."

"I don't know. I smell a little Ahi tuna. Something's fishy." Tee-Tee tooted up his lips. "Well, look, I'm pulling up to my house, and Bernard is here."

"I thought y'all were broke up."

"We were, but one night I let 'im come over and put that thang down on me, and it's been curtains ever since."

"You are such a whore."

"Aaaaaaaaaw! I don't know about you, but I'm about to get drunk, get naked, and be somebody. Talk to you later, girl. Smooches!"

***

State lay flat on his back with his hands behind his head, listening to XM Radio's Heart & Soul station. The warm air circulating through the vent next to his bed quietly kissed his bare chest. It had been a long, tiring day filled with contract negotiations, artist development, and artist showcases, but sleep still evaded him. State loved what he did for a living, but being the hottest CEO in the music game came with a lot of pitfalls. Success, to him, was like suicide, because once you succeeded, you had to prepare to be crucified. Every other day, he was being hit with lawsuits, rumors, jealousy, and betrayal. Niggahs faked loyalty and friendship just to be in his inner circle, while women forgot love and commitment just to spend one night in bed with him. The same people who built him up found it their mission to bring him down. Niggahs that had been around from the beginning swore that he'd changed, but to State, who worked as hard as he did to stay the same?

Sure, his life was crazy, but State wouldn't trade it for the world. With the negativity came the positive, and State couldn't ignore the fact that right now, he was winning more than ever. He was number one on Forbes magazine's Hip-Hop Cash Kings list, racking in an estimated $47 million in 2009, bring his estimated net worth to $350 million dollars. State had it all. He had the hottest chick in the game wearing his chain, a successful and lucrative career in the entertainment industry, and a mistress on the side. Hell, what more could a thirty-three-year-old man ask for?

He had the best of both worlds. Ashton was his angel, his heart. When he was with her, he felt high. He wanted to be good for her. He wanted to be the man she deserved. The love she provided was something money couldn't buy, but somehow Dylan never strayed far from his mind. Like Ryan Leslie, he was addicted. He loved having her around. With Dylan, he was guaranteed a good time. All she wanted was his time and attention, and State was more than happy to give it. Plus, the sex was phenomenal. She was like a Dell computer: she lived in his lap. He yearned to hear the erotic moans of pleasure she screamed into the air.

The sound of his cell phone ringing interrupted his thoughts. Assuming it was Dylan, State picked up his phone expecting to see her name on the screen. To his surprise, Ashton's appeared.

"Hello?" He answered groggily, pretending to be asleep.

"I'm sorry, baby. I didn't mean to wake you. Were you asleep?"

"Yeah, but it's cool. What you up to?"

"I just got out the shower. The show was great tonight. The concert was sold out. Tomorrow we'll be on our way to Dublin," Ashton said excitedly. She was still high from her performance.

"You tired?" State asked.

"Yeah, but I gotta hit the gym. I can't wait to see you, though. I miss waking up to your big ol' face," she teased.

"I miss waking up to that fat ol' ass." State laughed.

"Shut up." Ashton giggled.

There was a loud knock on State's door.

"Who the hell is that at the door this time of the morning?" Ashton's attitude quickly changed.

State made up a lie real quick, knowing good and well it was Dylan at the door. "Calm down. Before I fell asleep I called downstairs to the concierge and told them to send the maintenance man up. The sink in our bathroom has a drip that's been annoying the hell outta me."

"Don't be on no bullshit, State, 'cause I swear to God I will get on a plane and come home in a hot second and kick everybody's ass."

"Go 'head wit' all that. Ain't shit going on but you. Go 'head and go to the gym. I'ma just holla at you later on."

"Okay," Ashton replied, hesitant to get off the phone. "I love you."

"I love you too," State said back then hung up.

He hated to do her like that. Lying to his wife was something he never really liked to do, but there was no way Ashton could know the truth.

State placed his feet on the Venantino marble floor and made his way down the steps. The last thing he was expecting to find when he opened it was Dylan with her coat unbuttoned, dressed in nothing but her lace panties and bra.

"You like?" She smiled seductively.

"Hell, yeah." He licked his lips. "But where the fuck are all your clothes?"

"I took them off on the way here."

"You wild as a muthafucka."

"Why you standing all the way over there? Don't be scared. Come closer." She reached for his hand and pulled him toward her.

State happily wrapped his arms around her and held her tight.

"You never saw me like this before, huh?" She whispered softly into his ear. She placed her hand on his growing manhood and massaged him.

"Bring yo' ass here." He pulled her into the house and kicked the door shut.

With her backside facing him, Dylan seductively peeled off her coat. Very tipsy, she placed her hands on her hips and began to saunter slowly toward his bedroom when she lost her balance, and her right heel collapsed over, causing her to stumble. Quick on her feet, Dylan caught herself and stood up straight.

"You okay?" State tried his best not laugh, but he couldn't help it.

"Pretend you didn't see that."

"I didn't." He enveloped her in his arms and kissed the nape of her neck.

Dylan drowned in his touch. Inside his bedroom, under the watchful eye of the moonlight, Dylan's back met with the sheets. Seconds later, she was fully naked. Maxwell's "Bad Habit" played as he removed his boxers.

With her legs pushed back, Dylan's pink clit stared him in the face, begging him to come forth. State couldn't deny it; she had the prettiest pussy he'd ever seen. The fact that it smelled like fresh strawberries enticed him even more.

Feenin' for him to taste it, Dylan parted her lips for him. With expert precision, he licked the center of her slit, causing her to shake and moan. State's head game was lethal and should've been illegal. Dylan's juices were flowing in a matter of seconds.

"Damn, you taste good," he whispered into the lips of her pussy.

"Ooooooooooooh, baby, don't stop," she whimpered.

"You like that?"

"Yes!" She squealed as he flicked his tongue across her clit even faster. "Ooooooh, yeesssss. Don't stop, baby. Don't stop."

The faster he licked, the more Dylan lost her mind. While sucking on her clit, State took two of his fingers and placed them inside her warm honey pot. The one-two punch of his tongue and fingers caused Dylan to go into service overload.

"Oooh shit, I'm cumming! Oooh, baby, I'm cumming." She bounced up and down, cumming all over his mouth and chin.

State loved it. Licking his lips, he wiped his mouth and made his way back up.

"Don't ever make me wait this long for some pussy. I've been thinkin' about this shit all day," he confessed, ramming his dick inside her warm, wet slit and hitting bottom.

As soon as he entered her, Dylan's thighs began to shake. All ten inches of his thick, luscious dick filled her insides. She barely had enough to room to breathe.

With her legs held in the crook of his arms, State squeezed his eyes shut and groaned. Dylan's pussy was the best. It was fat and always dripping wet, just how he liked it. That night, she was so wet that it was hard for him to keep his dick from slipping out.

"Oooooh . . . baby . . . fuck me! Fuck me!" Dylan continued to beg while rotating her fingers across her clit.

"Cum for me, baby! I want to see you cum!" State ordered, pinching and massaging her nipples.

"Aaaaaaaaaaaaaaaah," Dylan squealed, feeling an orgasm near. "Baby, you feel so good. Ooooh."

"You feel good too, baby." He slowed down his pace, hitting her with only rough, slow pumps.

"Oooooh . . . baby . . . that's my spot!" Dylan screamed, clawing the sheets.

"You love me?" he questioned, feeling the nut build up in the tip of his dick.

"Yes," she moaned.

"You wanna have my baby?"

"Yes."

"A boy or a girl?" he groaned.

"A girl." Dylan shrieked as she and State came at the same time.

Spent from the night before, Dylan sat upright in bed with the sheets covering her hard nipples. State's room was immaculate. Everything was top of the line. The walls were a calming shade of gray, while his platform bed was brown with a yellow headboard. By the bed was a beautifully crafted portrait by Robert Geveke.

State stood before her with only a towel draped around his defined waist. He'd just gotten out of the shower. Beads of water trickled down his chest, slowly landing in the place she wanted to bury her face. Flashbacks of the thick ten inches of wonder he possessed sliding in and out of her mouth filled her mind. The thought caused Dylan's mouth to water and her pussy to soak with sticky cream. State was so delicious.

Just looking at him ignited a flame deep inside her heart. There wasn't anything about him she didn't adore, and in a perfect world, they would get married, have beautiful babies, and grow old together; but nothing in life was perfect, nor was her relationship.

Dylan still couldn't conjure up the nerve to tell her friends they were back together. Plus, all of the lying and sneaking around she'd been doing was starting to wear on her nerves. Tried of living a lie, Dylan made it up in her mind that now was the time to tell the truth.

"I'm thinking of tellin' the girls that we're back together," she announced suddenly as State took off his towel and placed on his boxer briefs.

"Really?" He stopped and paused. "What made you decide that?"

"Come on. You know how they feel about you."

"They, as in Billie, you mean?" State turned and shot her a look.

"Yeah." Dylan put her head down.

"Well, if it makes you feel any better, I haven't told anyone either."

"That's because you don't have any real friends. All you have is industry friends, also known as associates."

"That's not true. What about C.I.?"

"He doesn't count. He's your cousin." Dylan laughed. "And if that's the case, why haven't you told him?" She eyed him quizzically.

"I don't know. I haven't put that much thought into it, I guess."

"Wow . . ." she replied visibly hurt. "That makes me feel good."

"Nah. I ain't sayin' it like that. I just felt that we should keep it between us," he said, trying to regain control of the situation.

"Oh."

"Look." He put on his Michael Kors dress pants then sat beside her. "Stop trippin' off that shit. If homegirl ain't wit' it, then fuck it. You gotta live yo' life for you. It ain't like you fuckin' her or are you?" he joked, placing his head back.

"Don't play wit' me." She playfully pushed him in the chest.

"I'm just sayin'. You ain't living your life for them. You gotta make you happy. And I know we had our issues in the past, but things are different now. I'm yours and you mine. Ain't no middle man. Hopefully your homegirl can get wit' it. If not, then, oh well."

"I guess you're right." She shrugged, still unsure.

"You know I'm right."

"What if after I tell them, we all get together for dinner and drinks?"

"I don't know about that." State shook his head while tying his tie. He didn't want to risk his extramarital affair getting back to Ashton.

"Pleeeeeeease. I really want you to know my friends better."

"I already know what I need to know about 'em. Billie's stuck up, and Tee-Tee's a fag."

"Heeeey!" She threw her pillow at him. "Watch your mouth."

"Well, it's true."

"Okay, then, I want them to get to know you better. They've only been around you a couple times, and I think if they spent more time with you, they would have a different opinion of you."

"I don't really care what they think about me."

"But I do. I want them to know that you're funny and charming and sweet."

"As long as you know that, that's all that matters."

"C'mon, State. Just do it for me." She batted her eyes.

"Look, I said no!" he snapped. "Damn . . . you gettin' on my nerves wit' that shit. I don't like them muthafuckas." He pointed his hand. "Them yo' friends. You go have drinks wit' 'em."

Dylan's mouth flew open. She was shocked. Pissed that he had the nerve to come at her crazy, she cocked her neck back and prepared herself to go into ghetto-girl mode, but before she could, State checked himself and apologized.

"My bad." He tried taking her hands, but Dylan drew them away. "I ain't mean to bark on you like that, but I ain't really feelin' being around yo' peoples like that."

"It's all good, 'cause by the way you actin', I don't want yo' ass around. You got me fucked up, talkin' to me out the side of yo' neck. And who gives a fuck about you not liking my friends? They don't like yo' ass either!" She snatched the covers off of her and tried to get up, but State pushed her back down.

"If you don't move yo' big ass out my way," she warned. Dylan played a lot of games, but not when it came to her friends.

"Stop being so damn dramatic. Look, if it'll make you happy, I'll go," he lied.

"Don't do me no favors."

"A'ight, you can chill wit' the Bonquisha-from-the-block shit. I said I'd go, and I meant it," he lied again.

"Mm-hmm." Dylan looked the other way and crossed her arms.

"We cool?"

"Yeah," she said, still upset.

"I don't like the way you said it. Are we cool?" State made her face him and placed his forehead on hers.

"I said yeah." She laughed.

"Well, act like it then." He pressed his lips up against hers and rotated between sucking her top and bottom.

"But check it: I'm finna shake. I'm running late as hell." He quickly kissed her lips once more. "Lock up before you go."

"I will. Have a good day."

"You too." He grabbed his cell phone and keys.

"And don't forget to call me!" she yelled after him.

"I'll think about it," he teased, closing the front door behind him.

"How could you be so heartless?"
—Kanye West, "Heartless"

Chapter 5

"Kyrese, come and help me with these bags," Billie said to her ten-year-old son as she entered through the front door of her spacious apartment.

She and her husband of eleven years, St. Louis Rams superstar Cain Townsend, along with their three children, Kyrese and twins Kenzie and Kaylee, had lived there for the past three years—until Cain announced he wanted a separation and he moved out. It was one of their many homes, and one of Billie's favorites. Unlike most NFL wives, she wasn't afforded the pleasure of having a maid or a chef. Cain felt since he was the breadwinner, she should be a stay at home mom—and in every sense of the word, she was. Billie couldn't even take a vacation without him. She took the kids back and forth to piano and karate lessons, participated in school plays, and kept up a nice home, all while presiding over numerous organizations. It was hard work, but somebody had to do it.

Billie waited at the bottom of the stairs for her son, who still hadn't come down.

"Kyrese! I know you hear me!"

"Ma'am?" He came stomping to the top of the steps.

"If you don't bring yo' ass down here and help me with these bags, I swear to God I'ma punch you in the throat!"

"Why can't Daddy help you?" he asked, taking the bags from her hands.

"'Cause first of all, I didn't know your father was here, and second, because I asked you, that's why." She shot him a look then walked up the steps and entered the kitchen.

Billie loved her kitchen. The space was huge, 1200 square feet to be exact. The custom designed cabinets were made of Wenge, an imported hardwood. Stainless steel countertops mingled with earth tones, including red, yellow, and orange glass tiles on the backsplash. A six-burner cooktop island sat in the middle of the room underneath an exhaust hood. The see-through refrigerator, two ovens, and a microwave were built into the wall.

"And where is Mrs. Robertson?" she asked her son, referring to their next door neighbor who sometimes helped her with the kids.

"Daddy told her she could go."

"Where is your father anyway?"

"In the room on the phone."

"When did he get here?"

"Ummm . . ." Kyrese thought. "About a half an hour ago."

"And where are your sisters?"

"In the sitting room watchin' *True Jackson VP* and they gettin' on my nerves."

"Kyrese, according to you, everybody gets on your nerves." Billie began unpacking the groceries.

"Nah, Ma, for real, straight up. Kaylee and Kenzie knew that I wanted to watch *Rob and Big* at eleven, but they gon' try and be ignorant and go in there and turn on the TV at ten fifty-eight, talkin' about they got there first."

Billie couldn't help but laugh. Kaylee and Kenzie were always trying to do something to aggravate their brother.

"I'll talk to them. Tell them to come here."

Kyrese placed his hands up to his mouth and yelled. "Kunta Kenzie and Kaylee, yo' mama want you!"

"I said go get them, not scream from the kitchen, boy." Billie thumped him in the back of his head.

"Ow, Mama! Dang, that hurt!" Kyrese massaged the sore spot.

"Yes, Mommy." Kaylee and Kenzie skipped into the room looking as angelic as ever, even though they were too grown for their own good.

That afternoon, they both wore pink sleeveless ruffle dresses that Billie had bought in Paris. Seeing all of her children together brought an instant smile to her face. To her, they were the cutest kids on earth. They all possessed honey-colored skin and long, wild, curly brown hair. To most, Kyrese was the spitting image of Jaden Smith, while Kaylee and Kenzie reminded her of Sasha Obama.

"First off, would you like something to drink while I'm in here?" Billie asked. "'Cause when I leave out, I don't wanna hear nothing about, *I'm thirsty, can I have this, can I have that?*"

"Chardonnay, please," Kaylee said matter-of-factly.

"Li'l girl, don't play wit' me."

"Aw, Mama, you're no fun. Get wit' it. Like Candy say, a li'l sip er' now and then ain't gon' hurt nothin'."

"Let's not forget Candy is crazy, and anyway, why are you two tormenting your brother?"

"Who, us?" They both placed their hands up to their chests and looked around, stunned. "Why would we do such a thing like that, Mommy?" Kenzie batted her eyes.

"Let your brother watch TV."

"But why?" Kaylee whined, jumping up and down. "We were there first!"

"Question me again and see what's gon' happen," Billie warned, giving her the evil eye.

"But it's not fair, Mommy!" Kaylee jumped in.

"Um, you heard what I said."

"Daaaaaaady!" They both ran from the room in search of their father.

"I don't know what you think that's gon' do!" Billie yelled after them. "Like he gon' whoop me!" She turned her attention back to Kyrese. "Go on in the room and watch that TV, boy."

"Thanks, Ma." He smiled.

Billie rolled her eyes and continued to put up the food. Seconds later, Cain entered the kitchen. The smell of his Gucci cologne intoxicated her nose. Billie turned around and faced him. Cain wasn't the finest man on earth, but every time she laid eyes on him, her heart would melt. He was a six foot, 230-pound chocolate quarterback with muscles the size of Zeus. Since the day they'd met in the quad during their freshman year of college, he'd made her feel that way.

But ten years into their marriage, things began to change. Someone finally saw the beauty she saw in him, and named him one of *People* magazine's most beautiful people. Homeboy flipped and lost his mind. In the off season, instead of spending time with Billie and the kids, he was often found out of town, club-hoppin' with his teammates. When they were together, the conversations they shared were forced, and when Billie tried to bring up her concerns about his behavior, the end result would be him grabbing his car keys and leaving.

Then the late night phone calls began, and the scent of another woman's perfume was left in his clothes. Things got so bad that Cain stopped coming home at night. Billie did everything she could to get their marriage back on track: counseling, dressing up in lingerie, fuckin' him in every position imaginable, and taking it in the ass. But nothing worked. Cain's heart just wasn't beating for her anymore. And the feeling of knowing that hurt like hell, but for the sake of their kids and her reputation, Billie pretended that everything was okay.

Then one day, Cain hit her with the hardest blow to her heart and announced that he was moving out and wanted to separate. That day, Billie swore that the entire neighborhood could hear her heart fall to the floor. A hurt like no other seeped through her veins.

She didn't understand how Cain could look at her and not see how much she loved him. Was this really what she'd worked so hard for? Had she really upgraded him to be the perfect man for some other woman to reap the benefits? Did she put up with all of his lies and broken promises for nothing? Didn't all the times he'd hurt her and put tears on her face count for anything? Didn't she deserve some kind of recognition for all of that?

For weeks after that, Billie lay in bed, crying and wondering why. For the life of her, she couldn't understand why Cain would want to be with someone else. All he needed was her. She was his wife and the mother of his kids. Hadn't she been enough? But then Billie thought maybe being just enough was the problem. She should've been more. So here she was, three months later, still wishing and praying that one day she would have her family back and Cain would come to his senses and return home.

"Wassup wit' you?" he asked.

"Nothing." She smiled, happy to be in his presence. "Did your daughters come and tell on me?"

"Yeah, they did. I told them I would whoop you later."

"Really? How about now?" She stuck her butt out.

"If you don't put that shit up . . ." He took a seat at the island and looked at her.

Billie wasn't a size four anymore, but no man could deny how pretty she was. She was a five foot eight inch diva with diamond-shaped eyes. Whenever she smiled, a slight glimmer of a dimple graced her left cheek. Her long, jet black hair and Chinese-cut bangs highlighted her high cheekbones. The black Fendi pinwheel cardigan and cream-colored short full skirt enhanced her size twelve curves.

Billie caught him staring at her and asked, "What, you see something you like?"

"Wouldn't you like if I did?" Cain slightly chuckled.

"Whateva. You know we gon' have to start planning the kids' party. Their birthday is in a few months."

"Damn, it's that time already," Cain replied.

"Oh my God!" Billie shouted, spinning around. "I forgot. Today I'm supposed to have lunch with Dylan and Tee-Tee. Will you watch the kids for me?"

"Nah, I got someplace I need to be."

"Where?"

"None of your business." He looked at her funny.

"Whateva." Billie waved him off. "I'll just ask Mrs. Robertson if she'll come back over. But if I may ask, what are you here for?"

"To see my kids," Cain answered, taking out his cell phone. He'd gotten a text.

"Mm-hmm." Billie resumed putting up the groceries. "What do you think we should do for the kids' birthday?"

"I don't know."

"I was thinking maybe this year we should have a circus theme. What do you think about that?"

"Yeah, that shit is fucked up," Cain answered as he replied back to the message.

"What?" Billie turned around. "Are you even listening to me?"

"Yeah."

"Well, what I just say?" She placed her hand on her hip.

"What the fuck? I'm listening!" Cain put the phone down, annoyed.

"No, you're not! You too busy fooling wit' that phone. Whoever that bitch is, she can wait."

"Yo', don't start," Cain warned, massaging his forehead.

"No, don't you start," Billie shot back. "I'm sittin' here tryin' to have a conversation wit' you about your kids, and you not even concerned. Why you even over here? All you do is sit and talk on this damn phone." She picked it up.

"You out yo' fuckin' mind." Cain snatched it from her hand, pissed. "I done told you about touching my shit."

Caught off guard by his reaction, Billie stood back. "Be easy, homeboy. Ain't nobody even trippin' off that damn phone. All I did was pick it up. You ain't have to snatch it from me."

"But that's the point. Don't pick it up. It's not yours. Just leave it where it is, 'cause if you see something you don't like, I don't feel like hearing a bunch of whining and complaining about it."

Swallowing the lump in her throat, Billie tried her best to remain cool.

"Cain, I don't care about you and them raggedy-ass hoes you fuck wit'," she lied. "Like I said, don't snatch nothin' from me."

"And like I said, don't touch my shit."

"Well, how about I don't like yo' stupid ass being here, so why don't you and yo' phone go home." She pointed toward the door, fed up.

"Whateva. I'm not gon' argue wit' you." Cain got up.

"Bounce, niggah!"

Not even concerned with the way she felt or the fact that he'd hurt her feelings, Cain grabbed his keys and proceeded to the door.

"I can't stand yo' stupid ass!" Billie picked up a pint of milk and threw it at him.

"What the fuck is your problem?" Cain ducked to dodge the milk. "Are you insane?"

"You're my problem!" She picked up a pack of lean ground beef.

"I ain't playin' wit' you, Billie! Don't throw shit else at me," he barked.

"Fuck you!" She reared her hand back as far as she could and threw the package at his head. This time, she hit him. Billie watched in delight as Cain's head bounced forward from the impact.

"You're fuckin' crazy!" he yelled, running down the steps.

"Let me be crazy then! You stupid muthafucka, I hate yo' ass!"

"The feeling is mutual," he shot, closing the door behind him.

"Stupid muthafucka," Billie said underneath her breath as her chest heaved up and down.

"So, you and Daddy at it again?" Kenzie asked, standing by her mother's side.

"Yeah, baby, but this time it's different."

The In Spot Dessert Bar and Lounge, located in the outskirts of the Delmar Loop, was a cozy hideaway for intimate gatherings and social networking. It was smoke-free and designed for patrons to chill with their friends or that special someone. Dylan and her girls often frequented the lounge to gossip, eat, and drink.

That afternoon, Lamar Harris and his band were performing there. While the band played their rendition of The Roots' "Rising Up," Dylan and her girls enjoyed their afternoon lunch, which consisted of cosmopolitans and Cobb salads.

"So, what's the T, ladies?" Tee-Tee unfolded his napkin and placed it into his lap.

"Shit," Billie said, taking a bite of her food.

"Oh my God, did you see those new gold Christian Louboutin robot ankle boots?" Dylan shrieked.

"Yes, girl! Those muthafuckas are fierce." Tee-Tee snapped his fingers.

"You know I'm on them, right?" Dylan confirmed.

"How much are they?" Billie asked.

"Twelve hundred ninety-five."

"Now, you know you don't need to be spending that kind of money right now."

"Fuck that. I will be the first person to rock those bad boys."

"Sorry to burst yo' bubble, but I saw Kim Kardashian in them last night at Home," Tee-Tee said. Home was a very popular club in St. Louis that celebrities frequented.

"Ain't that about a bitch," Dylan said with a pout. "Speaking of Kim K, did you hear that she and Reggie Bush broke up?"

"Yep." Tee-Tee smirked. "And please believe I'ma be on the first flight to New Orleans this afternoon, 'cause that bitch ass ain't got nothing on mine." He stood up and smacked his backside.

"You two are ridiculous." Billie scrunched up her face. "There is far more going on in the world besides the crap y'all talk about."

"We can't help that our lives revolve around fashion, celebrities, and boys," Dylan defended herself.

"Don't forget Suri Cruise," Tee-Tee jumped in.

"See what I mean? Ridiculousness." Billie rolled her eyes.

"I do have something else I wanna talk about," Dylan said.

"Please don't tell me Paula Abdul is back on *American Idol.* I swear I wouldn't be able to take it," Tee-Tee pleaded.

"No, silly. Um . . ." She inhaled deeply. "I didn't want to say anything until I was absolutely sure that it was real this time, but . . . I'm back wit' State . . . but this time it's different," she stressed.

"Booyah! I told yo' ass!" Tee-Tee raised his arm and thrust his finger in Billie's face.

Billie didn't even bother to respond. Instead, she sat back and shook her head.

"What?" Dylan cocked her head to the side.

"Nothing." Billie waved her off. "That's all on you. You're a grown-ass woman. You can do whatever you wanna do."

"I know I can do whatever I wanna do, but I still felt as if y'all should know."

"Why? What we think don't matter anyway." Billie uncrossed then crossed her legs again.

"Yes, it does. Look . . ." Dylan sat upright. "Things between us are different this time." She tried to convince herself.

"And how is that?"

"I mean, they just are." Dylan shrugged.

"If it's so right this time, then why have you been sneaking around behind our backs?" Billie countered.

"Why you so negative?" Dylan replied because she had no answer.

"I'm far from negative. I just see the reality of the situation. You stupid and State's a liar, so I guess y'all belong together. All I got to say is when he play yo' ass again, and oh, he is going to play you, don't come cryin' to me."

"I won't, but let's not forget how we warned you about Cain's trifling, cheating ass, but you upped and married the niggah anyway and had three kids by his lousy, I-wanna-leave-you-for-a-VH1-*Rock of Love*, Kim-wig-wearing, I-wanna-sing-sounding-like-Billy-Bob-Thornton-bitch ass, so don't call the kettle black, POT!"

"Ooooooooooooh, no she didn't," Tee-Tee instigated. "You gon' sit there and take that?" He looked at Billie.

"First of all, you need to shut up," she advised, then turned her attention to Dylan. "I know you ain't tryin' to compare my eleven-year marriage to your on again/fuck again/off again so-called relationship." She raised her hands and imitated air quotes. "Do you even know what that niggah look like in the daytime?"

"All right now, that's hittin' below the belt." Tee-Tee stepped in as people began to look.

"Bitch, you shouldn't even wanna see that tore-down-ass niggah of yours in the day. The moonlight shouldn't even hit his ass," Dylan shot back.

"Ugly and all, I ain't never had to go get no script. Let's see . . . what was yours for again?" Billie placed her index finger to her chin and thought. "Chlamydia or gonorrhea?"

"Bitch, it was a simple bacterial infection, and you ain't have to go there," Dylan spat, angry as hell as she threw down her napkin. "Gon' sit up there and say he ain't never gave you nothing. Hell, we don't know if he gave you something or not. You coulda been keepin' that on the hush-hush like you did everything else. One minute you happy, and the next you gettin' a goddamn divorce!"

"Haaaaaaaaaaaah!" Tee-Tee screamed, placing his hand on his chest, cracking up laughing. "Now it's a party!"

"That's really how you feel?" Billie replied, crushed.

"Yo' jealous ass the one who started it," Dylan countered.

"Well, I'm finishing it," Tee-Tee chimed in. "Now, both y'all need to stop before somebody start cryin' or bleedin'."

"Fuck her. I'm outta here." Dylan scooted back and got up out of her chair and left.

"Shit, fuck her too." Billie followed suit and walked out of the restaurant, heated.

"Oh, heeeeeeeeell no! I know these bitches didn't stick me wit' the goddamn bill. They got me fucked up," Tee-Tee said out loud to himself, pissed as he reached inside his purse for a hundred-dollar bill. "I will hurt both of they feelings and kick they asses at the same time, retarded bitches." He placed the money on the table, stood up, and spotted a cutie coming his way. "How *you* doing?" Tee-Tee reached out his hand for a shake. "My name is Tee-Tee. Dick'em Down Diva, if ya nasty."

"I'm ready to roll . . . Girl, I'm with you."
—Rihanna, "G4L"

Chapter 6

The one place Dylan could find solace when she was upset or feeling down was one of her favorite boutiques, Giselle. Being around gorgeous, one-of-a-kind designer dresses, shoes, and handbags always brightened her day. For the first time in a long while, she needed that comfort. She and Billie had argued before, but never the way they did back at the restaurant. There was always a line they never crossed with one another, but that day the line became invisible.

Things were revealed that neither knew the other felt. Dylan never knew that her best friend viewed her as stupid. She'd been called a lot of things in life, but never stupid. A part of her wondered if Billie was jealous. She and Cain had been separated for several months, and she hadn't even attempted to move on. It was like she was bitter and mad at the world. Cain's infidelity had become every man's mistake. Dylan knew what it felt like to be alone with no one there to hold you and promise that everything would be okay, so she sympathized with Billie's plight. But just because Billie didn't have anybody in her life didn't mean that Dylan couldn't follow her heart and be happy.

"Now, you know yo' ass owe me." Tee-Tee walked into the store, stopped, and pulled out a receipt. "Twenty-five dollars and thirty–two cents."

"Really, Tee-Tee?" Dylan spun around, still upset. "You seriously gon' sit up here and sweat me over twenty-five fuckin' dollars? Here." She grabbed her purse. "Let me give you this money before I have to punch the shit outta you."

"Is she talkin' to me?" Tee-Tee looked to the side and asked one of the salesgirls. "'Cause I could've sworn this bitch mistook me for a punk. She must not know 'bout me."

He reached inside his bra and revealed a switchblade. "Now, let me tell you one thing." He walked up on Dylan with the knife in his hand. "Don't let the platform Gucci's and the three hundred–dollar sew-in fool you. Respect my gangsta, 'cause in about ten-point-two seconds, I'ma go *Kill Bill* on dat ass. Please believe I got a jar of Vaseline and some high top sneakers on deck. Now, try me."

"Boy, put that damn knife up." She jerked back.

"Okay now." He rolled his eyes. "I love you, God knows I do, but don't make me come outside myself, Dylan."

"I'm sorry, cousin." Dylan gave him an apologetic hug. "That trick made me mad."

"Both of y'all was wrong."

"I ain't even do anything," Dylan whined like a child.

"And the best actress in a drama series goes to . . ." Tee-Tee placed his hand up to his mouth and yawned.

"Seriously?" Dylan shot him a look.

"Yes! She shouldn't have called you stupid. That was wrong, but you ain't have to go in on her marriage. You know that's a touchy subject for her."

"I understand that." Dylan sat down across from him. "But what about the shit she said to me? She ain't have to bring up my infection."

Tee-Tee tried not to, but he couldn't help but laugh.

"You gotta admit that was funny," he said.

"Fuck you." Dylan laughed too. "But for real, what am I

gon' do? 'Cause I'm not leaving State alone no matter what she say or how she feel, but I also want to keep my friendship."

"I mean, the only thing you can do is talk and put everything out on the table."

"I guess." Dylan sighed. "I just hope we can get past this."

Three A.M. was fast approaching, and Billie hadn't slept a wink. For hours, she'd tossed and turned under the covers. The argument she and Dylan had replayed over and over again in her mind. All day long she'd wanted to call and apologize, but her stubborn pride just kept getting in the way. Plus, she wasn't ready to make nice. Dylan had said things she wasn't sure were forgivable. She knew how her separation from Cain affected her. Many nights went by where Billie cried on her shoulder. For Dylan to say the things she did had to mean that she already felt that way.

That shit didn't come from nowhere, but Billie still couldn't place all the blame on Dylan. She'd dished out her own tray of insults that she was sure burned like hot coal. Every part of her wanted to be supportive of Dylan and State's relationship, but the concerned friend within her couldn't muster up an attitude of acceptance. Yet and still, she and Dylan had been friends for too many years to count. Like her marriage, she wasn't willing to lose a friendship she'd invested time, love, and loyalty into. Pushing aside her complex feelings, Billie picked up the phone and dialed Dylan's number.

"Hello?" She answered on the first ring, wide awake.

"So, I guess you call yourself still having an attitude?" Billie questioned jokingly.

"Girl, nah, you know I can't stay mad at you forever. I

thought you were still upset wit' me. I was gon' call you tomorrow." Dylan sat up.

"I was . . . am, but you're my sister, and I love you despite your flaws."

"That's good to know." Dylan chuckled, rolling her eyes to the ceiling. "I love you too, Billie, and I'm sorry for everything I said."

"I'm sorry too. I should've never called you stupid. That was wrong. I just had a fucked-up morning and took it out on you."

"What happened?" Dylan quizzed.

"The usual. Cain and I got into it."

"Oh." Dylan sat quietly, unsure if she should say what she thought.

"And I know what you're thinking." Billie read her mind. "I should file for divorce and move on with my life . . . but it's just not that simple. He's my husband, and I have to believe that somewhere deep down inside he still loves me. Like, who could just walk away from an eleven-year marriage as if it were nothing?"

"Sweetie—"

"No," Billie cut her off. "Please don't give me the you-can-do-better speech, 'cause I already know I can. I'm strong and I'm intelligent, but for some reason, when it comes to Cain, I lose all sense of self."

"I know how you feel," Dylan said, thinking of State. "Well, at this point, you have to do what's best for you. I mean, it's only been a couple of months. Who knows? Cain may come to his senses and beg for your forgiveness. Then you'll renew your vows and live happily ever after."

"I wish everyone was as optimistic as you." Billie smiled. "Now, what are we going to do about this whole State sitchiation, as Tee-Tee would say? Why are you back with him?"

"I know it's a mess, but, Billie, there is just something about him that I cannot let go of. Like, he was the father of my baby, and yeah, he ain't want me to keep it, but that shit don't go away. Like, I love him, and I wanna see us work this time."

"And you really think it will?"

"I mean, I hope so," Dylan responded optimistically.

"I guess," Billie said, still weary.

"I really want all of us to get together for dinner. I feel like if you got a chance to sit down with him and see his personality, then you'd understand why I care for him so much."

"I just don't like his ass. Ugh." Billie balled her fist. "But for you, I'll do it."

"Thank you, thank you, thank you. Trust me; you won't regret your decision."

The day of the ill-fated dinner had finally arrived. They were to have drinks at 609 Lounge then travel next to door to the sushi restaurant Blue Ocean. Dylan was dressed to the nines in a hippie-inspired Diane Von Furstenberg long-sleeve, flowy, brightly colored sheath dress that hit mid-thigh. To cinch in the waist, she wore a black leather belt. Instead of showcasing her signature bob, she rocked her hair to the back with an eighteen inch weave. An Indian-like headband with flowers and feathers enhanced her spring-inspired makeup. To complete the ultra unique outfit, she rocked a Carlos Falchi pleated clutch purse and extreme cutout sandals.

Dylan had never been more nervous in her life. Bringing Billie and State together was like the ultimate *Clash of the Titans*. In one corner you had Billie, the Oprah Winfrey of the social scene, and in the other, State, the Bill Gates of hip-hop. With all of that money and ego in one room, there was bound to be a conflict of personalities. But Dylan was determined to stay hopeful and pray that somehow, some way, the two most important people in her life would get along.

Checking the clock on the wall, Dylan wondered what could be keeping State. They'd made an agreement that he was supposed to pick her up by seven. It was now 7:50 P.M. Tired of waiting, she picked up the phone and called him.

"Wassup," he answered.

"Where are you?" Dylan spoke, frustrated.

"Just leaving the office. Why, wassup?"

"What do you mean, wassup? Tonight we're having dinner with Billie and Tee-Tee, remember?"

"Aw, damn." He faked like he'd forgotten. "My bad. I forgot, babe."

"It's okay," she replied, looking down at her feet. What Dylan really wanted to say was, "How could you forget? We've been talkin' about this all fuckin' week!"

"Well, just meet me at the restaurant then," she said. "I'll take a cab."

"I'm already runnin' late, babe. Why don't you just go by yourself?"

Breathing in deep, Dylan told herself, *Don't spazz out on him. Don't spazz out.*

"But everybody's expecting you," she reasoned, gathering her emotions.

"I know, but I gotta go home and take a shower, then find something to wear, and besides that, it looks like it's about to rain."

"Are you fuckin' kidding me, State? You know how important this is to me," she spat, heated.

"I understand that, but they're your friends. It'll be cool wit' just y'all."

"And a partridge and a pear tree," Dylan shot, fed up. "Whateva, State. I'll go by my damn self, but before I do, let me introduce you to someone I just met. His name is dial tone." She hung up before he could respond.

How could I have been so stupid, to believe that things would be different the second time around? His ass ain't gon' never change. And why the fuck is it raining? Dylan thought as she exited the cab. Pissed off beyond belief, she placed her head down and ran into the lounge. The sound of Jay-Z's song "Run This Town" bombarded her eardrums. To the left of her, sitting on large black leather ottomans, were Billie and Tee-Tee.

"Where in the hell have you been?" Tee-Tee rolled his neck with an attitude. "We've been waiting on you since seven-thirty."

"I'm sorry." She walked over and air-kissed both of his cheeks. "I had to catch a cab."

"Why? Where is State?" Billie placed down her drink, ready to go off.

Dylan wanted to tell the truth. She wanted to admit that Billie was right and that State hadn't changed. But to see the looks on their faces and to hear the "I told you so" would be too much for her to take. Unwilling to succumb to defeat, Dylan parted her lips and said, "He's coming. He's just running a little late."

"Oh, 'cause I was gettin' ready to say . . ." Billie picked up her drink and took another sip.

"You look cute," Dylan said to Tee-Tee, trying her best to avoid the conversation.

"Thank you, girl," he responded, doing the cabbage patch. "Let me give you a better view." He stood up and pretended to pose for a camera.

Dylan thought she was out there with the way she dressed, but Tee-Tee took style to a whole 'nother level. He wore his hair in a low and close platinum blonde buzz cut. On his face he donned a pair of Maison Martin Margiela shades and candy apple red lipstick. On his body he sported a red long sleeve fitted shirt, but what set off the top was the fact that it had a trail of fringes on the sleeves. For him to be a man, Tee-Tee had a body most women would kill for, and he loved to show it off. To showcase his voluptuous behind and thighs, he rocked a pair of extra-tight lime green skinny leggings, and purple five-inch stilettos.

"You are fierce, darling!" Dylan gave him two snaps in a circle. "Strangé-strangé."

"Will the real Amber Rose please stand up?" Tee-Tee rolled his torso like a belly dancer. "Don't I look just like her? All I need is a li'l angry brown chipmunk to be my Kanye West."

"You are a mess."

"Oh, I forgot to tell y'all Angel called today," Billie announced.

Angel was Billie's younger brother and Dylan's secret crush. Since junior high they'd been sworn enemies, but beneath the surface lay a deep attraction between the two of them.

"He said that he wanted us to come to L.A. in May for the announcement of his fight."

"All right! I miss boo." Tee-Tee sat back down and smacked his lips.

"Now, you know Angel is Dylan's man."

"Yeah, okay." Dylan side-eyed her. "Where did that come from?"

"My mouth, heffa," Billie challenged. "Everybody knows you got a thang for my brother."

"You must be smokin'," Dylan said, trying to keep a straight face.

"Anyway, what you want to drink?" Tee-Tee asked her.

"I'll have whatever you're having."

The next thing Dylan knew, an hour had gone by and she was on her third cranberry and Absolut. State was nowhere to be found, and her friends were starting to get suspicious. Dylan wondered if the anxiety she felt could be read on her face. Why did State have to go and prove Billie right? More importantly, how could she have been so wrong?

"Okay, let's all quit pretending that it's not a big-ass elephant in the room," Tee-Tee blurted out, unable to hold it in anymore. "Is State coming or what?" He looked Dylan directly in the eye.

"Uhhhh . . ." She paused then shrugged.

"I knew it." Billie chuckled and shook her head. "I told you his ass wasn't shit."

As Dylan felt an ocean of tears burning the rims of her eyes, she glanced out the window and spotted State parking his car.

"There he is!" She pointed and shouted, happy that he showed up.

"Shut the front door." Tee-Tee gasped, surprised.

Yeah, sure he was an hour and a half late, but for him to even attempt to come through on his promise was a huge accomplishment for their relationship. It solidified that what she'd been praying for was coming true. He was trying to change, and this time, he wasn't going to play with her heart.

State opened the lounge door and time stood still. An unexplainable confidence exuded from his skin. He made women hotter than Jamaica. Everything about him was dangerous; but the sweetest thing about him was that he was all hers.

"All right, Clark Kent." Tee-Tee licked his lips.

"Wassup?" State softly kissed Dylan on the mouth.

Being around her and her peoples was like playing with fire, but State couldn't let Dylan look like a fool in front of them, especially Billie. He knew Dylan would be hearing her mouth for weeks if he didn't show up. Plus, he'd hurt her enough in the past to last a lifetime.

"Hi." She spoke and gave a broad grin.

"How y'all doing?" He gave Billie and Tee-Tee a head nod.

"Better now, honey." Tee-Tee winked his eye.

"Sorry I'm late." State ignored him and sat down. "So, what y'all drinkin'?"

"Um, I'm having an apple martini," Billie responded, flabbergasted that he'd actually come.

"Let me get you another one." State signaled a waitress.

Even though she'd secretly hoped he wouldn't show just so she could be right, Billie gave Dylan a warm smile. She hadn't seen her friend smile so brightly in months, and to know that State was the one who made her feel that way encouraged her. Maybe some men could transform themselves into what their woman wanted them to be. Maybe the time they'd spent apart had changed State into a better human being. It was obvious in the way he gazed into Dylan's eyes that he cared tremendously for her. There was no way Billie could hate on that.

Over drinks and sushi, Dylan and her loved ones shared memories, stories, and laughs.

"This has been fun," Billie stated. "I think we should all get together again at my place."

"Really?" Dylan's eyes grew wide with excitement.

"Yeah, really."

Overjoyed, Dylan indulged in what appeared to be the promise of a bright future.

***

After having drinks and sushi, Dylan returned home and immediately drifted off to sleep. She hadn't been asleep three hours before she heard a loud knock at the door. Unable to move an inch, she lay still, praying that whoever was at the door would get the hint and go away. But apparently the person knocking was determined for someone to answer.

Aggravated that she couldn't sleep in peace, Dylan snatched off her Egyptian cotton covers and stomped into the living room. With one eye closed, she peeked through the peephole. To her displeasure, she saw her mother causing the ruckus.

"Oh my God. Not now." She winced. *If I pretend like I'm not here, will she go away?*

"It would be nice if you would open the door. I can hear you breathing." Candy put her eye up to the peephole as well.

"Damn it." Dylan spoke underneath her breath. Reluctantly, she placed her hand on the knob and turned.

"Tyra mail!" Candy yelled with her arms in the air.

"Tone it down!" Dylan imitated her. "What are you doing here so soon?"

"I told you I would be here, so here I am," Candy said as she passed by her and entered the house.

In the year since they last saw one another, nothing had changed about her mother. She still possessed the stunning looks of a beauty queen, but to Candy, the old adage "less is more" wasn't true. To her, the more cleavage you showed, the better you looked, and at four o'clock in the morning, she had them on full display. The burgundy V-neck Juicy Couture shirt highlighted her thirty-six double D breast implants well. Dylan could hardly stare her mother in the eye. Her eyes kept traveling back to her mouth. Candy had so much collagen in her lips that she looked like a blowfish.

"Chunky, can you grab those bags for me?" she said over

her shoulder as she took off her shades and placed down the one Louis Vuitton bag she was carrying.

"Sure." Dylan clenched her jaw tight.

Expecting to see one or two suitcases, Dylan stepped into the hallway to find five. *Now, wait a minute. How long this chick think she's staying?* she pondered.

Once all of the bags were inside, Dylan closed the door behind her and wondered if she had made the right decision on letting her mother stay.

"So this is your new place . . . hmm." Candy twisted up her face while gazing around.

"And what is that supposed to mean, hmm?"

"Nothing. It's . . . very you. I mean, I can't get wit' all these Forever 21–ass colors, but you gotta live here, not me."

"Whateva." Dylan waved her off.

"Okay now, girl, you better watch yo"self. I'm still yo' mother."

Barely, Dylan thought as she heard something bark.

"What the hell was that?"

"Oh, girl, my new doggy." Candy reached down and unlatched the lock on the bag she brought in. "Ain't she cute? I named her Fuck 'em Gurl."

Dylan eyed her mother and wondered if she had not only bumped her head, but lost her mind in the process.

The dog was precious. She was a winter white malti-poo, but that still didn't change the fact that Dylan hated all animals, including dogs.

"Before I flip out, I'm going to take into consideration that you weren't much of a mother to me as a child, so you might've forgotten that I *hate* dogs!" she said with a menacing stare.

"Ugh, you ain't gotta make that face when you talk. It's really not all that cute, and while we're on the subject, what the heck is going on wit' yo' head?" Candy ran her hand through Dylan's hair, which was all over her head. "Hot night? Get it? Hot . . . night?" Candy simulated giving head, with her fist coming toward her mouth and her tongue poking her jaw.

"No, and stop!" Dylan yanked her head away.

"I swear you's a grump in the morning. Just like that ol' ignorant-ass daddy of yours."

I do not have time for this shit, Dylan thought, feeling like she was about to cry. The last thing she wanted to hear was how much she reminded her mother of her deceased father, who Candy hated so much.

"Look, just make yourself at home and keep that damn dog away from me. I'm going back to bed."

"Well, ain't you hospitable. I ain't come here to sleep. I came to kick it. Where the party at?" Candy snapped her fingers and threw her hips from side to side.

"I just got home, Ma. I'm tired."

"It's cool. Go 'head, 'cause I'ma make it do what it do, baby. Just point me in the direction of my friend Jack. I know he round here somewhere." She went into Dylan's kitchen and began opening up the cabinets. "Where he at?"

"Candy! It's four in the damn morning. You don't need nothing to drink."

"Girl, please. Ain't nothing wrong wit' a li'l early morning sip."

"This is not happening to me," Dylan said to herself. "I don't have any Jack Daniel's. All I have is a bottle of Moët and a bottle of Cîroc in the refrigerator."

"Moët?" Candy held her head back in pure disgust. "Who in the hell want some damn Moët? Moët is for muthafuckas who can't handle no liquor. And Cîroc, don't nobody want that 'take that–take that' Bad Boy 2009 bullshit. That niggah Jack'll put some hair on ya pussy."

"All right." Dylan closed her eyes, outdone. "I'm officially over this. When I wake up, we'll go to the store. Is that okay?"

"I guess I got no choice, chunky ass."

"Wait, do you see my heart on my sleeve?"
—Adele, "Best for Last"

Chapter 7

State's downtown high rise apartment was the epitome of a young bachelor's pad, but with swank elegance and style. Although very spacious, it was still inviting. Dylan could most definitely sense a woman's touch here and there. Following his busy work day, State and Dylan often found themselves meeting up there for drinks and quality time. Today was no exception. Now more than ever Dylan needed a place to escape from the world. Being around Candy and Fuck 'em Gurl was driving her insane.

Candy, being the night owl she was, generally stayed up until the wee hours of the morning watching Cinemax After Dark movies with the volume up high. When asked why she watched them, she said she had to keep up with all the new booty moves. It also didn't help much that she listened to the worst music in the world on blast.

Dylan was a connoisseur of hip-hop and R&B. She loved artists like Electrik Red, Ryan Leslie, The Clipse, and J. Cole. Candy, on the other hand, liked that ol' processed, bubblegum music. Every morning, she threw on a mix tape which consisted of Pleasure P, Ron Browz, Lil Boosie, and Dorrough, and popped her ass.

Then there was Fuck 'em Gurl. Dylan had never seen so much piss and shit in her life. Every five seconds she was stepping in piss and then having to tell Consuela to clean her hardwood floors with vinegar so the smell wouldn't stick. For some reason, Fuck 'em Gurl preferred Dylan's bed as a resting place.

Dylan was determined to gain peace of mind and get away from the madness. Thankfully, she had State.

As he sat at his desk taking business calls and Skyping to his business associates in New York, Dylan lay back on his futon listening to the sweet sounds of Aretha Franklin on her iPod. She wished that State would hurry up and finish. They hadn't seen each other in a week. He'd taken an impromptu trip to Ukraine for what he told her was business. She didn't know that State was really there visiting Ashton. Back home, he buried himself in his work. One of his biggest artists was preparing to release his third album, and he had a talent showcase as well as an open house auditions for an all-new boy band he was putting together for a reality show.

Dylan loved seeing him in his element, barking out demands. State was always in such control. She admired that most about him.

With his back facing her, he smoked a cigar. State had just finished wrapping up his Skype session, and was still talking on the phone to C.I. Dylan simply couldn't control herself. Pulling out her earphones, she sat up and began to slowly unbutton her blouse. State had no idea what she was doing behind him. As soon as her shirt was off, Dylan stood up and unzipped her jeans. The cool sensation from the floor sent chills up her spine. Quietly, she sauntered over to him, dressed in nothing but her panty and bra set.

The outline of his broad shoulders heightened her yearning for him. Bending over, she let her arms fall over his shoulders as her lips met with the side of his neck.

"Yo'," he said, caught off guard by Dylan's sudden desire

for him. "Let me call you right back. "What are you doing, miss lady?" he asked as soon as he hung up.

"Nothing." She grinned, making her way around the chair.

Leaning against his desk, she cocked her head to the side and shot him a look filled with lust.

"Wait a minute." State closed his eyes and laughed. "Why don't you have any clothes on?"

"I don't know. I guess I was a little hot." She licked her lips suggestively.

"You wild as a muthafucka, ma."

"Come spend some time with me. I miss you."

"I miss you too, but I got a lot of work to do," he said, scooting up his chair, pushing Dylan out of the way.

"I know you do," she responded, standing up straight, slightly annoyed by his blatant disregard of her. "But I got a lot on my plate too. You know my mother's in town, and she's driving me nuts. Plus, she brought this dog with her who constantly pees everywhere. And do you know that that damn dog peed in my one-of-a-kind Lanvin sandals? And then on top of that, I haven't been gettin' any sleep. I just need a vacation," she groaned, while State ignored her and continued working.

"Are you even listening to a word I'm saying?"

"Yeah, just let me finish this." He focused on the paperwork in front of him.

"What all do you have to do?" Dylan picked up some of the files he had before him. "Maybe I could help."

"Nah, I'm good, but thanks." He took them out of her hand. "This not really yo' thing. Why don't you go sit and be pretty? Better yet, why don't you put back on your clothes and go fix us something to eat or something?"

Is this niggah tryin' to call me dumb?

"How about we both go and find something to eat? Or better yet, order in." She leaned down and tried kissing him again.

"Yoooo, chill out!" He pushed her away, aggravated with her presence. "Go . . . sit . . . doooooown somewhere!"

Shocked by his reaction, Dylan stood paralyzed. She'd already looked past the fact that he hadn't touched the brownies she'd brought over, but for him to be rude to her was downright unacceptable. Sure, he had a lot going on, but hell, he was the one who asked her to come over. She could've easily stayed at home and dealt with Ren and Stimpy, but no; like always, when State called, she jumped. As a matter of fact, every time they chilled with one another, it was always at his place. Anything they ever did was always on his time and his terms. Where they ate, what they drank, where they slept, when they fucked—it was all his decision. Dylan never got a say.

Maybe that was her fault because she never spoke up. Dylan feared that if she did, she'd become less than the perfect woman she'd built herself up to be. Everything about her was supposed to be easy and uncomplicated. Now that she had him, she wasn't willing to rock the boat, but being a Stepford Wife was proving to be too difficult. Any time she went outside the norm of what State wanted her to do or to be, there was a problem.

Never wanting to be viewed as weak or meek, Dylan silently walked across the room and grabbed her things.

"Where you going?" he asked.

"Home." She placed on her shirt. "I'ma let you finish doing your work."

"Yo', my bad for yellin' at you." He reached out and took her hand. "I got a lot on mind, and I guess I'm just a little overwhelmed."

"It's cool, but let me explain something to you. I don't know who you think I am, but please believe you got me fucked up."

"And what's that supposed to mean?" He cocked his head back.

"It means don't you ever in your life speak to me that way again. Just because I'm nice to yo' ass don't mean that you can treat me any kind of way. Do you understand?"

"The question is do you understand how much you making my dick hard right about now?" He positioned her hand on his dick and kissed her lips roughly.

"I'm happy I made you feel that way." She gave him a peck on the lips then stepped back, not in the mood. "But I gotta go." She put on her jeans then slid on her shoes.

"Word? That's really how you feel? I said I was sorry."

"I'll see you later, State." Dylan swung her purse over her shoulder then left without saying another word.

Dylan bobbed her head and sang as she put the finishing touches on a freshly rolled blunt. She'd done enough stressing to last her a lifetime in the last several months. She for damn sure wasn't going to do that tonight. If State wanted to act a monkey, he could do it by his damn self. Dylan for damn sure wasn't beat for his shit. She had her own stuff to deal with, the main one being how to get rid of her mother.

Thankfully, she was gone that night. Candy was out in the streets doing God knows what, but that was all right. As long as she didn't get a collect call from jail, Dylan was more than fine with her being gone.

Once the blunt was rolled perfectly, Dylan lit it and inhaled deeply. A wonderland of magic and pleasure filled her mind.

This was what she needed. This is what she called fun: a night at home alone with the music up high while getting high.

Forget State. His stank attitude was not going to ruin her night. Dylan loved him, but she wasn't going to let him treat her any kind of way. Candy might've been a lot of things, but she ain't raise no fool, and Dylan was determined not be a fool for State again. No, this time she would do things differently.

Scooting back, she leaned her head against the back of the couch and zoned out. One of her favorite songs from Jay-Z's *Blueprint 3* album was playing. "Real As It Gets" featuring Jeezy was her shit. The beat, mixed with the weed, had Dylan feeling like she was on another planet where debt didn't exist, heartache was a mystery, and anything you desired was yours for the taking.

Dylan heard the sound of heavy panting and looked down. To her displeasure, Fuck 'em Gurl was sitting beside her with her tongue out, gazing up at her.

"What the hell are you lookin' at?" Dylan spat as if the dog could answer. "If you didn't piss everywhere, maybe I could like you." She rubbed the top of Fuck 'em Girl's head as the doorbell rang. "Lord, please don't let Candy have lost her key again," Dylan said out loud, getting up. "Who is it?"

"Delivery for Dylan."

Delivery, she thought. *Ooooh, maybe it's the skis and the Tori Spelling jewelry I ordered off of HSN the other night.* She opened the door.

"Hi, are you Dylan?" the deliveryman asked.

"Yeeeeeees." She clapped her hands, excited.

"I have an order of bread, mussels, lobster ravioli, and seafood risotto from Mihali's for you, courtesy of a gentleman named State."

Now, why did he have to go and do something so sweet so soon? she thought. *I wanted to be mad at him for at least another hour.*

"Thank you." She graciously smiled, taking the bags.

The right thing to do as soon as she shut the door would've been to call State and thank him, but the hunger pains in her stomach outweighed proper etiquette. Dylan scurried across the room into the kitchen. The aroma coming from the bags had her drooling, but just as she was about to dig in and do some damage, the phone rang.

"Damn!" Dylan balled her fist tight. Sliding across the floor in her socks, she picked up the phone.

"Hello?" she said, slightly out of breath.

"You still mad?" State asked.

"Maybe."

"Well, I'll say it again: I'm sorry. I never wanted to upset you."

"That's good to know."

"A'ight, Dylan, you can stop actin' like you a part of the *Bad Girls Club*."

"Who said I was actin'?" she opposed.

"Did you get the food?" He changed the subject.

"Yes, so can we wrap this conversation up so I can go eat?"

"You got me fucked up if you think you gon' eat that food without me. Come open the door," he demanded.

"You are not outside."

"Just open the goddamn door."

Hanging up in his ear, Dylan unlocked the door and stared into State's puppy-dog eyes.

"Yo' ass been smoking?" he asked.

"No, my mother was earlier," she lied.

State hated smokers.

"Why you so mean to me?" He reached out and pulled her into him by the waist.

"Yeah, right. I need to be asking you that question."

"You know I love you," he said sincerely while running his hand over the top of her head.

"No, you don't." Dylan looked down at her feet, afraid he might see the hope in her eyes.

"Look at me." He placed his hand underneath her chin and made her look at him. "Don't tell me how I feel. If I tell you something, that's what I mean."

Unable to speak, Dylan choked back the tears and nodded.

"Now tell me you love me too."

"I love me too," she joked.

"Yo' ass can't never act right." State chuckled.

"No, seriously, I love you too."

"I know you do. Now, let's go eat this food. I'm hungry as a muthafucka."

Two weeks later, Dylan and State, along with her mother, made their way over to Billie's for dinner. Dylan was overjoyed. State was really making an honest effort to be involved in her life. It felt good that they were finally building a future together. She was no longer chasing pavements, flying in circles, waiting for her heart to drop.

"How much longer we got to get there? My damn foot fallin' asleep," Candy complained from the backseat.

"Just a few more minutes, Ma," Dylan replied, already feeling a headache coming on.

"Well shit, State, put the pedal to the metal. My stomach startin' to growl, and Lord knows if I don't get something in there soon some shit gon' start coming outta me that might fuck up ya appetite."

"And nobody wants that." State chuckled.

"I don't know why you think she's so funny," Dylan whispered. "Her behavior is embarrassing."

"Be easy." He caressed the side of her face with the back of his hand. "I think she's cute."

"In what way?" Dylan screwed up her face.

"What y'all up there talkin' about?" Candy yelled.

"The weather," Dylan threw over her shoulder, wound up.

"State, this car of yours sho' is nice. Yeah, buddy." Candy traced her index finger across the plush leather seats of his Mercedes Benz G500. "You ridin' like a big shot! You know I used to date a niggah that drove one of these."

"Look, we're here," Dylan announced, relieved.

Once the car was parked, they all got out and headed to the door. A twinge of nervousness ate away at the lining of her stomach as she rang the doorbell. Things could either go extremely well or horribly wrong. She silently prayed that the night would be something she'd never forget.

"They're here," Billie shouted over her shoulder as she opened the door. "Hey, sweetie." She air-kissed Dylan's cheek.

"Hey, girl." Dylan air-kissed her back.

"Y'all come on in." Billie ushered them inside.

"Now, this is nice." Candy glanced around in awe. "Simple and straight to the point. Dylan, you need to take decorating advice from Billie."

"I like my own style just fine." Dylan groaned, taking off her jacket.

"How you doing, State?" Billie spoke coldly, still wary of him.

"I'm good. You?"

"Fine. I'm glad you came. We're going to have a good time. Let me introduce you to a few people." She escorted him into the living area. "These are my girls, Kenzie and Kaylee."

"Wassup?" State smiled.

"Hiiiiiiiiiii." The girls spoke in unison, with huge grins on their faces.

"I'm sure you remember Tee-Tee," Billie said.

"Wassup, man?" State gave him a handshake.

"You don't want to know." Tee-Tee took a quick look down at his crotch then back at State.

"Yo', you trippin'." State quickly took his hand away.

"I'm sorry about that," Billie apologized. "He ain't got not one bit of home training."

"Girl, boo." Tee-Tee clicked his tongue and waved her off. "State, this is my part-time lover, Death Row, but you can call him Bernard."

"Wassup wit' you?" State extended his hand.

"Not a damn thing." Death Row tooted up his nose and wrapped his arms around Tee-Tee.

"Bernard, you so crazy." Tee-Tee kissed him on the lips then turned his attention back to State. "Don't mind him none. He just don't want nobody else to get at me."

"Don't nobody else want you." Dylan shot him a look.

"Miss Candy!" The twins rushed over to her.

"Hey, sugar mamas! I missed y'all." Candy bent down and wrapped them up in her arms.

"We missed you too," Kaylee said.

"Miss Candy." Kenzie tapped her on the shoulder.

"Yes, sugar?"

"Did you bring us a present like you did the last time?"

"I sure did." Candy unzipped her purse. "But first tell me . . . where do you wanna work when you grow up?"

Without missing a beat, the girls screamed, "Hooters!"

"That's what I'm talking about!' Candy cheesed, pulling out two matching Hooters tank tops.

"Whew-whew-whew-whew!" The girls ran around in a circle, lifting up their shirts, revealing their stomachs.

"Ma, are you out of your mind?" Dylan stepped in.

"What? Every child gotta have a dream."

"Can we put 'em on now?" Kaylee begged, jumping up and down.

"I don't think so," Billie said.

"But why not?"

"'Cause I said so." She shot them both a look that could kill.

"Huh. Now you see what we got to put up with." Kaylee rolled her eyes.

"O. O. C. Out . . . of . . . control." Tee-Tee waved his index finger in the air, laughing.

"Laughter only encourages her," Dylan said with a grimace.

"It's okay, girl," Billie assured. "I'll take the tank tops away while they're asleep."

"Don't throw them away, though. Later on tonight they can be put to good use." Dylan winked.

"You are such a whore."

"Shhh. Don't tell nobody."

"Well, look. Y'all have a seat. Dinner will be served shortly," Billie announced.

"Yo', Billie," Candy called out.

"Yes, ma'am?"

"Girl, don't be ma'am-ing me. Shit, I'm too young for all that. Where is my main man Kyrese?"

"With his father."

"Well, I'll be doggone. I wanted him to teach me how to do the Stanky Leg. I already got the Ricky Bobby down pat." Candy did the dance then stopped and did a jailhouse pose for the frame.

"Shoot me now." Dylan looked up at the ceiling.

"Candy, you a mess, girl. Come sit down wit' me." Tee-Tee patted the seat next to him.

Candy happily obliged his request. She absolutely adored Tee-Tee.

"How you been?"

"Baby, if I was any better, I would swear it was a setup."

"I know that's right. So, you seein' anybody?"

"You know, for a minute there I was in between gigs, ya dig? But I been doing this li'l Internet dating thing and done found me a nice li'l fella."

"That's wassup! Now, tell me, what you think of Bernard?" Tee-Tee and Candy eyed him from across the room.

"Aw, baby, you know I likes me a ruff neck, an old crazy muthafucka. A niggah that'll growl at ya. Grrrrrrrrrrrr!" She laughed. "Pull ya weave out! Make you give him a blow job just 'cause you looked at him the wrong way type of niggah."

Tee-Tee fell out laughing.

"And, sugar, that there is all man," Candy continued. "If he wasn't batting for yo' team, I would be all over that lush tenderloin, 'cause homeboy got it going on."

"Miss Candy." Kenzie and her sister came over giggling.

"Yes, sugar." Candy held her hand.

"What's a blow job?"

"That's simple, sugar. Fifty bucks, two dinners, and a watch."

While Dylan tried to pretend she hadn't heard the conversation between the twins and Candy, State checked a text message he'd just received on his phone. After reading the message, he closed his phone and gazed off into space.

"I am starving," Dylan leaned over and said. "I hope we're having steak. I'm in a red meat kind of mood. Are you ready to eat?" she asked State. He didn't answer.

"Hello." She waved her hand in front of his face.

"My bad." State finally looked up.

"Mm-hmm." Dylan pursed her lips and rolled her eyes. "You enjoying yourself so far?"

"Yeah, your people are cool. I mean, yo' mom and homeboy are kinda out there, but it's cool. I'm enjoying myself, but yo' . . . let me go make a run real quick."

"A run where? We just got here, and plus dinner will be served any second now." Dylan searched his eyes, confused.

"I'll be right back." He stood up and placed his phone in his pocket.

"So, whatever you're about to do can't wait until later?" Dylan said in a whisper so no one else could hear.

"Yo', don't start trippin'. I said I'll be right back." He quickly kissed her cheek. "Billie, I have to run out for a quick second, but I'll be back."

"Okay." She smiled then turned her attention back to the chef.

"Please don't take too long," Dylan whispered so no one would hear the desperation in her voice.

"I won't," he assured.

"You will not hurt my pride if right now you decide that you are not ready to settle down."
—Brownstone, "If You Love Me"

Chapter 8

State drove down I-70 wishing that he could rewind time. It wasn't right to leave Dylan at a moment's notice, but when Ashton texted him saying she got a break in her schedule and that she'd be home in less than two hours, he had no choice but to bounce. There was no way he was gonna let his wife come home to an empty house, so he left Dylan to face the critics alone. It was fucked up that her feelings would be hurt, and State knew sooner or later he'd have to deal with the consequences of his actions, but Ashton was his main priority.

For the past four months, they'd done nothing but Skype and talk over the phone. He missed his wife like a fat kid loved cake. He had to have her. And yeah, the fact that he was living two different lives was becoming too hard to juggle, but State wasn't ready to give up either woman just yet. He had an appetite for destruction, and both women were like five-star meals.

Ten unanswered phone calls and an hour and a half later, Dylan sat at the table, unable to eat, with an empty chair beside her. She didn't want to look up from her plate. She was afraid that if she did, the reality of the situation would be too hard to ignore. This all had to have been a horrible dream, because no way had her "boyfriend" left her nearly two hours before at a dinner party and not even cared enough to answer his phone to explain why. That shit wasn't real. Nobody does stuff like that. Oh, but wait, State did. Just like before, he'd build up her trust and emotions only to let her down, and Dylan, being completely head over heels in love with him, fell for it each and every time.

"Honey, are you all right?" Billie wrapped her arm around Dylan's shoulder.

Dylan took her eyes off of her plate and realized that she was the only one left at the table. Everybody else had retired into the living area.

"Yeah, I'm fine."

"You didn't eat any of your food. Are you sure you're not hungry?"

"Uh-huh. I just wanna go home."

"Do you wanna try calling State again?"

"No . . . it's no use. He's not coming back. Can you just have your driver drop us off? I gave mine the night off."

"Sure, sweetie. No problem." Billie kissed her on the forehead then excused herself from the room.

Despite her outer demeanor, on the inside, Billie was pissed. For her friend, she'd let her guard down and accepted State into their inner circle. She'd opened her home to him without reservation, only for him to shit on it all. Billie knew he hadn't changed one bit. State was still the same lying, two-timing, dirty-dick, sack-of-shit niggah in her eyes. She just prayed for Dylan's sake that she'd wise up and realize that State would always remain the same, despite what his mouth claimed.

***

"This State. You know what to do." His voice mail message clicked in again. Fed up and disappointed, Dylan snapped her phone shut. That was the twentieth time that night she'd heard his voice mail greeting. Determined not to call him anymore, she turned off her phone and placed it on the table next to her. A warm spring breeze swept through the window.

Dylan lay on her chaise lounge chair with Fuck 'em Gurl in her lap. Somehow, she'd grown fond of the dog. She didn't even mind when she climbed into her bed to sleep at night. Dylan now expected her to. Rubbing Fuck 'em Gurl's back, Dylan gazed at the sky. The stars that night seemed so close that she could reach out and grab them one by one. Normally, when she was depressed, Dylan baked or perused the racks or Internet for her next can't-live-without purchase, but that night, not even retail therapy would solve her problems.

With the persistence of a stalker she'd tired calling State all night, only to get no answer. A part of her wished she could say his behavior was out of character or unexpected, but it wasn't. State was being typical State. Nothing about him had really changed. Dylan was the one who had tricked herself into believing that this time around, after time apart, his word would hold true. But State was never there for support. He never was around for her birthday or holidays. He never volunteered to meet her family and friends. He never thought twice about her aborting their baby, but yet and still, there was this so-called love, want, and need for her in his heart that he just couldn't escape. None of it added up, and Dylan knew it.

She knew that something major was missing between them. Maybe it was the fact that she loved him more than he loved her, or the fact that he never invested as much of himself into their relationship as she did. Dylan just wished he'd see how much she cared for him. If he recognized that, maybe, just maybe, he would appreciate her more and treat her better.

Dylan lay on her side, curled up in the fetal position, in a state between asleep and awake. The ever present sinking sensation in the pit of her stomach caused her to toss and turn all night. She'd never felt more nervous. It didn't help that her mind kept replaying the night before over and over again like a bad pop song. She just wished that she could pinpoint when and where things went wrong. She and State hadn't really gotten a chance to talk, so she couldn't have been getting on his nerves. Maybe it was Tee-Tee and Bernard. Maybe they were too over the top for his taste. It was no secret that State only tolerated them for Dylan's sake. She knew he didn't agree with homosexuality.

Better yet, was it all too much too soon for him? Committing to Dylan had always been their biggest problem. If that was the case, she would have to let him go, because this time she wasn't looking for a casual affair. She wanted a relationship that was based on truth, not lies. Dylan wasn't the silly little naïve girl she used to be.

She knew State had a lot of girls on his dick. She knew that he would one day get too comfortable and want something new. The trait was in his blood. Every man before him and since him had done her the same way. Dylan had always been able to get a man, but never keep a man. Maybe it was because on the inside she felt that love wasn't in her reach. The basic principle of love started with family, but Dylan never had that need fulfilled. Her own mother didn't love her, so how could a man with no real obligation fulfill that void? She just hated that like before, she'd let down her guard and gave in to empty promises.

Suddenly, a thought came to her mind. State didn't start acting weird until he received that text message. *Hell naw,* Dylan thought, rising out of her sleep.

"That niggah got a text message from another chick and left my ass. I wonder, was it that one chick? I bet it was . . . muthafucka. That got to be it because if it was just business, he would've said so. I swear to God, if that big-head muthafucka played me to the left for another bitch—"

The phone interrupted her conversation with herself. Dylan wondered who it could be. It was eight o'clock in the morning. The only people who called her that early were bill collectors, who she hated. At one point, she was a valued customer, but now all they did was send her hate mail.

Picking up the phone, she checked the caller ID and saw State's name glaring back at her. Every fiber in her being, every beat of her heart wanted to say fuck him, but the big part of her that loved him needed to know point blank what his excuse was so she could somehow feel better.

Before she answered, Dylan decided to play him like he'd played her and not answer his calls. Instead, she pressed ignore and sent his ass to voice mail. State, being the persistent man he was, continued to call back, even though he was fully aware he was being forwarded to voice mail. Ten unanswered phone calls and two voice mail messages later, Dylan felt inclined to finally pick up the phone.

"Hello?" she said with an obvious attitude.

"Are you conscious? What the fuck is on yo' mind?" State barked.

"What do you want, State?" Dylan replied dryly, unfazed.

"Why you ain't answering the phone?"

"Same reason you didn't last night."

"Really? That's how you feel?"

Dylan held the phone and didn't respond.

"My bad about last night. I got caught up."

"I just bet you did," she mocked.

"Straight up." He turned the wheel on his car and pulled away from the curb. "What you got going on today? You wanna go have breakfast or something? We need to talk."

"And the sad part is you're serious." Dylan laughed, amazed. "I'ma call you back." She hung up before he could reply. "He got me fucked up if he think he gon' call me and say my bad and that be it."

She snatched the covers off of her and stood up as State tried calling back again. Dylan stepped out into the hallway and noticed her mother coming out of her room as well.

"Who is that steady callin' here like a goddamn stalker?" Candy rubbed her eyes.

"State." Dylan walked past her and proceeded down the steps.

"Have you talked to him?" Candy followed her.

"Yes," Dylan said, entering the kitchen. "Consuela!"

"Yeezzzz," Consuela answered, irritated.

She'd just started her shift and was already ready to go home.

"Can you please iron the blue Gucci tank top and printed cigarette pants that I have hanging up outside of my closet? Oh, and grab those red Mary Janes and my cream fedora with the blue band around the top. Also, once you're done with that, run me a hot bubble bath, set out all of my makeup and hair products, clean up my room, then start cleaning up downstairs."

"And I need you to run out and get me some Jack," Candy joined in. "And some toenail clippers. My big toe been killin' me."

"*Perras perezoso.*" Consuela rolled her eyes, calling them both lazy bitches.

"So, did he apologize?" Candy took a seat at the kitchen island.

"Kinda sorta." Dylan opened the refrigerator and pulled out a bottle of cranberry-raspberry juice.

"Well, what the hell does 'kinda sorta' mean?"

"It means he said, 'My bad. I got caught up.'"

"You got to be fuckin' kidding me. Now, ain't that a load of monkey shit."

"You want some?" Dylan grabbed herself a glass from the cabinet.

"Yeah, but put a li'l splash of Absolut in mine."

"Why can't you just be normal?" Dylan rolled her eyes as Fuck 'em Gurl ran into the kitchen.

"Girl, please." Candy waved her off. "That niggah there is a trip, but you the damn dummy."

"And how am I to blame for this?" Dylan screwed up her face.

"'Cause if you would've kept that damn baby like I told you to, you wouldn't be having all these problems. Ain't no way in hell I would've had an abortion just 'cause that niggah said he wasn't ready and that he ain't want you to have it. Fuck that! That niggah woulda had to pull that muthafucka up outta me.

"Like I told you before, a baby outweighs er'thang else. You woulda had that niggah in yo' back pocket fo' life, ya feel me? Anything you wanted, before you thought about it you woulda had it, but since you used yo' heart instead of yo' head, guess what you are to him?"

"I'm sure you're going to tell me." Dylan sighed.

"It means that in State's eyes you're still the chick he just got feelin's for, a.k.a. Miss She Ain't Going Nowhere. That baby could've been our meal ticket. State is worth three hundred and fifty million dollars. Dylan, we would've been set fo' life. All them money problems you having right now . . . gone!" Candy pointed her index finger going down. "Wham!"

"Hold up." Dylan waved her hands in the air. "How you know that I'm having financial issues?"

"Girl, get over ya'self. You put all ya damn mail on the refrigerator. Plus I was here one day the mail ran."

"Oh my God, Ma! Do not open my mail!"

"Shit, girl, get ya panties out ya ass and get over it. Instead of gettin' mad wit' me, what you need to be doing is thinkin' about what I told you. Hell, why you think I had you?"

"Are you fuckin' kidding me? I'm outta here. Come on, Fuck 'em Gurl." Dylan left the room, fed up.

"How do you spell Dylan?" Candy yelled behind her. "M-E-A-L T-I-C-K-E-T!"

Decked from head to toe in Gucci, Dylan roamed carelessly throughout Neiman Marcus. Buying stuff she didn't need was the only thing she could think of that would make her happy. The stuff her mother said really had her thinking. Did State only see her as his Miss She Ain't Going Nowhere? Was she the one woman in his life that he knew he could always run to? Dylan certainly hoped not. She hoped that his feeling for her were more than that. But what if her mother was right for a change? If so, she was only setting herself up for failure. The last thing Dylan wanted was to be left on the losing end of the stick again.

Tired of pondering her circumstances she picked up a Judith Leiber clutch purse. Her cell phone started to ring. By the ring tone, she knew it was Billie.

"What up, hooker?" Dylan said.

"Good afternoon to you too, Dylan. Where you at? I just tried callin' your house."

"At Neiman's."

"Yo' ass ain't gon' never learn."

"Whateva. What you doing?"

"About to run out to the museum board's monthly meeting, but I wanted to call and make sure you weren't over there on suicide watch," Billie said, applying another coat of lipstick.

"I'm good," Dylan lied.

"Has he called you yet?"

"Yeah, he did this morning, but I don't even care," she lied again.

"What he say?" Billie was dying to know.

"Same ol' same ol'. He got caught up, his bad."

"Wow, isn't that original."

"Girl, fuck State. Ain't nobody thinkin' about him," Dylan spat, knowing she didn't mean it.

"That's what your mouth say, but how do you really feel?" Billie pressed.

"I mean, it is what is. He played the fuck outta me. And you were right. The same shit he pulled the first time around, he's doing all over again. Except this time, I'm not putting up wit' it. Shit, I deserve more. Plus, I'm just through with the situation." Dylan tried to convince herself.

"I most certainly hope you are, 'cause I don't want to see you get your feelings all into it only to go through the same ol' played-out bullshit all over again. All that carrying on about how much he love you is a bank full of bullshit." Billie put on her heels. "It's obvious that his feelings are not deep into it, 'cause if it was, he wouldn't have done you like that. Hell, I wouldn't be surprised if he was wit' another chick last night."

"Right," Dylan agreed, praying that wasn't the case. Her heart wouldn't be able to take it.

"Anyway, next week I want you to go wit' me to pick out the twins' birthday gifts. You know they love the way they auntie dress."

"Yeah, maybe we'll do lunch afterwards at the Four Seasons," Dylan responded, still trippin' off what Billie said about State being with another girl.

"Sounds like a plan. And, Dylan, please don't spend a lot of money," Billie advised.

"I promise I won't." She crossed her fingers.

"A'ight, well, I'll holla at you later."

"Billie, no one says holla."

"Oh, well, I'll get at cha then." Billie tried to be hip.

"Bye, girl." Dylan snapped her phone shut. "Excuse me." She stopped a salesgirl.

"Yes."

"How much is this?" She held up the clutch purse.

"One thousand five hundred and ninety-five dollars."

"I'll take it."

"I'm tryin' hard to hold on to us,
but it seems like you don't wanna stay."
Ledisi, "Turn Me Loose"

Chapter 9

In order to keep her mind off of State, Dylan avoided any time she would have to spend alone with herself. Instead, she drowned herself with unnecessary shopping, costly massages, social events, and countless glasses of champagne. Escaping thoughts of State worked during the day, but when it was time to go to bed at night, he invaded her mind. Dylan hated every second of it. She wanted nothing more than to erase the memory of his sly grin, the way he pulled her into him at night and held her close. The lips of her pussy ached for the sensual lick of his tongue. She missed riding up and down on his dick while his fingertips toyed with her hard nipples. But all of that was over now. He'd try calling, sending flowers, texting her non-stop, and sending emails, but Dylan was determined not to let him back in her life.

With her signature bob flat-ironed to perfection, Dylan gave herself one last look in the mirror. Pleased with the way she looked, she blew herself a kiss then turned off the bathroom light. Dressed to kill, Dylan grabbed her new $250 shades, purse, and keys, and then left out the door. She was headed to Saks Fifth Avenue to meet up with Billie.

After taking the elevator down to the first floor, she got off and headed to the front entrance, where her driver, Tony, was to be waiting. To Dylan's surprise, Tony wasn't there. In his place stood State, leaning against his Maybach with the biggest bouquet of flowers she'd ever seen. *Shut the front door,* she thought. *I'm not ready for this. I don't even have my speech memorized. Maybe if I turn around and go back inside he won't notice me.* She closed her eyes and eased backward.

"Dylan!"

Goddamnit!

"State." She opened her eyes and smiled. "I didn't even see you standing there. What are you doing here?"

"Shit, you been duckin' and dodging me all week." He approached her. "What else was I supposed to do but swoop down on dat ass? I told you we needed to talk."

"Whatever you have to say is gonna have to wait, 'cause I'm on my way out." She tried to pass him.

"I get it." He stopped her. "You're mad, but what I have to say can't wait. It's real important that we talk today," he stressed.

Dylan could see the urgent need in his eyes. The evil bitch in her wanted to give him her ass to kiss, but the mere thought of him groveling at her feet persuaded her to hear him out.

"You gon' have to make it quick. I'm already runnin' late as it is now," she huffed, glancing down at her Cartier watch.

"Let's go back inside then and have drinks at Café Eau."

"All right." Dylan shot him a look that could kill, but as soon as her back was turned and they began to walk, a wicked grin graced the corners of her lips.

Billie wasn't the type of mom who threw parties; she threw events. For weeks, she'd been planning the twins' birthday soiree. Imagine MTV's *My Super Sweet 16* but for second graders. The twins were only turning eight, but the world famous DJ Clue would be on the ones and twos, spinnin' their favorite tracks. There was to be a runway show, a tattoo artist giving fake tattoos, a performance by Miley Cyrus, and every girl in attendance would leave with their very own custom-designed American Girl doll.

For Billie, planning the party served as a much-needed distraction from her dwindling marriage. Nothing she said or did made Cain want her or remember how much he used to love her. It was like he'd forgotten when they bought his and her towels, how they used to do the Kid 'n Play, or how he used to walk and hold her hand. She'd tried calling him on some peaceful shit to see where his head was at, but Cain didn't have two words for her. He always hit her with "I'ma call you back," but he never did.

Billie had even gone so far as to cook his favorite meal, meatloaf and mash potatoes, and dress up in sexy lingerie, but Cain was so unfazed that he ate, thanked her for the meal, then left without even looking at her twice. Billie prayed to God that being together for the twins' birthday as a family would bring them closer. It was the last trick she had up her sleeve. If it didn't work, she knew her marriage would be over for good.

Once her Audi R8 4.2 was parked, Billie opened the driver's side door and placed her heel on the pavement. Stepping out, she secured her shades over her eyes, shut the door, and set the alarm. Billie walked briskly toward the entrance of Saks. She was running late. She hoped that Dylan hadn't been waiting long.

She didn't even make it to the curb when she was stopped by the hottie bartender that was eye-fuckin' her at The Pepper Lounge.

"Excuse me." He touched her arm gently.

"Yes?" She smiled, placing her hair behind her ear.

"You're Billie Townsend, right?" He swallowed hard.

"The one and only," she gushed.

"Billie Townsend, you've officially been served." The hottie handed her an envelope.

"What the fuck?" She hastily opened the envelope and pulled out the contents.

"I'm sorry," he said before walking away abruptly.

Billie's heart raced a mile a minute. Her hands shook uncontrollably as she unfolded the papers, anticipating her fate. Nervous as hell, Billie focused her attention on every word. It read: *Petition for Dissolution of Marriage.*

A flood of tears covered Billie's eyes like clouds did the sun, causing her vision to blur. In a matter of seconds, her entire world had come crashing down around her, and there was nothing she could do about it. She couldn't cry her way out of it, buy her way out of it, or lie her way out of it. The one thing she'd dreaded most had finally come to fruition. For months she knew the word divorce was in his mind. She just hoped it would never escape through his lips.

More than ever, Billie needed her friend to be by her side. Wiping her eyes, she pulled herself together, inhaled deeply, and entered the store in search of Dylan's shoulder to cry on.

Tranquil jazz music served as Dylan and State's backdrop as they sat at the bar trying their best to avoid what was on each of their minds. It didn't help that Billie kept blowing her phone up with text messages that said **911 Bitch** and **Answer the fuckin' phone. It's an emergency.**

Whatever she wanted could wait. Dylan had to deal with State first. All week she'd been preparing to give him a piece of her mind. There was no way in hell she was going to miss her opportunity. Homegirl was gonna kick his ass and dish out the details later that night over cocktails with Billie and Tee-Tee. She had to make him see that he wouldn't be able to serve up bowls of bullshit as an early bird special whenever he felt like it, and she would not graciously eat it up every time.

By the gloomy look in his eyes, Dylan could tell it was time for his punishment to come to an end. Once State apologized, she'd hit him with a smack of lips, a roll of the neck, and as an added bonus, a finger wag to the face, all while spittin' some of the nastiest shit he'd ever heard. State would take her by the hand and sincerely apologize once more, and then they'd head upstairs to her place. He'd lift up her skirt, bend her over the kitchen sink, and fuck her until she begged for more. But before any of that could take place, one of them would have to speak first.

"So, State." Dylan threw her hair to the side and crossed her legs. "What's going on? You wanted to talk, so talk."

"You just gangsta wit' it. Straight to the point, huh?" he remarked.

"I'm just sayin', what's going on?"

"Look, man." He turned and faced her. "The reason I left like that the other night is because shit between us is just moving way too fast. I mean, I'm kickin' it wit' yo' peoples, and somehow, some way, we ended up boyfriend and girlfriend again—"

"Hold up. What are you tryin' to say?" Dylan asked, completely caught off guard by his choice of words.

"I don't know." He gazed deep off into space. "Maybe we should chill out for a minute."

"You say what now?" She placed her hand up to her ear and eased closer.

"I think we just need some time apart, see if this is something we really wanna do."

"What do you mean, 'see if this is something we wanna do?' I know what I wanna do! You the confused muthafucka," she yelled, causing people to stare.

"Chill," State said seriously. "I know you can't be happy wit' the way things are between us."

"What are you talkin' about?" She eyed him, confused.

Her phone rang again. It was Billie.

"Hold up. Let me get this real quick." She excused herself and stepped off to the side. "Wassup?"

"Where the hell are you at? I been standing in here waiting on you for almost forty-five minutes," Billie spat, aggravated as hell.

"Look, I'ma have to get wit' you another day. Me and State in the middle of something important right now."

"Okay." Billie held up her hand like she was giving the Hippocratic Oath. "Where is Ashton Kutcher, 'cause I swear to God I'm being punked. Either I'm losing my mind, or you're just as dumb as I thought you were. Which one is it, Dylan? 'Cause I know damn well you not throwin' me shade for the same wack-ass niggah that left you and yo' mama stranded in my living room a week ago. Like, are you that fuckin' desperate?"

"Whateva, Billie." Dylan tried her best not to react to the ruthless venom Billie was hittin' her with. "Think what you wanna think. I'll talk to you later." She hung up and placed her phone on silent mode. "Now, what were you sayin'?" she asked, returning to her seat.

"On everything, I'm not tryin' to hurt you, but I feel like you all on my neck, and I need a minute to breathe," State said.

"On yo' neck," Dylan repeated in disbelief.

"Calm down. I ain't sayin' it like that."

"Then what the fuck are you sayin'?" Her nostrils flared.

"Check this out." He took her by the hand. "I love you, I do, but right now I just think I need some space. Plus, I'm gettin' ready to be gone for a minute on business in New York," he lied.

State was really going with Ashton to finish the last leg of her tour.

"What's a minute?"

"A month, maybe two."

"I see." Dylan snatched her hands back, shaking her head.

For the umpteenth time, life was repeating itself; except this time, State was the one letting her go.

"And this is something you really wanna do? 'Cause frankly, this is all coming out of the blue to me." She fished for answers.

"Yeah, I really think this is gon' help us in the end."

"Help you, you mean? 'Cause this for damn sure ain't helpin' me. You fuckin' killin' me right now with this shit," Dylan confessed, barely able to breathe.

"And that's the last thing I wanted to do, but let me just get my head together, be single for a minute. While I'm doing that, you do you and see other people too," State lied again, still unable to tell her the truth.

"So, that's what this whole thing is about? You wanna see other people?"

"No," he groaned. "What I want for us is to be happy. When I get back, we'll see where we're both at and go from there."

At a complete loss for words, Dylan sat silent. State seemed to be running from all of the answers and leaving her with too many questions. It wasn't fair. He needed to let her know what it really was that he wanted to do. He needed to tell her the truth instead of always leaving her alone to fill in the missing spaces of their relationship.

With the curtains drawn shut, Billie sat in bed wondering if she begged and if she cried, would it rewind time? The world around her continued to go on as if she hadn't been shot point blank in the heart. This just couldn't be her fate: long, drawn-out days pretending to be okay, and sleepless nights alone, wondering why.

For the life of her, she couldn't understand why Cain would want to be with someone else. All he needed was her. She was his wife and the mother of his kids. When they'd met, she didn't know his name or that he played ball. None of that mattered. His sly grin and charming ways had her sewed up. Every day she thanked God for him, not knowing that the man she would one day marry would be a crazy fool.

But it was okay. He'd be the one in the end to regret his decision. It was just fucked up that right now she was the one suffering. Cain was out with his new woman doing God knows what, while she lay cooped up with tears the size of raindrops falling from her eyes. It wasn't fair, nor was it her fault that she slipped up and fell in love with an iceberg. And no, her pity party wouldn't last forever, but right now she needed time to piece together the reasons why her marriage had fallen apart.

Maybe it was all the time he spent on the road that tore them apart, or the fact that she drowned herself in numerous charities and committees to forget the fact that Cain hadn't touched her or said he loved her in years. Or maybe it was the fact that Billie didn't know when to pick and choose her battles. Everything Cain did was always a problem. She never made him feel like anything he did was right or good enough. But then again, she nagged and complained so much because he wasn't meeting her needs. At times she hated him for the tears he put on her face, but at the end of the day, he lived inside her heart and in the eyes of their children.

Oh, the children, she thought. Billie had no idea how she would break the news to them. The mere thought of it caused her to break down and cry even harder. As a mountain of pain escaped through Billie's eyes, her bedroom door slowly creaked open.

"I thought I told y'all not to come in here," she yelled, thinking it was one of the kids.

"Calm down, Lucifer. It's me, Tee-Tee." He walked in carrying a tray of food.

For the past week, Billie had been telling everyone she was sick with the flu so she wouldn't have to face anyone. To her, facing the public was like admitting defeat.

"Why the hell you got it so dark in here? Bitch, you ain't a vampire, and this for damn sure ain't *Twilight*." Tee-Tee placed the tray down and walked over to the curtains, pulling them back. A beam of sunshine lit up the entire room.

"Tee-Tee, if you don't close my blinds in ten point two seconds, I'ma jump out of this bed and punch you in the throat," Billie warned.

"I dare you. As a matter of fact I double dog dare you. I want you to jump. Y'all hoes gon' quit fuckin' wit' me. I see now I'ma have to show you better than I can tell you." He snatched the covers off of Billie. "Get yo' ass up! These kids done called *Nanny 911* on yo' ass, and now I'm here, so we about to get shit moving." He snapped his fingers. "And don't try to say you're sick again, 'cause Kenzie's grown ass already told me you been fakin' the funk. Had me thinkin' you over here wit' the swine flu. I done made you homemade soup for nothing. Well, actually, it's Campbell's, but you get the point. Get up!"

"Uh-uh, Tee-Tee. Stop. Not now." Billie turned over and pulled the covers back up.

"What the hell you mean, 'uh-uh?'" He placed his hands on his hips. "The twins' birthday party is a week and a half away, and we gotta go meet with this caterer today at twelve, so what do you want to wear?" He walked to the other side of the room and began to ransack Billie's walk-in closet. "Oh, what about this laROK high-waisted jumpsuit with the back out?" Tee-Tee held up the outfit and spun around on his heels, excited.

When he turned around and noticed Billie's swollen eyes for the first time and the thousands of tears that had rolled down her face and dried, his heart instantly sunk to his feet.

"Honey, what's wrong?" He ran over to the bed and sat on the edge. "What happened?"

"Cain." Billie sobbed uncontrollably.

"Cain what?"

"He wants a divorce." Billie's chest heaved up and down as she continued to cry.

"When you find this out?" Tee-Tee was surprised.

"Last Saturday."

"What the hell? Why you ain't call and say nothing?" He caringly rubbed her forehead.

"'Cause I'm not talkin' to Dylan's funky ass, and I ain't wanna bother you. I know you over there shacked up wit' yo' boo."

"Girl, please. Fuck Bernard. He ain't nobody. You my girl. Remember, hoes before bros," he joked.

"You stupid." Billie laughed for the first time in a week.

"So, you didn't see this coming?"

"Yeah . . . no . . . I don't know." She threw up her hands. "I guess I always figured we would work it out somehow. I mean, we cuss and fight each other all the time, but after a while I figured, hell . . . that's how we love. I ain't never think his ass would buck and leave me, especially not for no white girl. But then time just went on and we stopped making love, and he stopped coming home, and the fighting persisted." She rocked back and forth. "Then I found out he started dating some chick from *Rock of Love*, and Lord knows I couldn't mentally deal with that. So, I made myself believe that as long as he continued to put me in front of that bitch and take care of me and the kids, everything was okay. And besides, I was raised that once you're married, that's it. You don't get divorced, no matter what."

"Who told you that lie?" Tee-Tee looked at her funny.

"My mother. When I was about ten, I started noticing that my father didn't come home on Friday nights, and it was just Fridays, which I found odd. So, of course, me being the nosey person I am, I asked my mother about it, and she said, 'Oh, your father plays poker with his friends on Fridays, and they play pretty late, so instead of him driving all the way home, he just spends the night there.' And so me being young and naïve, I was like, 'Oh, okay.'" Billie shrugged her arms.

"But then a year later, Friday nights started turning into Saturday and Sunday. And I will never forget"—Billie gazed off absently into the distance—"waking up in the middle of the night to my mother hysterically crying into the phone. I wanted to know what was wrong, so I got out of bed and went to her room. She didn't even know I was outside of her door, but I listened to her beg"—Billie's lips quivered as tears streamed down her cheeks—"my father to come home and to not do this to her."

"That's when I put two and two together and realized that my father was seeing someone else. I stayed up that whole night by my mother's door, praying that my father would come home and make my mother's pain go away, but he didn't. He didn't come home until that afternoon. And do you know that when he did, my mother had the biggest smile on her face I had ever seen?" Billie looked at Tee-Tee and shook her head. "It was as if the night before hadn't even happened.

"Years later, I confronted her about it, and she simply said to me, 'My darling, when you love someone as much as I love your father and you make vows in front of God and everyone you love, you never leave that person, no matter what.' And I believed her."

"That's some deep shit." Tee-Tee exhaled.

"I thought that no matter what Cain did to me or no matter what we went through, that I was supposed to stay. And look at where that got me." Billie looked around her room. "Here, lookin' stupid as hell. I can't believe I didn't leave his trifling ass a long time ago."

"Well, Billie, you can't dwell on what you should've did now. Now is the time for you to move forward. You can't stop living because of this. You have three bad-ass kids out there that need you. And if that ain't motivation enough for you to get up, then I don't know what to tell you," Tee-Tee joked.

"You gon' quit talkin' about my kids."

"You know I'm tellin' the truth." He smiled.

"Whateva." Billie rolled her eyes. "Where my goddamn soup?"

"Right here." Tee-Tee got up and set the tray on her lap. "You want me to feed you?"

"If you come anywhere near my mouth, I will stab you."

"Ugh. Why you gotta be so violent?"

"People like you make me violent," she teased.

"So, have you told the kids yet?"

"Nope." Billie took a sip of the soup. "They just think we're into it again."

"So, y'all been over here going at it, huh?"

"Every time we're around each other," Billie said honestly.

"So, Billie, I always wanted to know." Tee-Tee eased all the way on the bed and sat Indian style. "Why didn't you feel comfortable enough to tell me and Dylan what was going on between you and Cain when it was happening? We up here thinkin' y'all Will and Jada. Like, we didn't know nothing was going on, then suddenly you hit us wit' the news y'all was separated. What's the T, bitch? I thought we were bosom buddies." He squeezed his implants together.

"We are." Billie chuckled. "I just didn't want y'all to look at me different. I'm always the one giving you two advice, but if y'all would've known what was going on over here, y'all would've been lookin' at me like I was crazy."

"You got that right." Tee-Tee slapped her thigh.

"I just wish this feeling would go away." Billie ran her hands up her face and began to cry again. "It's like it's a hole in my chest."

"It will eventually. It just takes time." Tee-Tee wrapped his arms around Billie. "But you have to stop crying. Crying isn't going to fix the problem."

Tee-Tee was right. Crying wasn't going to solve a damn thing and Billie knew it. She was stronger than her tears. And no, this wasn't love or life. What she and Cain had was reckless, and Billie deserved more. At this point, she just needed to demand more.

"And it kills me to know
how much I really love you."
—Melanie Fiona, "If It Kills Me"

Chapter 10

The smell of sugary treats baking in the oven brought a smile to Dylan's face for a brief second. She'd been up all morning making homemade cookies in the shape of the Chanel logo for the twins' birthday party that afternoon. She wasn't quite sure if she was still invited due to the fact that she and Billie hadn't talked in more than a week. She'd tried calling her numerous times, but Billie would never pick up the phone. It was obvious that she was still upset with her, but Dylan didn't think she would cuss her out in front of the kids if she showed up unannounced.

Dylan was determined to do whatever it took to get her friend back. She'd let her down in the worst way by allowing her own selfish needs to come first. If she had been the friend she was supposed to be, she could've been there to support Billie in her time of need. Now things were all fucked up. Billie was getting a divorce, and Dylan had lost her best friend and boyfriend all in one afternoon.

Dylan needed the distraction of a bunch of rowdy Bébé's kids to get her focused and back in order. Sure, she hadn't shed one tear, but she and State's impromptu break up in fact hurt her to the core of her soul. They'd talked a couple of times since he'd left, but distance had already begun to put a strain on things. Their conversations were forced and met with continuous silences. After a few minutes, one of them would say they'd call the other back, and that would be that.

Dylan didn't know what to do. State was the man she longed for. She craved everything about him, the bad and the good, and to love him on top of that did nothing for their time apart or her self-esteem. All she could think about was what was it about her that couldn't make him commit? Why was it so hard for him to factor her into his life in some kind of way? She did everything a woman in her position could do. She didn't make him home-cooked meals, but she could bake her ass off, and brought him yummy delicacies all the time. She was never too far from his reach. Whenever he called, she came running. The sex was always on point. The way they contoured their bodies into Cirque de Soleil-like positions, and licked, screamed, and bit one another was wickedly delicious.

Maybe distance will make the heart grow fonder, Dylan tried to tell herself as she opened the oven door. The tray of cookies that had been baking for twelve minutes was done. Bobbing her head, she placed them on top of the stove and sang along to Ledisi's get-to-steppin' anthem, "Turn Me Loose." Dylan couldn't sing a lick, but the words to the song resonated deep with her. "*I called you yesterday, but you're too busy to have a conversation*," she sang.

"Oh my God. How long are you going to listen to this depressing-ass shit?" Candy sauntered into the kitchen with her third glass of Jack in hand.

"Until I'm tired of listening to it," Dylan snapped back.

"Ugh. I don't know where you got to be so damn sentimental." Candy sat at the island. "Last time I checked, I ain't raise no punk. Shit, if the niggah don't want you no more, then fuck 'im. Shit . . . next! There are plenty more rich, successful, fine—did I mention rich?—men out there. State ain't the only baller in the sea. You better throw yo' cast in and hook you a new one."

"Are you finished?" Dylan stopped and looked at her.

"As a matter of fact, no, I'm not. I need to holla at you about something."

All Dylan could do was laugh. She already knew that when her mother needed to holla at her, money would somehow be involved.

"I was wondering when this conversation was gonna take place. I have to give it to you. You waiting a month to ask me for something is a record," she said, cutting out more cookies.

"Watch yo' mouth, li'l girl," Candy warned. "Now, I got this business venture that I want you to back me on. See, I know this guy in Bangkok that's starting this edible dildo company called Eat a Dick. I'm tellin' you, Chunky, it's gon' be huge. All I need is for you to let me borrow fifty grand—"

"Excuse me?" Dylan cut her off. "What did you say? 'Cause I know I didn't just hear what I thought you said. All those face lifts you've had must've affected your speech."

"Listen, now." Candy tried to get her refocused. "I know you a li'l bit in debt, but if you give me the fifty Gs, I can become a silent partner, right? Then I can pay you back all the other money I owe, and then you can pay off some of yo' debt. I'm tellin' you, D, you help me out with this, and we gon' be large and in charge, big boy!" Candy threw her hands up in the air as if to say "Now what?"

"I'm not giving you fifty thousand dollars to blow on yet another one of your get rich quick schemes. Whatever happened to the thirty thousand I gave you to invest in that placenta skin care line, or that fifteen thousand dollar gambling debt you collected in Atlantic City that I had to pay off? Oh, and let's not forget the seventy-five thousand you squandered on creating that wack-ass turquoise jewelry collection. I mean, who in the hell wears turquoise?"

"So, let me get this straight. You're tellin' me no?"

"And the lady with the silicone boobs wins a cookie!" Dylan threw one at her mother.

Quick on her feet, Candy caught it and took a small bite.

"Let me hit you wit' something, li'l girl. I don't need yo' money. Candy got connections. My name run deep in the streets. Instead of sittin' up here sounding like a goddamn cat wailing and baking doggie treats, you need to get like me. See . . . I already learned my lesson. After ya daddy, couldn't no man get in this heart, but you young, dumb, and full of cum. And frankly, you being a li'l bitch right about now." Candy quoted her favorite line from *Menace II Society*.

"Who you think you talkin' to?" Dylan shot, ready to go off.

"You, fire crotch. While you think you know everything, what you need to realize is that love is a magical comfort food for the weak and uneducated. Yeah, it makes you feel all warm and relevant for a while, but in the end, love only leaves you weak . . . dependent . . . and fat." Candy threw the half-eaten cookie back at Dylan. "Now, take that in ya ass!" she spat before storming off.

After all of what her mother said, all Dylan could think was, *I know this bitch ain't tryin' to call me fat.*

Over two hundred of Kenzie and Kaylee's best friends filled the City Museum. The City Museum was an eclectic mixture of a children's playground, funhouse, surrealistic pavilion, and architectural marvel made out of unique found objects. The attractions consisted of enchanted caves, an aquarium, shoelace factory, and more. Kids were screaming, laughing, and running everywhere. It was barely controlled chaos, but

Billie was enjoying every minute of it. Kyrese was off play-ing with his friends, and by the smiles on her girls' faces, she knew they, too, were satisfied. They'd eaten way too much cotton candy and had one too many snow cones, but Billie didn't mind. It was their day.

Although she was keeping a close eye on the kids, Billie was having some adult fun too. All of her family and friends were there, including her industry friends. Big of Big Enter-tainment records and his wife Unique were there, along with their daughter. Tee-Tee's other homegirls, Gray and Heidi, came with their kids as well. For some reason, Gray's uncle in-law Clyde had insisted upon coming too.

Billie didn't mind his presence, but his whole look was bringing down the ambiance of the party. The man looked a hot-ass mess. It was ninety degrees outside and he wore a rhinestone fedora, a pair of 1996 fake Versace shades, tan crocodile blazer, a crushed velvet button-up, polka dot wide leg slacks, and Stacy Adams. Besides his outfit, there was just something off about him. If he decided to act up, Billie was sure to sic security on him.

"Hey, girl!" Mina Gonzalez spoke. She was Billie's friend, a fellow member of the PTA, and owner of Mina's Joint Salon and Spa, where Billie got her hair done.

"Hey!" Billie stretched her arms wide for a hug. "I'm so happy you came. Where is Miss Lelah?"

"Girl, over there playin' already wit' my friend Mo and her kids."

"How's the hubby?"

"Scrumptious. I swear, it's been almost fours years, but ev-ery day is still like Christmas."

"That's what's up. Well, enjoy yourself. I gotta go see what's going on with this magician."

"All right, go 'head," Mina assured.

Billie walked across the room and dialed the magician's cell phone number but got no answer. "If this muthafucka don't get here soon . . ." she said out loud to herself.

"Okay, I need you to calm down, psycho mom. If who don't get here?" Tee-Tee asked, fixing her hair for the third time.

"Get yo' goddamn hands out of my hair." She smacked his hand away. "And I'm talkin' about the magician. He's twenty minutes late."

"Oh, hell no." Tee-Tee twirled his index finger around in a circle. "I know you ain't got my babies no damn magician."

"What's wrong wit' a magician?"

"Girl, magicians ain't nothing but an organized ring of pedophiles."

"You're an idiot." Billie waved off the idea.

"I'm tellin' you. What you think gon' appear when he start doing them tricks? Little girls' panties."

"I'm done talkin' to you." Billie started to walk away only to stop dead in her tracks.

"What's wrong wit' you?" Tee-Tee came up and stood beside her.

"What the hell is she doing here?" Billie and Tee-Tee watched as Dylan and Candy entered the building. "I thought I told you to take her ass off the guest list."

"Stop being like that." Tee-Tee hit her softly on the arm. "She's here now. Just hear her out."

"What up, nephew?" Candy yelled, happy to see him.

"Hey, Auntie." Tee-Tee hugged her. "What you all dolled up for?"

Candy was scantily clad in a hot pink freak'em girl dress that hung low in the front, displaying her full cleavage, and Cinderella stripper heels.

"I'm meeting the fella here I was tellin' you about from the Internet." Candy searched the room for him, but didn't see him.

"That's what's up." Tee-Tee smacked her on the ass.

"So, if you'll excuse me, I got to go find my next victim. But before I do, y'all work this shit out." She pointed her finger back and forth between Billie and Dylan.

"What it do, boo?" Tee-Tee smacked his lips and stared Dylan up and down. "You look hot."

"Thank you." She turned to the side and dipped down then stood back up. "Billie, you look cute too. I love that dress."

Billie didn't even reply. Instead, she shot her a nasty look.

"Okay, I'm just gonna say it." Tee-Tee raised up his hands as if someone had told him to freeze. "I sense a little tension between you two. Bam! It's out there."

Billie finally spoke up. "Bitch, I don't like you."

"C'mon, Billie, stop," Dylan whined. "Be my friend again. I've called you I don't know how many times, sent you flowers, and look." She held up the box. "Since you wouldn't let me do the cake anymore, I made the girls these sugar cookies designed in the shape of the Chanel logo, and even made you your favorite kind of cookie, peanut butter cups."

Billie still wouldn't budge.

"And I'm sorry that I wasn't there when you needed me. That was a fucked up thing to do, and I feel like shit about it. Plus, if it makes you feel any better, State broke up with me."

Billie stomped her foot on the floor. "I told you he was gon' drop dat ass! Yes!" She balled up her fist and thrust her hand back. "I love it when I'm right!"

"Well, damn, you ain't got to be that excited." Dylan pouted.

"Aw, shut up and give me my goddamn cookies. We got work to do." She took the box from Dylan's hand.

"And I thought I was touched," Tee-Tee said, linking arms with Dylan. "C'mon, let's go find your mother."

"Do we have to?" Dylan continued to pout.

"Yes. I wanna see who yo' new daddy gon' be."

To both Tee-Tee's and Dylan's dismay, they found Candy talking to none other than Uncle Clyde.

"This is some bullshit," Dylan said under her breath once she saw what he was wearing.

"Uh-uh, girl," Tee-Tee disagreed. "This shit here is priceless. Auntie! Introduce us to yo' friend."

Candy hadn't been this upset since Dylan crushed her dreams of being a silent partner in Eat a Dick. Clyde looked nothing like his profile picture on Black Planet. On there, he looked like an older, more distinguished Boris Kodjoe. In person, he resembled a played-out Charlie Wilson. And his outfit, well, he might as well have gotten dressed in the dark.

"Clyde, this is my nephew, Tee-Tee, and my daughter, Dylan."

"What it do, he/she?" He raised his hand for a handshake.

"He/she? Who the hell this country muthafucka think he talkin' to? Baby, this right here is all woman." Tee-Tee slid his hand down his body to emphasize his words.

"You ain't got to get all nasty," Uncle Clyde shot back. "I'm just callin' you what ya is, boy!"

"Oh, let me get the hell away from this coon before I have to cut his ass." Tee-Tee marched off, having had enough.

Unsure of what to do, Dylan reluctantly spoke. "How you doing, Clyde?"

"Better now that yo' fine-ass mama here. Shit, she make me wanna spend all my bill money." He roughly grabbed Candy by the waist, pulling her close.

"On that note, it was nice meeting you. I'ma let you and Candy have some alone time."

"Uh-uh, Dylan. Stay." Candy quickly took a hold of Dylan's hand.

"Uh-uh. That would be rude." Dylan sneered, snatching her hand back. "See you two lovebirds later."

"Now that broke-ass is gone, why don't me and you creep off in the back and do what big boys and girls do?" Clyde kissed Candy's cheek. "Girl, you look better than a bacon and egg sandwich."

"Um, let me go get a drink first." She swiftly got away before he could object.

An hour later, the magician had arrived and performed. The kids had danced, got fake tattoos, and custom-designed their own dolls. Candy had given Clyde her ass to kiss and moved on to a new target, and Billie had put off singing "Happy Birthday" as long as she could. Cain still hadn't showed up, and after lying and telling the girls he was coming for two hours, Billie decided that she was done with protecting her kids from their father's negligence and inconsiderate behavior. They'd have to learn the truth about him sooner or later.

With everyone gathered around, she lit the candles on their cakes, which were designed in the shape of a purse and a high heel shoe, and started singing. Halfway through the song, Billie got the second biggest shock of her life. Out of the corner of her eye, she noticed Cain creeping in, hand in hand with his reality-show-reject girlfriend.

"Oh, no he didn't," Dylan whispered, spotting him too.

"Oh, yes he did," Tee-Tee said.

"You gon' be okay, friend?" Dylan asked.

"Mm-hmm."

Billie couldn't wait for the song to be over so she could chin-check his ass. Homeboy had a lot of nerve bringing his skank whore to her kids' birthday party. It was cool if he didn't want her anymore. Billie would have to learn to deal with that, but to subject Kyrese, Kenzie, and Kaylee to his immature, idiotic actions was a whole 'nother story.

"Happy birthday dear Kenzie and Kaylee . . . Happy birthday to you! Yay!" Everyone clapped and cheered.

"Handle this for me." Billie handed Dylan the knife to cut the cake. "I'll be right back."

Chunks of vomit rose in her throat with each step she took. What Cain saw in that woman she'd never understand. The chick looked like her ass was on steroids. Everything from her stringy pony hair to her surgically enhanced face was fake, and she dressed like an overgrown, confused Barbie. Billie could not believe that she had the audacity to even come, let alone wear a pink cowboy hat, rhinestone choker, pink-and-black leopard print bra, black tutu, and patent leather thigh-high boots.

"Have you lost your fuckin' mind bringing this trick here?" she hissed.

"Yo', don't come to me with that mess," Cain barked. "Me and you ain't together no more."

"You've made that abundantly clear."

"Billie, I know that this is hard for you," the confused Barbie chimed in. "But today is about your kids—"

"Hold up." Billie placed the palm of her hand in the woman's face. "Who the hell told you to speak, trashbox?"

"See, I'm not puttin' up with this," she said to Cain. "You better check her."

"Who gon' check me, boo?" Billie rolled her neck and looked her up and down. "Nobody told you to come, trashy."

"I told her to come, and whether you like it or not, you gon' have to deal wit' it," Cain shot.

"Over my dead body." Billie rolled her neck and crossed her arms over her chest.

"Well, you better call the coroner, 'cause she ain't leaving," he challenged.

"Daddy!" The twins ran over, interrupting their showdown.

"Wassup, bubble butts?" He scooped them up into his arms.

"What took you so long?" Kaylee questioned. "We've been waiting on you."

"I had to pick up my friend Becky. Say hi."

"Uh-uh. We don't know her." Kenzie screwed up her face.

"And why she so orange?" Kaylee added.

"Okay, let's go get some cake and open presents." Cain ignored their comments. "Daddy got something special for you. C'mon, Becky." He signaled with his head.

"You better hurry up. Your owner's callin' you," Billie spat.

"Ugh. Whateva." Becky rolled her eyes.

"Whateva to you too!" Billie shot back.

"You okay, girl?" Dylan rushed over.

"I can't stand his stupid ass."

"Just remember that today is about the girls. You've planned an amazing party. Don't let him ruin that."

"You're right." Billie placed her hands down to her side and exhaled.

There was no way she would allow Cain to continue to bring her down. No person would have that much control over her life. Fuck him. Unfortunately for Billie, even after she pulled herself together, things continued to spiral out of control. She'd just finished watching the girls do their annual father and daughter dance with Cain to the song "Pretty Wings" when she was graced with even more bad news.

"I cannot believe this," she scowled, snapping her cell phone shut.

"What now?" Dylan asked.

"Miley Cyrus's publicist just called and said she can't make it."

"Are you kidding me?"

"Huhhhhh, this is some bullshit. The girls are going to be so disappointed when they find out." Billie paced back and forth, trying to figure out what to do.

Unbeknownst to her, Uncle Clyde had overheard her entire conversation and decided to take it upon himself to fix the problem. Before she knew what had hit her, he had stepped onto the stage and moved toward the mic.

"'Cuse me! 'Cuse me!" He tapped the microphone with his index finger.

"What the hell?" Billie looked around frantically.

"Oh my God." Gray placed down her plate.

"Gather 'round, children. Gather 'round," Uncle Clyde instructed.

All of the kids rushed the stage, excited. Once everyone was settled, Uncle Clyde decided to speak.

"Mic check. One, two, one, two." He placed his mouth directly on the microphone, causing a loud, screeching nose to echo through the room. "My bad. Check it. My name Uncle Clyde. Now, I got some bad news. Riley Cyrus will not be performing this evening."

"Awwwwww." The children groaned.

"But don't fret. Uncle Clyde is here to save the day. See . . . love is a many splendid thing." He walked from one end of the stage to the other. "But when the person you done used all yo' daytime minutes on 'cause she wanna have phone sex play you out like chump"—he locked eyes with Candy—"for a Richard Gere-lookin' muthafucka, you tend to look at things a li'l differently. So, listen closely, kiddies. You might learn something. DJ Blue, hit it!"

"No-no-no-no-no-no-no-no!" Billie said in horror as the music cued.

Suddenly, the sound of a piano and a beat machine filled the air. Uncle Clyde, with his head down, dramatically stepped up to the mic and took it off the stand. Everyone was silent as he began to the sing the eighties classic, "The Beautiful Ones" by Prince.

"*You make me so confused.*" He pointed angrily toward Candy then fell down to the floor. "*Do you love me, baby? I gotta to know . . . I gotta know.*" He ripped his shirt open and exposed his chest hair. Licking his index finger, he toyed with his right nipple. "Yeahhhhhhhhhhhhhhhhhh!" Uncle Clyde screamed while lying on his stomach, humping the ground.

"Mommy, he's scaring me," Mina's daughter Lelah whined, hugging her tight.

"Am I dead?" Billie asked helplessly.

"I don't know, but this has to be the funniest shit I have ever seen in my life." Dylan laughed hysterically as Uncle Clyde did a pelvic thrust.

"Billie, I am so sorry." Gray took her by the hand and apologized. "I told Gunz I didn't want to bring him. He's always embarrassing us."

"At this point, I don't even care anymore." Billie shrugged her arms, giving up.

"Let me go get his crazy ass off this stage," Gray said.

"Can somebody just grab my purse for me?" Billie tried her best not to cry. "I got a bottle of Jack in there."

"Oh no, Billie, not you too," Dylan pleaded.

"This is what my life has become. My husband has left me for a—" Billie pointed in Becky's direction. "Hell, I don't even know what that is." She started to cry.

"Don't cry, friend." Dylan took her into her arms and held

her close. "That fake-ass Ken and wannabe Barbie ain't even worth it. And neither is State punk-pussy ass," she said as tears filled her eyes. "Fuck all of them."

"Okay, this is just too much." Tee-Tee jumped in, stopping their pity party. "Y'all two are the loneliest, saddest hoes I have ever seen in my life, and frankly, I'm sick of it. Suck it up, bitches, and I know just the way you can do it. We're going to L.A.!"

"I've lost the use of my heart, but I'm still alive."
—Sade, "Soldier of Love"

Chapter 11

Los Angeles was the home of the young and the reckless, the rich and the famous, Hollywood hot spots, media moguls, and paparazzi run-ins. Some called it Silicone Valley, while most referred to it as the land of broken dreams. The drug of choice was fame. Hollywood starlets frequented The Ivy, but only ate salads and drank Chardonnay. If you didn't drive a BMW, Benz, Ferrari, or Porsche, you were nobody. Texting on your BlackBerry was considered the normal form of conversation.

At the age of fourteen, Dylan, her mother, and husband number four lived there for two years in the ever famous 90210 zip code. Dylan loved the city of bottle-blondes and Mystic tans. She made it her business to visit at least twice a year.

That Thursday afternoon, Dylan, Billie, and Tee-Tee sat lounging by the pool at The Beverly Hills Wilshire Hotel. Dressed in their flyest swimwear and floppy hats, they sipped on margaritas and did what they know best: talk shit and gossip. But neither Dylan nor Billie could pretend that good conversation, dope outfits, and potent drinks could replace the never-ending ache in their hearts.

Although with her closest friends, Billie felt more alone than ever. Her entire life was changing before her eyes, and there was absolutely nothing she could do about it. It was a harder pill than she thought she could swallow, to come to the conclusion that Cain just didn't love her anymore. *Like, damn, is this really the end?* she pondered, taking a sip from her glass.

Dylan sat beside her, rubbing sunscreen lotion into her skin, gazing absently at the pool, wondering what State was doing at that exact moment. The last time they spoke, two days after the party, she asked how things were in New York. He said rainy and humid. The next thing she knew, he placed her on hold, and after waiting longer than normal, she finally said fuck it and hung up. Like Billie, she too wondered, *Is this really the end?*

"Um, don't y'all be sittin' over there gettin' quiet on me," Tee-Tee warned, wagging his finger.

"Will you shut up? Ain't nobody doing nothing," Dylan shot back as her cell phone started to ring. After checking the ID and seeing that it was Morty, she decided not to answer.

"Right?" Billie co-signed.

"So, you gon' sit up there and look at me wit' me a straight face and say that y'all ain't over there cryin' on the inside thinkin' about those two low-lives in yo' life," Tee-Tee debated.

"No!" they both said at the same time.

"Yeah, right." He sucked his teeth. "And next you'll be tellin' me the sky is green. And where in the hell is yo' brother?"

"Here he come now." Billie pointed to the left of her.

Dylan and Tee-Tee looked in that direction and spotted Angel. It was as if he were walking in slow motion. The sun seemed to be making love to his smooth skin. Everything from his hair follicles down to his toenails was on point. Sex instantly came to mind when looking at him. He looked like the type of niggah that would fuck the living daylights out of you and afterward, never even call again. Angel was the type of man every woman dreamed about.

Everything about him screamed heartbreaker and to keep it moving, but Dylan couldn't take her eyes off of him. He was six feet two, 220 pounds, with skin the color of golden wheat grass. A blue Yankees cap cocked to the left covered his bald head, but enhanced his eyes, which were like pear-shaped diamonds. His full and luscious lips were surrounded by a perfectly lined and trimmed goatee. But the best part of him was his rippled physique. His body was perfectly crafted, like the African warrior he was, and the tribal tattoo that began at his right wrist, traveled up to his shoulder, down his muscular chest, past his pelvis, and ended at his foot, enhanced it even more. Dylan would never admit it, but there were times when she fantasized about him while playing with herself at night.

"Good God almighty." Tee-Tee clutched his chest. "Boxing does a body good."

Angel was dressed in nothing but a pair of white-and-blue striped swim trunks and flip flops. A cotton towel was draped leisurely over his shoulder.

Thoughts of how his tongue would feel on hers entered Dylan's mind. Her cheeks burned bright red, but then a twinge of jealousy hit her when she saw a makeup-less, long-legged Selita Ebanks look–alike reach out and take his hand. The chick was disturbingly good-looking to the point that Dylan felt intimated.

"What's good?" Angel greeted them.

"I didn't know you were bringing someone." Billie cocked her neck back, standing up for a hug.

"Hi to you too, Billie." He gave her a warm hug. "Billie, this is Miliania. Miliania, this is my sister, Billie, better known as the ignorant one."

"Also known as the ass-kickin' one." Billie stuck out her hand for a shake. "Hi."

"Hi." Miliania giggled, unsure if she was playing. "How are you?"

"Fine, and you?" Billie responded skeptically. She was very overprotective of her brother. Gold diggers, skanks, and skeezers seemed to come out of the woodwork once they heard the words heavyweight champion.

"What up, Tee?" Angel shortened his name. He refused to call a grown-ass man Tee-Tee.

"Hey, baby doll." Tee-Tee pursed his lips and winked.

"Buckshot." Angel finally looked Dylan's way. He'd tried to avoid eye contact for as long as possible because he knew once he laid eyes upon her, the feelings he'd tried to bury for years would arise. Dylan was nothing like the women he was usually attracted to. She was self-centered, materialistic, and superficial, yet behind all of that was an innocence that not even designer duds could hide.

"That joke is as old as . . ." She pointed, trying to come up with something quick.

Fuck, she thought.

Pissed that she couldn't come up with anything to say back, Dylan said, "Aw, go kill ya'self, why don't you."

"Dylan!" Billie gasped.

"What?" She rolled her neck. "He started it."

"So what? That was mean. You need to apologize."

"I'll apologize all right . . . when hell freezes over. You know I'm sensitive about the back of my damn head."

"Calm down. I was just fuckin' wit' you and you know it." Angel laughed. "Whoever fixed your hair did a good job, Halle Scary."

"See!" Dylan threw her hands up, frustrated.

Angel enjoyed every second of it. He loved getting Dylan riled up. He couldn't stand that she always tried to play it so cool, like nothing affected her, when really she was as sensitive as a toothache.

"Well, look, it ain't no more lounge chairs over here, so we gon' head over to the other side of the pool," Angel said. "I'ma get at y'all in a minute, though."

"You make sure you do," Billie replied as he walked away. She wanted to find out as much info as she could on Miss Miliania.

"It's good to see you, though, Dylan." He ran his eyes over her toned legs.

"Mm-hmm," she replied, transfixed on his washboard abs. Thankfully, her shades covered her eyes.

"Angel new boo hot." Tee-Tee popped his lips.

"She look a'ight," Dylan scoffed.

"Quit hatin'. You know shorty is a ten."

"More like a six-point-five."

"No you ain't hatin'," Tee-Tee said, surprised.

"Chile, please. I'm far from a hater," Dylan adjusted her hat. "I just call 'em like I see 'em. Plus, I don't trust women who don't wear makeup. I always feel like they're hiding something."

"Mm-hmm. Sounds to me like somebody just took a sip from the jealous cup." He looked over at Billie and winked.

"Tee-Tee, get over yourself. Why would I be jealous of a chick I don't even know?"

"'Cause she got yo' man."

"Yeah, okay." She twisted up her lip. "Homegirl look like a goddamn BMW."

"BMW?" Billie scrunched up her forehead.

"Yeah . . . body made wrong."

"You wrong for that." Tee-Tee laughed hysterically.

"And anyway, to imply that I'm jealous means that I would have to care about who Angel dates, which I clearly don't, so *Boop!*" Dylan pointed her index finger in his face.

"Whateva. Tell it to the mirror later on tonight," he countered.

"Okay, I'll give it to you. Homegirl is cute, but trust me, and we all know this for a fact: Where there is a beautiful woman, there is a man who is bored as fuck."

Nearly two thousand people, including news reporters, television crews, journalist, and fans filled the Staples Center for the official announcement of the Carter vs. Sanchez fight. The historic fight would go down November 14 at the MGM Grand in Las Vegas. Up on the stage, each fighter, along with their camps, sat on opposite sides of the podium with fierce expressions on their faces. The game of intimidation was in full effect, and Angel was the king at it. He was the type where you could never really tell what he was thinking or feeling.

He always played his cards close to the vest. Maybe that was what Dylan found so intriguing about him. She'd never tell him that, though. Angel was the one man who, in her eyes, was off limits. He was her best friend's brother, and if things didn't work out, she'd still have to be around him. On top of that, she'd have to deal with Hurricane Billie if she was the one to break his heart. Besides that, Angel wasn't the faithful type. He'd had more women in and out of his bed than Hugh Hefner. Hell, State was enough to deal with, and she couldn't even keep him under control.

After the promoter announced the upcoming bout, questions were asked and photos were taken, everyone in favor of

Angel headed that night to L.A.'s premiere hotspot, Katsuya, to celebrate. The place was packed and jumpin'. DJ Samantha Ronson got the crowd hyped. Numerous celebrities from Tobey McGuire to J-Lo and Marc Anthony were there.

While Billie and Tee-Tee mingled, Dylan stayed behind and posted up by the bar, not amused by any of it. Sure, she was excited for Angel, but not even her Brian Atwoods suede Lola pumps could get her into a festive mood. She missed State terribly. Any and everything around her reminded her of him.

Across the room, Angel eyed her while finishing up an interview. Normally he wouldn't gave a damn about Dylan pouting in the corner, but that night he felt the strong urge to comfort her. He understood that she had a man, but by the somber expression on her face, it was obvious he wasn't making her happy.

"Excuse me," he said to the ESPN sports reporter.

Dylan was so lost in memories that she didn't even notice him coming her way.

"Why you over here lookin' sad?" Angel spoke in a deep tone.

"Huh?" She looked up from the ground.

"You heard me. You act like somebody stole yo' bike or something."

Dylan smiled and released a slight chuckle. "You know damn well I'm not a bicycle kinda girl. And anyway, why do you care? Shouldn't you be somewhere hemmed up with what's her name?" Dylan patted her thigh, trying to conjure up the memory.

Angel turned his head and laughed.

"What?" She eyed him.

"You know damn well you know her name," he challenged.

"Yeah . . . okay," Dylan sneered, nervous.

Angel was dangerous. He possessed the kind of beauty chicks stupidly threw away their pride for, and Dylan would gladly be one of them. The custom-made grey Hermes crocodile skin hooded jacket, white tee, distressed jeans, Air Yeezy sneakers, and Vestal Plexi watch screamed big bucks, but it was the man inside the clothes that made Dylan so wet.

"But nah, for real, I know when something up wit' you. Dylan Monroe never plays the bar. What City do to you now?" He gave her a broad grin.

"First of all, his name is State, and how you figure I'm trippin' off of him?"

"'Cause every time I see you, you always got a fucked-up-ass look on your face. I mean, ain't you tired of lookin' sad? You too pretty for all that. Don't let a muthafucka take yo' smile away, especially not a lame-ass niggah like him. And I know we ain't never been that close, but I figured you were smarter than that to let a muthafucka keep on hittin' you with the same tired bullshit time and again, but I guess not." He shrugged.

Infatuated by the fact he thought she was pretty, but pissed that he'd tried to play her on the sly and call her stupid, Dylan stood up straight and said, "Like always, you have no idea what you're talkin' about. Me and State are better than ever. As a matter of fact, once he gets back from New York, we're thinkin' about moving in together," she lied. "So why don't you mind your fuckin' business. Go listen to 'Eye of the Tiger,' drink some egg yolks, or whateva weird-ass shit you steroid-using muthafuckas do."

"Word?" Angel massaged his chin. "That's wassup, but let me hit you with this real quick." He got into her personal space. The sweet smell of his breath tickled her nose he was so close. "You can feed yourself, my sister, and anybody else that nonsense, but I know wassup." He looked down at her titties, which were pressed up against his chest, then back up to her face.

"Oh, really," she challenged.

"Just by lookin' at you I can tell that you ain't benefiting from being wit' him. If you can look me in the eyes and tell me you gettin' what you need in your heart,"—he placed his lips up to hers and lightly ran his thumb across her right nipple—"in your head . . . in the mall . . . in the bed, I'll never say anything else to you about him."

Dylan was speechless. In a matter of seconds, he'd reduced her to a mere puddle. Angel had conjured up feelings in her she never felt before. She'd never felt sexier and more wanted. Angel was all the medicine she needed to cure her broken heart, but she belonged to another.

"Since you can't answer that, does he spank you?" His lips softly touched her ear. "Does he bite . . . does he hit it just right? Is the sex so good that he make you wanna cry?"

Dylan wanted to speak. The words were there but refused to come out. Angel wasn't playing fair. He knew that she was going through changes. With each second that went by and he touched her body in forbidden places, she grew more and more confused.

"That's what I thought." He stepped back. "And while you tryin' to flip off at the mouth with a bunch of foul shit, you need to go holla at your so-called man, who you thought was in New York."

"What?" Dylan blinked her eyes, confused.

Angel pointed with his head in the direction of State, who was holding a conversation with someone. A mixture of emotions hit Dylan at once. A part of her was overwhelmed with joy and excitement to see him. It had been almost a month since she last saw his face. But then the other side of her wanted to know what the hell he was doing in L.A. He hadn't told her a damn thing about coming there. *Oh my God! How romantic! He's here to surprise me,* she thought.

"If you'll excuse me . . ." Dylan shot Angel a look over her shoulder while walking away.

With the meanest walk she could muster up, she headed over in State's direction. Questions needed to be answered, and only he could give them to her. He had no idea she was coming toward him. The sight of him captivated her like the last time they ran into one another at the Wale concert. Dylan didn't understand why, but she was a slight bit nervous. For some reason, being in State's presence always made her feel off kilter.

"Hey, you." She tapped him on the shoulder then stepped into his view.

State was at a loss for words. In a million years he never expected to see Dylan.

"Hey." His voice cracked. Frantic, he searched the room nervously.

"I wasn't expecting to see you here." Dylan eyed him suspiciously.

"Me either. Wassup wit' you, though?" He hit her playfully on the arm.

"Umm . . ." Dylan stalled, wondering what was going on with him.

State was behaving totally out of character. Since she spoke, he hadn't even looked her in the eyes, and he seemed extremely jumpy.

"I mean, what are you doing here? The last time I talked to you, you were supposed to still be in New York," she quizzed.

"Yeah . . . see, what had happened was, uh . . . I heard about the party and decided to come down. But yo', that ain't even important. Me and you need to talk."

Dylan's heart instantly stopped beating. Any time State uttered the words "we need to talk", bad news for her was near. But before he could say what he needed to say, R&B singer Ashton appeared out of the blue. At first Dylan was thrilled to see her, but when Ashton wrapped her arm around State's waist like he was her man and State didn't budge, Dylan began to feel faint. Sister girl was so caught off guard and overwhelmed, she could have sworn she saw a couple of purple monkeys run across the room.

"You gon' introduce me to your friend?" Ashton gave Dylan a once over glance.

"Ashton, this is my homegirl, Dylan. Dylan, this is my wife, Ashton."

Dylan's focus immediately went to Ashton's left hand. To her shock and utter disappointment, not only was there a ring on her finger, but it was the same one Dylan and State had custom designed a year before for her. It all made sense. Ashton was Ash.

Dylan couldn't breathe. With each breath she took, the room got smaller and smaller. It was like she was in a dream where she was falling and wanted desperately to wake up before she hit the ground. *No way is this happening*, she thought, rubbing her forehead. *This niggah is married and his wife is a superstar dressed in one-of-a-kind Dior, and I'm in a lousy T-shirt and jeans.*

"Dylan, you okay?" he asked, concerned, but the words she wanted to convey like *Fuck you, you low down dirty dog* wouldn't come out. Instead, tears stung her eyes, dying to spill out onto her cheeks; but she knew that she couldn't let them see her cry.

"Yo', Dylan," Angel said out of nowhere, taking her hand. "Come get a drink wit' me."

He'd seen the entire fiasco go down and had seen enough. Dylan had a mouth on her and oftentimes spoke out of her ass, but he had too much love for her to let her get played out.

With her hand in his, Dylan floated towards the exit. She knew physically it was impossible, but her whole entire being seemed to have teleported to another realm. Her body morphed from human flesh to an oasis of tears. A sea of emotions traveled through her veins. She felt like Jello, like shit, like mud, like a sucka, like a plaything, but more than anything, like a fool.

Angel pushed open the doors and led her outside. The warm air soothed Dylan's skin, bringing her somewhat back to life.

"Oh my God, oh my-God, oh my God." She took her hand from his and massaged her temples as a headache came on.

"Calm down." Angel tried to take her hand again, but Dylan yanked away.

"I will not calm down! That funny-lookin' muthafucka is married, and that bitch has on my ring!" Dylan screamed, crushed.

"I get that." Angel glanced around, embarrassed. "But screaming and making a scene ain't gon' do nothing but get yo' ass locked up. And trust me, you are way too fine to be going to jail. Taxi!" He raised his hand and hailed down a cab.

"How could he do this to me?" She stared Angel in the face as the cab stopped in front of them. "Huh? What did I do to make him treat me like this?" A river of tears fell from her eyes.

"I wish I had the answer to that, beautiful." Angel gazed deep into her bloodshot eyes and brushed back the hair that was stuck to her cheek. "Just go back to the hotel, chill out, and blaze one. I'll be there to check on you in a minute." He held her face and looked into her eyes.

"Okay." Dylan nodded before getting into the cab.

Once she was gone, Angel headed back inside.

"Hey." Billie stopped him. "Have you seen Dylan?"

"I just put her in a cab."

"Why? Is she drunk? Is she sick?" she asked, worried.

"Nah, never that. She just ran into ol' boy she fuck wit'."

"Who, State?"

"Yeah."

"I thought he was in New York."

"So did yo' homegirl. Apparently he and his wife are here."

"You say what now?" Billie placed her index finger behind her ear like she hadn't heard right.

"Yeah . . . dude straight got a wiz, and you won't believe who it is."

"Who?"

"Ashton."

"The tone deaf, non-singing bitch?" Billie's eyes grew wide.

"Yeah, but let me wrap up this shit. I told Dylan I'd check on her in a minute."

"Okay. I'll get Tee-Tee."

Billie marched through the crowd, heated. She'd felt it from the start, but to know for a fact that she was right about State didn't settle well in her soul, mainly because her being right meant that her best friend would in turn be in a great deal of pain. Pissed off, she stopped her search for Tee-Tee and began to look for State instead. She'd tolerated his crap on behalf of her friend long enough, and if Dylan didn't cuss his ass out, she sure in the hell was going to. Billie spotted him and Ashton on the dance floor.

"Excuse me." She interrupted them.

"Yes?" Ashton answered with an attitude.

"Bring it down, homegirl." Billie pointed her finger in her face. "Can I have a word wit' you?" she said to State.

"Sure." He spoke up quickly. "Baby, give me a second." State gave Ashton a speedy peck on the lips.

Once they were out of listening distance of Ashton, State tried his best to speak first, but Billie wasn't having it.

"No! You don't get to speak. For some odd reason or another, my friend has put up wit' yo' tired ass for the last three years, despite you repeatedly treating her like shit!" She pointed her finger into his chest. "But let me tell you one thing: no more. As of today, you two are done. You stay the fuck away from her. Do you hear me? If I even hear about you breathing within a five mile radius of her, I will tell Miss R&B Queen over there everything." Billie gave him a robotic smile. "Do I make myself clear?"

State didn't respond. He simply hit her with a look that said she had him fucked up then walked back toward Ashton. Little did he know Billie was hot on his trail.

"Oh, and by the way," she said to Ashton, "nice ring. A friend of mine used to have one just like it."

"Impossible," Ashton scoffed. "My ring is one of a kind."

"Hers was too."

"Love, you said you'd never go away, but
you're gone, and I'm right back where I used to be,
wondering if you really were for me."
—Ledisi, "I Need Love"

Chapter 12

With her cell phone in her hand, Dylan stepped onto the hotel balcony, trembling. She felt like under her feet was air made of glass. It cut her deep and made her bleed for him. This time, she couldn't give into pretending and forgive him. All she wanted to know was how long had this been going on. Was this some recent shit, or had he been married the whole time they'd been back together? Crying uncontrollably, she dialed his number, but State didn't answer, so she left him a message.

"Like . . . I'm trippin', right, because you couldn't be married. I mean, married? It don't . . . really make any sense. I mean, it's not like we weren't supposed to be seeing other people, but . . . you knew what this is . . . you know what it was," she said desperately into the phone. "Like, just please tell me that this isn't true," Dylan cried, hanging up.

If she had the courage, she would've jumped off the balcony. That's how much pain she was in. She didn't understand how State could treat her so bad when she'd done all she could to love him wholeheartedly. Dylan had never loved a man like she loved him, so how could he discard her feelings as if they were an empty paper bag?

A comforting breeze drifted by as Dylan sat on the ground, leaning her back against the wall. With her knees up to her chest, she cried a gallon of gasoline tears. Each one scorched her skin like hot flames. This was the part of love she hated, when you were left with only you and a bunch of what-ifs, whys, and what-have-I-done-wrongs. It just sucked that from that day forward, Dylan wouldn't be able to cry enough or ponder it enough to get over his unfaithfulness. She just wished she understood why she let him do these horrible things to her. Everyone had warned her that she'd be left in this position, but no, she was so dead set on making State be the man she'd always wanted him to be. Now Dylan was faced with the harsh reality that State was who he'd always been: a liar and a cheat.

Not able to stay in L.A. a second longer, Dylan caught the red-eye out the next day. Billie and Tee-Tee begged her to stay, but she just couldn't. Dylan needed to be alone to gather her thoughts, but the more time she spent with herself, the more depressed she felt. She wanted to face the truth, but living in denial felt better. The entire ride home on the plane, she drowned herself in alcohol. By the time the plane landed, Dylan was past tipsy.

But this was nothing new for her. Dylan cherished the dark part of her life 'cause being in the center of drama was all she knew. She never felt comfortable when things were good. She hated when the sun shone down on her, 'cause it never lasted long.

Inside the security of her home, she placed her bags down by the door. Finally, she could be unhappy in peace, without Billie and Tee-Tee trying to lift her spirits.

"Consuela!"

"Yeeezzz," she huffed, wiping her hands on a towel.

"Can you get my bags for me and take them upstairs please."

"*Sí.*"

"Has anybody called?"

"*Sí.*" Consuela struggled to pick up one of the heavy suit-cases.

"Who?" Dylan asked, going through the mail.

"Jour accountant, Morty."

"What the hell does he want? He's been blowing my phone up the last couple of days."

"I don't know."

"Where is Candy? Let me guess. Somewhere around here with a glass of Jack in her hand, drunk like me." Dylan laughed.

"Jour mother not here. She left days ago."

"Left and went where?"

"I don't know. I jus work here, unfortunately."

Perplexed by the news, Dylan headed up the steps to her mother's room. The bed was made and all of her things were gone—clothes, shoes, wigs, fake eyelashes and all. Dylan couldn't decide whether to be happy or sad. She'd kinda gotten used to Candy being around; but with everything that was going on, maybe it was a good thing that her mother had bounced. The last thing Dylan wanted to hear was that she was stupid and "I told you so."

The only thing Dylan was concerned with was Fuck 'em Gurl. She'd really grown to love the dog, and now that she was gone, Dylan didn't know who she'd turn to when she needed comfort.

Jet-lagged and even more depressed, she walked down the hall to her bedroom. Surprisingly, Fuck 'em Gurl lay in her favorite spot on the middle of Dylan's bed. Overjoyed, Dylan ran over to the bed and scooped her up.

"Hey, baby. I missed you." She kissed Fuck 'em Gurl on the head. "You look so pretty."

After playing with Fuck 'em Gurl for a while, she put her down and took off her shoes. Dylan was tired as hell. The bed was calling her name, but so was the blinking red light on her phone, letting her know she had a voice mail message.

Pressing the number one, Dylan learned she had fifteen new messages. Silently, she prayed that at least one of them was from State.

"I don't even see why I continue to call you," Morty barked into the phone. "It's obvious that you don't care about your finances, but I still don't understand why you withdrew such a large sum from your account without consulting me first. I mean, c'mon, Dylan. Fifty thousand dollars!"

After that, Dylan didn't hear a thing Morty said. She hadn't withdrawn fifty grand from her account, but she knew who did. Pissed, she disconnected the call and dialed her mother's cell phone number. To her surprise, the number was disconnected. All of her life, Dylan associated her mother with a lot of things—a lousy mother, a freeloader, and a drunk—but never did she think she was a thief. Dylan didn't think that things could get worse, but obviously they could. In a matter of twenty-four hours, she'd been dumped by State and robbed by her own mother. If things didn't get better quick, Dylan was sure to snap.

Dylan couldn't go anywhere, listen to anything, or see anything without being reminded of State and Ashton's secret marriage. Each entertainment show, radio show, newspaper, and magazine was talking about it. Dylan was in hell. All of her favorite gossip mags had them on their cover. They'd given interviews with everyone from *US Weekly* to *OK!* magazine. Even Page Six in the *New York Post* had an article on how they kept their love a secret, and details on their quickie wedding in Vegas.

Dylan knew it was suicide to feed into the media frenzy, mainly when she knew State wasn't the dedicated, faithful husband he'd made himself out to be. Yet something in her needed to read every word that was written, so she got dressed and headed to the newsstand down the street from her building. Feeling exposed to the world and like every person walking down the street knew her shame, she stood at the newsstand dressed all in black.

Heavy raindrops poured down from the sky, tap dancing onto her Louis Vuitton Arc en Ciel umbrella as she glanced at each cover, each one killing a piece of her soul softly. State and Ashton appeared so happy and content with one another. Dylan wished she hadn't noticed, but State gazed into Ashton's eyes the same way he did hers. She felt lower than low. In the past two weeks, she'd died a hundred times. All she wanted was closure, but State was too selfish to give it to her. He wouldn't answer any of her calls.

"Ma'am, you've been standing here forever," the loud Italian gentleman behind the stand said. "Are you gonna buy something or what?"

"Yeah, I'll take anything that has him on it." She pointed.

After buying six magazines and five newspapers, Dylan hailed a cab and headed to Billie's apartment. There was no way she could face this alone. On the way there, she couldn't help but flip through some of the gossip rags. Suddenly, it all made sense. State was never going to make her his wife. Dylan was a well-known party girl, but by no means a star. State was all about enhancing his career, and Dylan had nothing to offer to make it better. Ashton, on the other hand, did. She was a successful singer—although she was notoriously talentless—a

Cover Girl model, and a media darling. Making Ashton his wife only made his social status go up. The public adored the alliance of two mega stars.

Minutes later, Dylan was at Billie's door.

"Explain to me why you're dressed like a cat burglar," Billie asked, letting her in.

"I'm in mourning," Dylan said in passing.

"Seriously, Dylan, it's the end of June and you have on a scarf draped over your head and tied under your chin like an old lady, Chanel shades— which, by the way, are fabulous—a leather jacket, leggings, and rubber boots. I know you're in pain, but what the hell is wrong wit' you?"

"I feel like I'm dying, that's what's wrong. The man I thought I would one day marry is married!" Dylan sat at the kitchen island and plopped her head down. "And here I am dressed like a goddamn spinster, while they're off globe trotting the world, planning their second wedding."

"Stop talkin' crazy. You are far from a spinster." Billie packed the kids' afternoon snacks.

"These magazines don't say so." Dylan reached into the bag and pulled them all out.

"What in the psycho hell?" Billie said, shocked. "Why did you go and waste money on this crap?"

"'Cause I wanted to know what was going on." Dylan took off her shades.

"You already know what's going on. That bastard fucked you for four months while he was married to someone else. You were his side pussy, and I'm sorry to stress it like that, but it is what it is."

Dylan understood everything that Billie was saying, but coping with that realization was another thing. What State did was unforgiveable, but there was no way they could've dealt with each other for three years and he not feel anything for her—or could he? In her mind, there was no way he could love Ashton more than he loved her. *He just couldn't*, Dylan thought as a single tear trickled down her face.

"Oh, baby cakes, don't cry." Billie ran over and comforted her.

"You just ever felt like your whole body couldn't breathe?"

"Every day," Billie replied sincerely.

"I just thought that one day he would stop with all the games and finally be ready to commit, and we would get married, or hell, I would be married to somebody by now." Dylan sobbed.

"Honey, the reason you're not married yet is because you're not single. Just 'cause you're technically alone"—Billie made air quotes with her fingers— "doesn't mean anything. You still hung up on State, Billy, Bob, Larry, and Joe. You haven't given yourself the opportunity to be set free in your heart by any of them. When God sends you your mate, there has to be room for him, and right now, Dylan, you don't have not an inch of space for someone new."

"Wow." Dylan sat back, shocked. "I never knew that."

"You would if you would take the time to listen to me sometimes."

"I do listen to you," Dylan objected.

"No, you don't, and another thing I wanted to tell you. And, Dylan, please believe I'm not tryin' to hurt your feelings, but how you gon' be somebody's wife?"

"What you mean?"

"Being a wife is more than 'I love you.' Love ain't gon' keep a roof over your head, the lights on, and food in the refrigerator. You have to be able to contribute. As a woman, you should know how to cook, clean up a house, and budget your bills, and honey, you ain't there yet. If you got married today, what would you be bringing to the table, mascara and lipstick? You're in debt. You don't even have a savings account, Dylan. You got a shit load of stuff that you need to take care of sista-girl before you even think about being somebody's wife. Quit tryin' to be a diva and prepare your mind to be a wife."

Dylan wanted to object, but what her friend was saying was the truth. "You're right. I do need to grow up. I just don't wanna." She pouted.

"Whateva. Now, pull it together before you make me cry. We are too fly for this sad shit." Billie rubbed her back then resumed packing.

Taking her friend's advice, Dylan gathered her emotions and stopped herself from crying. Then suddenly, she heard a loud thump come from upstairs.

"What is all that noise?"

"Girl, Angel and the kids." Billie closed the refrigerator.

"You didn't tell me he was here." Dylan shot up.

"I didn't know you would care." Billie looked at her funny.

"I don't." Dylan untied her scarf.

"Mm-hmm."

With lightning speed, Dylan reached inside her purse and pulled out her compact mirror. "Fuck!" she screeched, looking at herself. Her hair was flat, and she didn't have on a stitch of makeup.

Bitch, are you insane? You don't leave the house lookin' like Cruella Deville, she thought, hearing the sound of heavy footsteps coming down the steps.

Unable to do anything else with herself, Dylan swiftly combed through her hair with her fingers and tucked it behind her ears as the kids and Angel entered the kitchen.

"Heeeeeeeeey!" She waved her hand.

"Hey, Auntie." The twins and Kyrese hugged her tight.

"Where y'all going dressed like ninjas?"

"Karate practice," Kyrese replied.

"Oh, 'cause I was gettin' ready to say Kung Fu chic is not in."

"So, the kids the only people you see?" Angel leaned his shoulder against the wall.

Of course I see yo' big fine ass. Got me over here cummin' on myself, she thought, admiring the white V-neck T-shirt, jeans, and six-inch wheat-colored Tims he wore. The only jewelry he rocked was a thin gold chain with a straight razor pendant on it, and a Nooka watch.

"Cómo estás?" she joked in a deep voice, mimicking Wendy Williams.

You are such a dork, she thought. Angel couldn't help but laugh at her silliness.

"Come on, y'all. We gotta go." Billie raced around the island, grabbing the snacks and her purse. "Oh, I forgot. The kids' books are due today at the library. Dylan, on your way home can you drop them off and pick out the ones that I have on this list?"

"Sure. It's not like I have anything else to do."

"Thanks, hon." Billie kissed her on the cheek. "And throw that mess away," she said, referring to the magazines. "Angel, I'll see you later." She closed the door behind her.

"Well, I guess I'll be heading out then." Dylan got up.

"You mind if I go wit' you?" Angel asked.

"I don't care. It's a free country."

"Let me go grab my keys real quick." He turned to go back up the steps, unaware that he garnered the kind of beauty that set him apart from the rest of the mere mortals of the world.

***

After a five-minute ride in Angel's Aston Martin DBS Coupe, Dylan and Angel roamed the aisles of the children's section at the St. Louis City Main Library. Dylan didn't frequent there often, but when she did, she always marveled at the stained glass windows and stenciled ceilings. So far, she and Angel had found every book on Billie's book list but one. Angel was so close behind her as they walked that she could feel his warm breath on the nape of her neck. The sensation soothed her and made her nipples sprout like buds.

"So, how long are you gonna be in town?" she asked timidly.

It was the first time in years that she and Angel had been left alone with one another.

"Until August. After that I gotta start training."

"What made you come home anyway?"

"You."

"Me?" Dylan spun around, astounded. Her back was now facing one of the shelves.

"I had to make sure you were all right."

"You act like I was on suicide watch," she joked.

"Nah, I just knew that you were hurt. What ol' boy did to you was fucked up."

"Yeah, well, I'll get over it eventually," Dylan said, unsure if she really could. "Speaking of boos, how does Miscellaneous feel about you hoppin' on a plane and leaving her behind?"

"Miliania." He smirked. "Didn't have anything to say. She's not my girl, and she knows that."

"Well, at least you're honest with her. Hey." She thought of an idea. "Since you're not exclusive with anyone, why don't I set you up on a blind date?"

"I'm good." He quickly nixed the idea.

"Why?"

"'Cause it's honestly a waste of time."

"Why you say that?"

"You know the whole dating thing—dinner, movie, whatever . . . it's really not my thing. I always find myself not really that interested, but still I can't help tellin' the chick how beautiful she is anyway."

"Wow, I'm shocked." Dylan crossed her arms. "You finally dropped the Rico Suave act and said something real."

"It happens sometimes. You just gotta stay on your toes."

"Frankly, I'm tired of standing on my tippy toes. I've been doing it for the last three years of my life. I think I'm starting to get corns," she joked.

"Check it. I'm gonna say this once and one time only, so listen closely." He took her by the arms. "Fuck State."

"What? So, that's it?" Dylan looked at him like he was retarded. "Just fuck him? I'm not even allowed to be pissed off."

"Nah, never that." He shook his head. "You're allowed to be pissed off. Any person in their right mind would be. But maybe if you'd relax half a second and stop lookin' so hard for the right man, then maybe . . . just maybe . . . you just might wake up one morning next to the right one."

"Yeah, 'cause it's just that simple," she scoffed. "This is real life we're talkin' about, Angel, not a Lifetime movie of the week."

"I didn't say it was easy, but you gotta realize that you're the one in control over the situation."

"And how is that?"

"'Cause you're mad smart, and you're crazy beautiful so now what?"

"What the fuck are you talkin' about? I'm a total airhead." Dylan laughed.

"Stop talkin' like that. You're one of the great ones."

"One of the great ones, huh?" Dylan smiled. "So, you're just sayin' all this to make me feel better, right? 'Cause that's what people do in situations like this, right?"

"Which is bad why?"

"It's not bad. I just wanna know do you mean anything that's coming out of your mouth?" She hoped and prayed to God that he did.

"I don't just say shit to be saying it. I mean, I do talk a lot of shit, but generally I mean what I say."

Dylan's heart fluttered like a butterfly. No man had ever spoken to her that way. They'd told her that she was fine and that she was sexy, but never smart. Dylan didn't even think she was that intelligent. She would never be the type of chick that wore white and didn't spill something on it, or didn't stutter when nervous. Yet with Angel, she felt elegant and surrounded by his embrace.

Face to face they stood, exchanging breaths. An animalistic chemistry filled the air surrounding them. Dylan's chest heaved up and down in anticipation of a kiss as he placed his hand on the shelf next to her face. This was it, the moment she'd fantasized about for years. Angel came closer, his lips inches away from hers. Unprepared but born ready, Dylan closed her eyes and puckered up her lips; but Angel didn't kiss her. Instead, he whispered into her ear, "I found the book."

Umm . . . okay . . . do I crawl into a corner now or later? she thought.

Opening one of her eyes, Dylan sucked her lips back in and watched as Angel stepped back with the book in his hand.

"Well, that was awkward." She stood up straight and opened her other eye. "I hope you don't think that I was . . . you know . . ." she laughed nervously. "Ain't nobody trippin' off you, Angel. I mean, you fine and all, but let's not get ahead of ourselves."

"So, you think I'm fine." He grinned.

"Man, please." She waved him off, laughing too.

Dylan was totally unaware that the layers of bullshit she'd built up for years were fading away, revealing who she really was at the core: a shy, insecure woman who just wanted to be loved.

"Let's go check out these books so I can go home. Wendy Williams is about to come on."

"If I tell you how I feel, will you keep
bringing out the best in me?"
—Sade, "Sweetest Taboo"

Chapter 13

For days, Dylan had tried her best to stay cooped up in her apartment, but Billie wasn't having it. She knew firsthand how being alone when dealing with a broken heart could lead to depression. She wasn't about to let her best friend go down that rabbit hole, so she insisted that Dylan spend as much time at her place as possible. So far, the constant company of her best friend, the kids, and Angel seemed to work.

Dylan found herself only crying once or twice a day, versus all day long. Her eating habits even improved. Instead of just drinking champagne and eating crackers, she ate three full meals, as well as a snack. Without Billie, Dylan didn't know where she would be. No matter the time of day, whether morning, noon, or night, she was there to talk and lend a helping hand. Often, the two found themselves staying up until the crack of dawn, discussing the relationship drama they'd been through and their hopes for the future. Dylan didn't quite know what her future would hold, but she knew it had to be brighter than her present.

One night, she helped Billie prepare for the museum's annual gala affair. Billie looked stunning in a one-shoulder canary yellow Carolina Herrera gown with a ruffled detail. Her long hair was swept up into a sleek ponytail, and her makeup was absolute perfection.

"Girl, if you don't snatch these kids up a new daddy, you better." Dylan joked, in awe of her appearance.

"Right, 'cause they sho' need one." Billie ran her hands down the front of her dress.

"Seriously, Billie, you look so pretty. You gon' walk up in that muthafucka and shut it doooooown."

"I hope so." Billie grinned.

"Yo'." Angel poked his head into the room. "Your driver's here."

"Okay, I'll be right down. Wish me luck." She turned to Dylan and crossed her fingers.

"Girl, you're gonna do fine on your speech. Just remember, take your time and speak from the heart," Dylan replied as they walked hand in hand down the steps.

"Kyrese, Kaylee, and Kenzie, Mommy's about to leave!" Billie yelled.

"Mama, can I go, please?" Kaylee begged, running into the foyer.

"No, and we already discussed this. This is a grown-up event."

"Well,"—Kenzie stood back on one leg and crossed her arms over her chest—"can you at least bring us a bottle of Moët back?"

"No, I cannot, grown ass," Billie snapped. "Now, y'all be good for Auntie and Uncle Angel."

"We will, Ma," Kyrese confirmed. "I got this. If Tia and Tamara here even think about actin' up, I'll be sure to give them a boot kick to the face."

"You put one foot on my babies and I'ma tombstone ya ass myself," Billie joked, referring to a wrestling move.

"Bet." Kyrese and Billie shook hands.

"On the real, though, y'all call me if you need me," Billie said to Angel and Dylan. "These three can be a handful."

"Will you leave already?" Dylan pushed her out the door.

"Okay, I'm going. Holla!"

"Oh my God." Angel hung his head and laughed at his sister's corniness.

"Does anybody still stay holla?" Billie questioned.

"No! Now, good-bye." Dylan closed the door before she could say another word. "Okay, now, who wants to make cupcakes?"

"Meeeeeeeeeeeeeeeeeeeeeeee!" The kids jumped up and down.

"All right then. Move it, move it, move it!" Dylan ordered, doing her best impersonation of a drill sergeant.

Two hours later, she and the kids, along with Angel, had baked thirty chocolate–chocolate chip cupcakes, played Wii Sports, G.I. Joe, and Barbies. Somehow, the kids ended up falling asleep. This left Dylan and Angel with the task of cleaning up the kitchen and playroom by themselves.

"Yo', I ain't never been this tired in my life." Angel stretched.

"Who you tellin'? Look at my nails." Dylan held up her hands. "They look horrible. I'ma have to go to the nail shop tomorrow and get a fill-in."

"Does everything that comes out of your mouth have to do with clothes, nails, hair, and makeup?" He looked at her.

"Pretty much," Dylan scoffed. "What else is there to talk about?"

"How about something a little deeper?" He fixed the pillows on the couch. "Like politics, religion—shit, something about your life. Something."

"You don't want to talk about my life." Dylan sat on the floor and began picking up the twins' Barbie dolls.

"Actually, I would. I mean, I've known you for what?" Angel sat down and thought. "Over ten years, and I don't really know that much about you. I know that you and yo' ol' bird don't get along that well, but that's about it."

"What more do you need to know?" She tried her best to avoid the conversation.

"I don't know. Whatever you wanna tell me."

"How 'bout I don't wanna tell you nothin'?" Dylan shot, feeling scrutinized.

"Figures." He got up from the couch, knowing she would respond that way.

"And what the hell is that supposed to mean?" She tuned up her face.

"It means that you always run from complicated situations."

"I don't run from shit."

"Except for the stuff that really matters." Angel picked up Kyrese's G.I. Joe tank.

"Since you think you know so much about me, did you know that most of my childhood I spent alone pretending that my Barbie dolls were my best friends? 'Cause I never really could make any real friends, due to the fact that at any moment's notice . . . when my mother felt like it . . . or some niggah played her, we would be moving to the next city, state, or continent.

"I remember one year in particular, I was transferred to about five different schools. That was the worst year of my life. That was the year my mother met Chauncey."

"Who is Chauncey?"

"Oh, one of Candy's many boyfriends." Dylan cocked her head to the side and exhaled. "One night, after him and Candy drank themselves to death, he snuck into my bedroom." Dylan bit her top lip and toyed with a Barbie doll's hair. "He snuck into my bedroom and put his hand underneath my cover and slipped his fingers into my panties. I remember just laying there, unsure of what to do. Like, naturally, the thought of screaming entered my mind, but I was more afraid of whether or not if I screamed Candy would believe that him touching me wasn't my fault."

While Dylan talked, Angel began to realize that the story she was telling him wasn't just a story, but a story one had to earn. For the first time since he'd known her, the superficial wall she'd built came tumbling down.

"Candy called the police, and that night she made the first promise to me that she never kept, that she would slow down on bringing so many men around me. And you know the sad part?" Dylan turned around and looked Angel in the eyes. "I believed her."

For a while, silence filled the room.

"So, that's a small portion of my life. Hopefully now you'll understand why sometimes talkin' about the insignificant,"— she made air quotes with her fingers—"superficial stuff in life feels better than talkin' about the deeper stuff."

"I feel you." Angel nodded his head, appreciating her more. Then a thought crossed his mind. He wondered if any other man had ever made it this far, which is why the next six words from his mouth changed the course of their relationship forever.

"You know, I've never told anybody besides Billie and Tee-Tee that story," Dylan said sincerely.

"I guess I'm not just anyone."

Finally Dylan got the phone call she'd been dying to receive. Unexpectedly, after weeks of hearing nothing from him, State called and asked her out for coffee so they could talk. Dylan wanted to be over it and pretend that an explanation didn't matter, but it did, and she couldn't deny it. So, at three o'clock that afternoon, she entered MoKaBe's coffeehouse. State was already there, sitting at a table for two.

Dylan's heart instantly rose to her throat once she laid eyes on his handsome face. Every emotion she felt and more came rushing back. She felt weak and unsure, like the night Chauncey touched her. What would come of this conversation? Would he say how much he missed her and that he and Ashton were getting a divorce, or would her heart be left splattered on the wooden floor?

"Hey, how are you?" He stood up and gave her a warm hug.

"As good as can be expected, I guess." She hugged him back, drowning in the scent of his cologne.

"Have a seat." He gestured with his hand. "I thought about ordering you something, but I didn't really know what you liked."

Dylan sat down, feeling as if she'd been stabbed in the heart one thousand times. How in the hell, after three years of dealing with each other, could he not know whether she liked coffee? Maybe that was a sign that what they shared wasn't that significant.

"That's fine. I'm not really thirsty or hungry anyway." She placed her bag down beside her.

"So, what you been up to?"

"Ummm." Dylan looked at him, confused.

Is this niggah serious right now? she thought, but ended up saying out loud, "Nothing really."

"Oh, you know I ended up signing that group from Atlanta."

"Really?"

"Yeah, we gettin' ready to start recording soon."

"Look, that's good and all, but let's cut the checks," Dylan spat, tired of being in limbo.

"You mean cut to the chase." He laughed.

"Whatever." She waved him off. "You know what I mean."

She wanted to laugh, but her heart wouldn't allow her to. "Like, how could you go from never wanting to be anyone's boyfriend to being somebody's husband?"

"I know. It fucked me up too."

"Like, I don't think I'll ever fully understand that. I mean, it doesn't make sense."

"I wish I could explain it. All I can honestly say is it just happened," he said, trying his best not to hurt her feelings.

"But that's what I don't understand." Dylan leaned closer. "What happened? All I know is I was pregnant, you proposed, we custom designed my ring, and then one day you changed your mind. Months later, I run into you, you feed me all this bullshit about how much you love me and that this time it's gon' be different and you ain't gon' keep on steppin' on my heart,"—she waved her hand back and forth—"but the whole time you're married. And you never think once of tellin' me." Dylan's lips trembled.

"Damn." State shook his head. "I don't even know what to say. I know what I did was fucked up, but one day it just hit me. I just woke up one day and I knew."

"Knew what?" Dylan asked, dying to know.

"What I was never sure of with you." State stared deep into her eyes.

Silence filled the space between them. Nothing more had to be said. Dylan knew exactly what he meant. State never felt the same way for her as she did for him. Their love was always off kilter, yet the feeling still remained that being with him was the closet to being in a serious relationship she'd ever experienced.

"I guess that's all then." Dylan reached for her purse.

"Don't end it like this." State grabbed her hand.

Dylan looked at him. "Wow." She shook her head and snatched her hand back.

Before State could utter another word of nonsense, Dylan got her bag and left him sitting there. The entire ride home, she sat in the back seat, thankful for having a driver so she could gaze out of the window, wondering how she had been so dumb and naïve to allow herself to fall for a man like State.

Numb to everything around her, Dylan returned home and decided to take Fuck 'em Girl out for her daily walk. She hoped that the fresh air would improve her mood, but Dylan was almost sure it wouldn't.

Dylan walked down Lindell Boulevard, oblivious to her surroundings. She was trapped in her own galaxy, but there were no stars or moon where she lived. Clouds of darkness and dust consumed her. She hated the fact that once again, she'd let State get the best of her. It wasn't fair that he could stop her heart from beating with a single word from his tongue.

Dylan was so lost in her own misery that she didn't even notice that the leash had slipped from her hand. Then she snapped back to reality and recognized that her hand was extended in front of her, but nothing was at the other end of it.

"Oh my God, oh my God, oh my God," she whispered, searching her surroundings for Fuck 'em Girl.

"Fuck 'em Girl!" She placed her hands up to her mouth and yelled. "Fuck 'em Girl!"

Other pedestrians on the street looked at her as if she was a crazy woman, but Dylan didn't care. She had to find her dog.

"Fuck 'em Girl! Come back to Mommy! Come here, baby." Dylan clapped her hands.

Frantically, she walked up the street and turned the corner. She prayed that at any moment she would spot her friend, her companion and comforter, but instead she was left with no dog and the empty sound from the echo of her voice.

"Fuck 'em Girl!" she wailed, with tears flooding her eyes. "Fuck 'em Girl!"

If Dylan weren't afraid of how the people around her would react, she would have just lay out on the sidewalk and cried. Her day was getting worse by the minute. No way in one day could the person she hoped would one day be "the one" tell her that she was never the one for him, and then she loses her dog.

Like, am I being punished? she thought as a couple eating outside at one of the restaurants eyed her in fear. Dylan stood crying hysterically. Tears rolled down her cheeks at the speed rain fell from the sky. On the verge of a nervous breakdown, she retrieved her cell phone from her purse and called Billie.

"What up?" Angel answered.

"Hey, is Billie there?" Dylan sniffed.

"Nah, what's wrong?" Angel asked, noticing the sound of distress in her voice.

"I was taking Fuck 'em Gurl for a walk and somehow I accidently let the leash go, and now I can't find her."

"Where you at?" Angel, without hesitation, got up and grabbed his keys.

"Around the corner from my place, by Liluma."

"Calm down. I'll be there in a second."

"Okay."

Ten minutes later, Angel arrived. Thunder struck the sky as he stepped out of his car. Brisk drops of rain fell onto his face and shoulders. Dylan stood soaking wet. Angel had never seen such a beautiful sight in all his days. The dress she wore clung to her skin like body paint, revealing her hard nipples and the outline of her waist and hips. Every ounce of him wanted to wrap her up in his arms and kiss all of her pain away, but the look of sorrow in her eyes told him that her pain went deeper than just losing her dog.

Unsure of what to say, Angel stood before her with his

hands inside his pocket while the rain made love to their skin. Before he knew it, Dylan's arms were around his waist and her face rested comfortably on his chest as tears from her eyes mixed with the rain. Dylan was so distraught that her chest heaved up and down. She'd cried a couple of times since returning from L.A., but each time, it was just a tear here and there. This was the cry that her body needed to feel whole again.

Angel placed his cheek on the top of her head and held her close to his heart. Nothing else seemed to matter. The world had somehow disappeared. The sound of the rain played as their background. Angel stroked her hair and realized that he could hold her that way forever.

Once Dylan calmed down, she reluctantly pulled away from his embrace and gazed down at the ground. "My bad. I ain't mean to . . . do all that." She wiped the rain and tears from her face.

"What's on the ground?" Angel placed his index finger under her chin and lifted her head. "I'm right here."

"Sorry."

"Stop apologizing."

"Sorry." Dylan caught herself and laughed.

"C'mon." Angel extended his hand.

"Where we going?" She placed her hand in his and noticed how well they fit together.

"To find this dog."

After searching the area for nearly two hours, Dylan and Angel finally gave up and decided to head back to her place.

"Excuse me," a woman said as they approached Dylan's building.

"Yes?" Dylan spun around.

"Is this your dog?"

"Oh my God, yes!" Dylan screeched, running toward the woman.

"I found her in front of my store." She handed over Fuck 'em Gurl.

"Thank you so much." Dylan took her and hugged her tight. "How can I repay you?"

"Your thanks is enough. You two have a good evening." The woman smiled and walked away.

"Mommy's so sorry for letting you go." Dylan kissed Fuck 'em Gurl all over her face.

"You happy now?" Angel smiled, happy to see her happy.

"Yes," she beamed.

"Good . . . now, how you gon' repay me?" He cocked his head to the side and admired her frame.

Dylan swallowed hard, licked her bottom lip, and said, "What you want?"

"What you givin'?" Angel slid his hands back inside his pockets.

Dylan's eyes zoomed in on his crotch. The bulge in his pants let it be known he was working with a python. "A dryer, a hot bath, and something to eat." She refocused her vision back on his face.

"A'ight, I see how you do, but it's cool. I'll take that."

Back inside her apartment, Dylan let Fuck 'em Gurl run loose while she searched the place for towels. She had no idea where Consuela kept that kind of stuff. When it was time for her to bathe, they always seemed to just magically appear. After ten minutes, she found the towels in a closet on the first floor.

"Here you go." She walked into her room and handed one to Angel.

"Thanks. Now I can get out these wet-ass clothes." He placed the towel down and began to undress.

Dylan didn't know if she should turn her head, shield her eyes, or walk away, but the sight of his succulent skin kept her frozen in place. As Angel pulled his T-shirt over his head, revealing two chiseled pecs, and six rows of perfectly crafted abs that she wanted to eat off of, Dylan ran her tongue across her lower lip, wishing that her lip was his.

Then he did the unthinkable and unbuttoned his jeans and let them fall to the floor. The Ken-doll slits that defined his waist called her name. Dylan swallowed hard. *This niggah is not playin' fair*, she thought as he wrapped his towel around his waist and took off his boxer briefs. Thoughts of falling to her knees and taking him into her warm mouth filled her mind. The towel couldn't hide how long, how big, or how thick he was. Dylan wanted all of him. Whatever he desired, she wanted to fulfill with her mouth, lips, and tongue.

"I'm gettin' ready to get in the shower." Angel handed her his things, oblivious to his effect on her.

"Okay, I'll be right here." She pointed to the bed. "Just let me know if you need anything else," she spoke, trying to recapture her breath.

"A'ight." He looked at her strangely.

Dylan held his things in her hands and waited until she heard the sound of the shower running. She didn't have the heart or courage to tell him that she didn't know how to wash clothes. Angel clowning her was the last thing she needed, so she ran down the hall to the guestroom and hung his clothes over the shower door so they could air dry.

"Here." She handed Angel a pair of hoopin' shorts once he got out of the shower. "And by the way, they're mine, so don't go tellin' my secret. Billie and Tee-Tee would clown me if they knew."

"Your secret is safe with me." He smiled, charmed by her sudden girl-next-door appeal.

After hopping out of the shower, Dylan put on an oversized T-shirt and lace boy shorts. Smelling like fresh raspberries, she walked out of the bathroom and found Angel sitting on the edge of her bed, watching television. The hypnotic scent radiating from her skin prompted him to look her way. Dylan was a vision of bliss. When she wasn't trying so hard to be the flyest chick in the room, she looked her best.

She didn't need M•A•C makeup, Roberto Cavalli dresses, or Stuart Weitzman heels to make her beautiful. The almond shape of her eyes, dazzling smile, small waist, juicy thighs, and delicate toes said it all. She was the shit, and none of the stuff she had piled in her closet was needed to prove it.

"Scoot over." Dylan pulled back the covers.

"Why?" Angel eyed her, confused.

"'Cause this is my side of the bed." She grinned.

"My fault." He got up and headed to the other side.

Comfortably under the covers with the lights off, they watched TV. Dylan wasn't sure if she should lay still or pull his dick out and suck it. She'd never, in her twenty-eight years on earth, just lay in bed with a man without some kind of sexual encounter going on. On edge from the silence and sexual tension that filled the room, Dylan pulled out her iPod.

"You wanna listen to some music?"

"Yeah." Angel turned off the TV.

As their legs touched, Dylan gave Angel one end of the earphones and placed the other inside her ear.

"I hope we like the same kind of music," she said.

"Just don't get to playin' a bunch of crazy shit and we cool," he assured.

"Okay." Dylan laughed, turning on Jay Electronica's "Exhibit C."

"A'ight." Angel bobbed his head. "That's what's up. I ain't think you would know nothin' about him."

"Boy, please. You talkin' to a faithful hip-hop head."

"Let's see what else you got."

"Okay." Dylan flipped to Blu & Exile, "Cold Hearted."

"You think you doing something, huh?" Angel turned his head and looked at her.

"I thought I told you I was hot," she joked.

"I bet you ain't got that 'Dreams' by J. Cole," he challenged.

"See, you got me fucked up." Dylan played the song.

"A'ight, Dylan, I fucks wit' you on the music tip. Who woulda knew we had something in common?"

"There is more to me than my love of couture."

"But that's all you show, though."

"You're right." Dylan nodded. "I guess that's something I need to work on."

"Yo', you wanna go to this party wit' me next week? My homey Bigg is celebrating his company's five-year anniversary."

"Yeah, I love a good party."

"Cool. I meant to ask you earlier, but it wasn't the right time. What else was bothering you?" Angel quizzed. "I know losing your dog had you fucked up, but it seemed like it was something more behind your tears."

"I met with State today." Dylan inhaled deeply. "He finally told me everything I needed to know."

"So, what now?"

"Nothing. He's with his wife and I'm moving on." She tried to convince herself to believe her words.

"Good. Who knows what God might have in store for you?" Angel said, speaking of himself.

"You're fly as hell, swagger right, brown skin poppin'."
—Keri Hilson, "Turnin' Me On"

Chapter 14

Never the one to be viewed as a thirsty chick, Dylan opted not to ride with Angel and had her driver drop her off at the Mandarin Lounge. The red carpet was on and in full effect as she made her way down. Everyone wanted a piece of her. The photographers had a field day as she twisted and turned, blowing kisses. There wasn't a camera that Dylan didn't love. She was having so much fun that she almost forgot she had an event to attend. After taking a few more pics, she blew the photographers one last kiss over her shoulder then headed inside.

Anybody that was somebody in St. Louis was there. Cash kings the Roberts brothers, fashionista Kimora Lee Simmons, and Jack Dorsey, the founder of Twitter, were all in attendance. With her brand new $495 neon yellow candy acrylic clutch by Jimmy Choo in hand, which she'd bought with a bad check, Dylan walked the room in search of Angel. She found him on the rooftop, sitting on a couch surrounded by women of all different races. The famous rap line by Biggie—*I like 'em brown, yellow, Puerto Rican or Haitian*—came to mind as Dylan screwed up her face, already annoyed. She did not come for him to be flocked by a bunch of ducks all night. For a split second, she thought about leaving, but Dylan quickly checked herself.

This thing with State and Ashton really had her off her

game. Dylan Monroe wasn't just that bitch; she was the queen bitch. A squawk of desperate, gold-digging pigeons wasn't gonna scare her off. With her shoulders back, she strutted toward Angel like she was the winner of *America's Next Top Model*. It didn't take much for him to notice her. When Dylan entered a room, she commanded attention. Plus, the sleeveless sequined mini dress she wore put every other chick's attire to shame.

Like most women, when dealing with a bad breakup, Dylan decided to do something drastic with her look. The asymmetrical bob she'd been rockin' was a thing of the past. Now she rocked her hair back and the left side of her head shaved low. The rest was cut just above her ear and flat-ironed straight.

Angel didn't look too bad himself. He was casually dressed in a grey cashmere cardigan, white tee, dark blue jeans that sagged low, and gray-and-blue Dior Homme sneakers.

"Wassup, beautiful?" He stood up to greet her with a hug.

"You." She took in his swagger. "I see you shining," she said, referring to the sea of women.

"That's nothing. C'mon, let's get a drink."

Angel didn't even bother telling the women good-bye.

"What you want to drink?" he asked her as they stood at the bar.

"Um, I'll take an X-Rated Flirtini, please."

"Cool. Baby girl," he said to the bartender, "let me get an X-Rated Flirtini and a Hennessy and Coke."

"Anything for you, sexy." The bartender smiled, licking her lips.

"OMFG." Dylan rolled her eyes. "This is ri-damn-diculous." She couldn't stand how chicks went "cuckoo for Cocoa Puffs" over Angel.

With their drinks in hand, Angel and Dylan found a table off in the cut and sat down.

"So, tell me," Dylan spoke up. "Are you always this cool, or do you ever show fear?"

"You have to understand; being fearless is a part of my job," Angel replied.

"So, nothing scares you?"

"Nope." He looked off to the side.

"That's a lie." She pointed her finger at him. "Everybody's afraid of something. Is it spiders?"

"I'm good with spiders."

"Failure?"

"Not a problem."

"Flying?"

Angel turned his head and grinned.

"Oh my God, you're afraid of flying?" Dylan exclaimed with her mouth wide open. She enjoyed seeing a hint of innocence in him.

"Yep, but don't go runnin' your mouth about it."

"I won't; that is, unless you piss me off," she joked.

"What are you afraid of?"

Dylan thought for a moment before speaking. "Calm."

"Before the storm?" he questioned.

"Nah . . . the storm I can weather."

Angel was put off by her confession, but admired her honesty.

"C'mon." He stood up and placed out his hand.

"What?" She looked at him perplexed.

"Come dance wit' me."

Angel didn't have to say another word. The dance floor had been calling Dylan's name since she got there. Three drinks and countless time on the dance floor later, Dylan and Angel danced cheek to cheek to Musiq Soulchild's soul-stirring hit, "Take You There." All of his adult life, Angel had avoided being the rebound guy, because he was a strong believer that how you began things would be how they would end, but unexpectedly, Dylan had captured his undivided attention. With each day that passed, it became increasingly hard for him to ignore the feelings of intrigue that his heart wanted to explore.

Common sense was telling him to take things slow, but the dangerous combination of her beauty and a couple glasses of Hen only put one thing on his mind, which was sex. He wanted to take her back to his hotel suite and lay her body down. He wanted to stare at her body while she was naked. He wanted to make her pussy bloom with every lick of his tongue. He wanted to hear her scream his name while he pulled her hair from behind.

Angel gazed deep into her hazel eyes. Dylan inhaled deeply. Everything he wanted, she wanted more. She wanted to drown in his sweat, to hold onto his back while he grinded in and out of her slowly. Neither could deny the attraction they shared anymore. It was undeniable. Before Dylan knew it, they were back at his hotel room, outside the door.

Angel couldn't wait a second longer. It was time to speed up the pace. He had to have her right then and there. Dylan stood pinned up against the door, helpless. Angel had her feeling things she shouldn't, like could this be the start of something new, and if so, would it last forever? At the same time, she hated that when he whispered in her ear, she came alive, and that she ached for the touch of his hand.

Leaning forward, Angel placed his nose in the crook of her neck. Chills ran up Dylan's spine as she closed her eyes and felt his tongue lightly slide up her neck to her earlobe. She wanted him deep inside her to the point that he would fill her up. On his knees, Angel pushed up her dress and ripped off her G-string.

"What you doing?" Dylan looked on in agony.

"Be quiet," he demanded. "You talk too much." Angel placed her thighs on his shoulders.

Pulling her close, he buried his tongue deep within the lips of her pussy. There was no other place in the world Angel would rather be than inside her dress and between her knees. In a snakelike motion, he swirled the tip of his tongue around her clit until her back arched. Dylan was so aroused that she unknowingly began to rotate her hips.

"Mmmmmmmmmmmmmmmm, yes," she groaned, running her hands up and down the door.

Making sure she knew it was not a game, Angel zoned in her on her clit and eagerly flicked his tongue across it at lightning speed.

"Shit, babe . . . mmmmmmmm . . . goddamn," Dylan shrilled in delight.

Nowhere near done torturing her, Angel gripped her waist and stood up. Dylan held on tight and wrapped hers leg around his back. Turned on to the fullest, Angel passionately kissed her lips. He was done with pretending that Dylan was nothing more than his sister's friend. The connection they shared went deeper, and both of them knew it.

Maybe their first time should've been in the sacredness of a bedroom and not outside his penthouse suite door, but honestly, Angel didn't give a fuck. He'd been waiting half his life for this moment, and nothing was going to stand in his way. Dylan, on the other hand, was scared shitless. She'd done it in a lot of places, but never somewhere as open as a hallway.

Angel could see the fear in her eyes. "You scared?" He antagonized her by dipping his fingers in and out of her warm tunnel at a slow pace.

"No." She moaned as he worked magic on her exposed clit.

"Stop lyin'." He grinned before he tenderly kissed her lips.

Dylan was in heaven. The taste of Angel's lips was as sweet as brown sugar. Enchanted by the friction he was creating in her pelvis, visions of Paris, Italy, Japan, Africa, and Rome flashed before her eyes. By her body movements, Angel knew he had her right where he wanted, so with his thumb, he applied more pressure to her clit. He wasn't going to stop until warm juices trickled down her inner thigh.

"Shiiiiiit, boy." She rubbed the back of his head, feeling lost.

Dylan didn't know whether to sing, hum, beatbox, or rhyme. There was no place for her to run or hide. His hands, lips, and tongue tricks had her trapped.

Ready to dive deep into her abyss, Angel unzipped his jeans. "What you want me to do with this?" he questioned, stroking his hard dick while looking into her eyes.

Unable to resist taking a peek, Dylan glanced down at it. Angel's manhood was long and fat. It was so big she was almost afraid it wouldn't fit.

"Put it in." She trembled, hoping she could handle all of it.

"Put it in and do what?" he asked, repeatedly inserting the tip of his dick deep inside her slit then quickly pulling it back out.

"Fuck me," Dylan said, feeling delirious.

Obliging her request, Angel entered her slit slowly. She felt so good that it took everything in him for his knees not to buckle. Intertwining his fingers with hers, he roughly stroked her middle. Dylan's body quaked with each thrust. Angel loved each second of seeing her so powerless. For once, she couldn't act so tough.

"We still just friends?" he whispered into her ear.

Dylan wanted to play hard and say yes, but she couldn't.

Angel had her all the way open. Anything he requested, she'd gladly give. She'd give him her last dime, fix him grits and bacon, whatever, as long as he didn't take his dick away.

"No."

"That's what I thought." He cupped her chin and kissed her roughly.

At that point, Dylan didn't even care if people in the other rooms heard her. She was dizzy with passion. She was so wet. Sweat dripped from her pores as Angel quickened his pace. He was going to give Dylan's body everything it was worth, which meant all of him. With her arms outstretched over her head, he pounded in and out, thrusting his hips from side to side. Angel was in so deep that Dylan felt as if she were breathing for him. Then suddenly, an orgasm rippled through both of their skin, causing them to call out for God.

Hours later, Dylan sat on Angel's lap, facing him, outside on his hotel room balcony. Strikes of thunder and rain echoed around them, but they were too caught up in one another to care.

Thirsty, Dylan parted her lips and allowed Angel to pour a shot of tequila into her mouth. Angel took a sip as well. With the bottle of tequila in one hand and Dylan's right ass cheek in the other, he gazed into her eyes. She reminded him of heaven. The rain dripping from the sky intensified her beauty, but the thought still remained: should he continue to play the field and live the single life, or dedicate all his time and energy to Dylan?

Angel wished the answer was as simple as one-two-three, but it wasn't. Relationships were a muthafucka, and Dylan had heartbreak written all over her; yet there was something about her that made him want to investigate more.

***

Rays from the beaming sun shone down onto Dylan's face as she lay on her stomach, sound asleep. She and Angel had gone at it all night, kissing, sucking, licking, and biting one another. He'd made her cum five times. State never got her to that point of no return. For him, her cumming once was enough. Dylan opened her eyes and welcomed the morning sun. For the first time in a long while, she woke up with a smile on her face.

Enthused to see Angel, she turned over onto her side; except he wasn't there. In place of him were a pillow and an empty space where he should've been. Wondering where he could be, Dylan got up and put on one of the complimentary robes and went to find him. Dylan searched the entire suite but couldn't find him anywhere. *Did this muthafucka bounce on me?* she wondered.

"I know this niggah didn't fuck me and leave," she panicked out loud.

Oh my God! He got what he wanted and jetted. You are so stupid. She paced the room. *Ain't no niggah that nice. He souped yo' head up and got the butt, and yo' naïve ass fell for it hook, line, and sinker. You ain't nothin' but another notch on his belt*, she thought, heading back to the bedroom to get her clothes. Dylan didn't even make it halfway down the hall before the hotel room door sprang open. Quickly, she turned around and found him walking in, shirtless, with a pair of hooping shorts on and Jordan 23s on his feet. Sweat glistened from his skin.

"How long you been up?" he asked, closing the door behind him.

"A couple of minutes. I thought you had left."

"Nah, I went down to the gym for my morning exercise."

"Oh." She slapped her hand against her forehead.

"Where did you think I was?" He came over and pulled her into him.

"Nowhere." She shook her head, playing off her insecurities.

"You miss me?" He kissed her neck.

"*Un poco,*" she said.

"Oh, okay, you gon' speak in Spanish on me." Angel laughed. "You hungry?" He let her go and grabbed the phone.

"Yeah," she said, speaking of his body and not food.

Every crevice and surface of Angel's physique was mouth-watering. All the chronic in the world couldn't even fuck with him. Once the order was placed, he refocused his attention back on Dylan, who was now sitting in a chair. Angel kneeled down before her and said, "I'm sorry you had to wake up without me."

"It's okay. I'm sorta used to it."

"Well, get unused to it, 'cause from now on, you're spendin' every mornin' possible wit' me." He undid the belt on her robe.

"What are you doing?" Dylan blushed.

Angel pushed open her robe, revealing her supple caramel breasts and flat stomach, and said, "Exactly what you want me to."

Dylan leaned back in the chair and prepared herself for takeoff. She couldn't deny it; since the night before, she'd craved the touch of his lips on her skin. It didn't matter which part. She just had to have him near. Dylan wondered if Angel could feel her heart tremble as his tongue met with the face of her pussy.

Agony was written all over her face. Angel was licking and biting her pussy with reckless abandon. Off into the distance, they both heard a soft knock at the door, and someone saying

"Room service," but Angel didn't stop. He wasn't going to, either. Not until Dylan came.

"Baby, we gotta get the door," she moaned, running her tongue over her top lip.

"Fuck that door," Angel said, sucking on her clit.

"But, baby," Dylan squealed, trying to move away.

"Be still." Angel pulled her back into his embrace.

He didn't care if the person on the other side of the door heard them through the walls. His priority was to make Dylan cum. Angel ran his hands up and down her thighs. His tongue had found solace in the slit of her cream–covered lips.

"Room service." The person knocked on the door again.

Dylan didn't know what to do. Angel held her thighs in his hands so tightly she swore his fingerprints would leave a mark. Besides, the cream lava building was too hard to ignore. At a loss for words, she found herself only able to utter one word as an earth-shattering orgasm neared.

"Yeees . . . yeees . . . yeeeeees . . . yeeeeeeeees . . . yeeeeeeeeeeeeeeeeeeeeeeeees!" Dylan screamed, channeling her inner Beyoncé. "Yeeeeeeeeeeeeeeess . . . yeeeeeeeeeeeeeeess . . . yeeeeeeeeeeeeeeeeeeeeeeeees!"

Pleased, Angel wiped his mouth and stood up.

Coming down from her orgasmic high, Dylan lay limp like a dead fish. She didn't know if she could take anymore. She'd never been that sexually pleased in her life. In less than twenty-four hours, she'd cum six times. But when Angel kissed her on the forehead and said, "Go get in the shower," then winked his eyes, she knew she could handle as much as he was willing to give.

***

The sensual, soothing smell of lavender oil descended through the air and into Dylan's nose. She, Billie and Tee-Tee sat with towels wrapped around their heads in a pool full of mud at The Face and The Body Spa. Spa treatments were a bi-weekly must for the trio, but Dylan didn't need a massage or a facial to make her feel relaxed. The constant attention Angel's hands, lips, tongue, and dick gave her body was all she needed.

"What in the Sam Hill are you over there cheesing about?" Tee-Tee grilled.

Dylan didn't even realize she had been smiling until he said something.

"Lookin' like a deranged-ass monkey. I'm tellin' you, Dylan, don't be over there on no funny shit. I will rise up outta this mud and drop kick yo' ass," he forewarned.

"Boy, ain't nobody even thinkin' about you."

"I'm just sayin'. I ain't never seen you grin this much."

"Normally I don't agree with Tee-Tee, but you have been actin' mighty weird here lately," Billie agreed. "For the last couple of weeks, ain't nobody seen nor heard from you. Are you and Consuela over there making bombs for Candy and State?"

"Girl, please, I don't have to do anything to State or Candy. They're gonna get theirs anyway. Like the Bible says, you reap what you sow."

"Okay, you're scaring me," Tee-Tee said with his hands close to his chest, pretending to cringe. "Since when you get so holy?"

"Shut up." Dylan slapped him on the arm, splattering mud onto his face. "Nobody's all holy. It's just the law of the land. When you do wrong to people, it comes back on you. Now, enough about me. What's going on wit' you, friend?" she asked Billie.

"Hmm, let's see. Cain and I are meeting with our lawyers next week to discuss the prenup."

"Oh. Are you going to contest it?"

"Of course I am. That bitch owes me more than the five thousand a month in alimony we agreed upon. Hell, that alone won't cover me and the kids' monthly expenses."

"That is true."

"I still want to know what the hell is going on with you," Tee-Tee said, looking at Dylan.

"Why it got to be something going on wit' me? A bitch just can't be naturally happy?"

"Not yo' sad ass. Since we were kids you've had something to complain about."

"Well, not anymore. I got good news," Dylan beamed.

"Oh shit! I knew something was up." Tee-Tee flung his wrist. "Yo' ass is back fuckin' wit' State, ain't you?"

"If she is, I'ma slap her so hard both of y'all gon' feel it," Billie shot, seriously.

"How little faith you two have in me. No, I'm not back with State. But I am seeing someone." Dylan bit her bottom lip and smiled.

"Who?" Tee-Tee held his breath in anticipation.

"Angel." She winced, closing her eyes.

"Eww." Billie tuned up her face.

"What you mean, 'eww'?" Dylan popped open her eyes.

"That's like incest."

"No, it is not," Dylan objected.

"I mean, don't get me wrong. I'm happy for you, but eww." Billie shook her body, repulsed.

"All I need to know is where the hose at, 'cause I'm about to chin-check this ho," Tee-Tee spat.

"What I do?" Dylan questioned.

"Don't . . . play . . . coy . . . with me . . . hussy!" He pointed his finger into her face. "You know damn well Angel is my man!"

"Ooooooookay." Dylan couldn't help but laugh.

"And you gon' laugh in my face? Bitch, don't try to act like you don't remember when we was eighteen and we made a deal that I would marry Angel and you would marry Ghostface Killah. Just 'cause we grown don't mean that you can go back on your word."

"Are you for real?"

"No . . . but, bitch, I'm still mad." He folded his arms across his chest.

"Are you mad at me too?" she asked Billie.

"No, of course not. I just know both of y'all, and it's very possible that one of you could hurt the other. And I don't wanna see that happen."

"You have nothing to worry about. I care for your brother a lot. I will in no way, shape, or form hurt him."

Since he began dating Dylan, Angel had grown tired of friends with benefits. He was at a point in his life where he wanted more than a casual one-night love affair. He was sick of second-guessing whether a chick liked him for him or for how fat his pockets were. For years, he'd made it up in his mind that his chances of love were over, but then Dylan came along and changed it. She was everything he always wanted but thought he'd never find.

She was funny, sexy, charming, and quirky—a little misunderstood, but he was, too, in a lot of ways. She didn't care whether the sky was blue or purple, which made being around her enjoyable.

The downside to loving her was that she didn't realize her own strength and abilities. Angel needed a woman who was secure in who she was, and Dylan was not.

Angel also didn't want to be the rebound guy. He didn't feel like dealing with every problem she had with another man. It was obvious every time he looked into her eyes that State was still in the back of her mind. He didn't want to be another man that ran from her life, but opening up was hard for him too. Angel refused to wake up one morning with his feelings shot point blank, but there was something about Dylan he couldn't leave alone. He wanted to show her trust and the beauty of being friends as well as lovers. Unlike past men in her life that just wanted to love her then leave her, Angel wanted to show her something deeper.

"So, you want our children to sleep in the bed with us, or on their own?" he asked as they visited the World Aquarium. So far they'd petted a star fish and touched a stingray.

"Where did that come from?" Dylan replied, caught off guard.

"Me, 'cause I wanna know."

"I never really thought about it." She shrugged her shoulders. "I never even really saw myself as a mother. Lord knows I don't wanna repeat what happened to me with my child."

"It won't if you don't let it happen."

"That's why I don't plan on having any kids," she admitted. "But then again, it would be pretty fun to have a little girl who I could play dress up with. Oh, and I can teach her how to apply makeup and how stores always get new merchandise in on Wednesday, and—"

"I swear, you's a trip." Angel laughed. "First you go from not wantin' to have kids to playin' dress up. Which one is it?"

"I guess in some kind of way I would like to have kids. Maybe that would help me get my life in order."

"I would think you might wanna handle that first before bustin' out a bunch of babies, especially if they're gonna be by me." He smiled deviously.

"Look at you, so sure of yourself." Dylan smiled too. "I'm sure there are plenty other women you would want to reciprocate . . . participate." She snapped her finger, trying to think of the word.

"You mean procreate?" Angel chimed in.

"Yeah, that." She giggled.

"I'll be glad when you realize that I ain't tryin' to be wit' nobody else but you."

Instead of replying, Dylan gazed down at the ground as they walked. She believed Angel when he professed his feelings for her, but at the same time, like Sunshine Anderson, she'd heard it all before.

"Word up, I'm tryin' to give you the safe combinations and all that. Like Fifty say: *Have a baby by me, baby, be a millionaire*," he rapped.

"You silly."

"I'm serious." He stopped walking and took her hand. "Here." Angel reached into his pocket and pulled out a Tiffany box.

"Is this what I think it is?" Dylan asked, petrified.

"No, but open it anyway."

Dylan took the box from his hand, wondering what could be inside. Gradually she opened it. Inside she found a Tiffany bracelet with round and marquise cut diamonds set in platinum. Dylan did a quick estimate in her head and calculated the bracelet had to have cost close to $14,000.

"Angel . . . this is too much." Dylan choked back the tears in her throat. Over the years, she'd fucked plenty of men, but none had ever gone out of the way to do something so special for her—not even State. He'd taken her shopping and on trips, but nothing about that screamed how he felt about her.

"The way I see it, it's not enough." He retrieved the bracelet from the box and placed it on to her wrist.

Dylan wanted to play tough and act like she didn't feel a thing, but from the second they met at the age of eighteen, he had her at hello. He didn't have to buy her diamonds to unlock her heart. Angel held the key from the start. Like Venus and Mars, their love was written in the stars.

"Thank you so much, Angel." She leaned forward and kissed him lovingly on the lips.

"Nah, thank you."

"For what? I haven't done anything."

"Stop short-changing yourself, ma. It's unattractive. You being in my life is enough for me to thank you for."

"This ain't love, this ain't human,
and this ain't real, so what the fuck is we doing?"
—Mario, "Spectacular"

Chapter 15

Coming in the house at four o'clock and five o'clock in ther morning had become the norm for State since Ashton returned home from her European tour. Lately she'd begun to irritate the fuck out of him. He never knew that one person could talk so goddamn much and about the most irrelevant shit. In addition to that, the amount they'd spent on their second wedding—with his money, of course—was ridiculous.

Ashton just had to have the nuptials take place at The Plaza Hotel in New York. Her dress was custom designed by Reem Acra. The three hundred guests that attended dined on food prepared by Wolfgang Puck. Serendipity 3, known for the world's most expensive chocolate sundae, catered the desserts, all dusted with twenty-three karat gold flakes. To cap off the night, there was a fireworks display. The total amount of the wedding was six million dollars.

On top of that, homegirl wanted a new ring because she felt as if the one she had wasn't big enough. State never knew that something he wanted so much could irritate him so bad. The more time he spent with Ashton, the more he realized that he'd made a huge mistake by marrying her. The non-stop arguing didn't help much either.

Before he left the house earlier that day, he and Ashton had gotten into a huge fight over how much money she was spending on redecorating the apartment. Ashton was bleeding him dry. She spent money the way she used toilet paper to wipe her ass. Nothing with her was real or of some kind of substance. Everything was fake and generic.

They didn't even make love anymore. He couldn't even vibe with her sexually. Any type of intimacy between them was strictly for getting a nut off only. And her over the top diva antics were driving him insane. His cousin told him not to let the shit bother him, but how could it not when Ashton was his wife? State didn't even care anymore. Fuck it. He did what he wanted to do. Who cares if he was drunk and the stench of another woman lingered on his skin as he made his way into their bedroom? Ashton would just have to deal with it.

Ashton sat up with her back pressed against the headboard, dressed in a white silk negligee. She'd been calling State's cell phone non-stop for the past six hours. Ashton felt bamboozled, hoodwinked. This wasn't what she committed her life to, limitless nights wondering where her husband was. State was the most heartless man she'd ever met. And yeah, she could have any man she wanted, but at the end of the day, she chose to be with him. There wasn't anything about State that she was willing to give up. Ashton was in it until the end.

"Where the fuck have you been?" she said with a menacing stare.

"Man, take yo' ass back to sleep." State waved her off, stumbling.

"If you weren't so damn drunk, maybe you would see that I haven't been to sleep!"

"And that's my problem because . . . ?" He looked at her. "Yeah, okay."

"I'm so sick of you." she spat, feeling as if she was about to cry.

"Yeah, yeah, yeah. Who gives a fuck?" He took off his shirt.

"We'll see how you feel when I leave yo' ass!"

"Please do!" State placed his hands together as if he were praying. "That's all I've been praying for."

"Maybe I will! It's not like I married you for love anyway," she lied, knowing her cruel words would hurt him as much as he was hurting her.

"What the fuck is that supposed to mean?" State asked, visibly saddened.

"Oh, please, don't act like you don't know. I'm only wit' you for the currency."

State stood with his shirt in his hand, shocked. He couldn't fathom that Ashton had enough balls to tell him that to his face as if it were nothing. She didn't even blink when she said it. She didn't give a fuck about his feelings. What she said cut deep, like surgery. State looked at her with hate in his eyes. The emotions he felt mixed with the tequila in his system made him want to kill her.

"So, bitch, you don't love me? All that punk-ass change I spent on that pussy-ass wedding and, bitch, you don't love me?" His raised voice frightened her.

"Bitch?" Ashton repeated, crushed. "Bitch, yo' mama's a bitch. A stank bitch at that, wit' her retarded-lookin' ass."

"Real talk, Ashton, I ain't never hit a girl, but right about now I could choke the shit outta you."

"Try it, muthafucka. I dare you." she rolled her neck. "'Cause as soon as you lay a hand on me, I'ma call the police on yo' black ass!"

"You know what?" State licked his lips, nodding his head. "Fuck you. I'm outta here. I ain't gon' be arguing wit' yo' ass." He put on his shirt again.

"I know you ain't gettin' ready to leave again and you just walked in the house." Ashton got out of the bed.

"Watch me," he said, heading for the steps.

"You ain't goin' nowhere!" she yelled, mushing him in the back of his head.

"Ashton, you better go 'head," he warned, getting up in her face.

"I know you fuckin' somebody else!"

"Now you really buggin'!" He turned his back to her.

"You don't even see how your lies are affecting me. This ain't how our life was supposed to be, State. You're the first dude I ever let get this close to me, but you ain't cracked up to who you was supposed to be. You always gone. You're never here wit' me!"

"Would you wanna be around you? All you fuckin' do is complain!" He poked her in the forehead with his index finger.

"Well, stop giving me shit to complain about and maybe I wouldn't!" she screamed, feeling like she was losing her mind.

"Whateva," State threw over his shoulder as he left.

"So, you really gon' leave?" Ashton called out to him from the top of the steps.

State ignored her and kept on going.

"Well, fuck you too then!"

Billie sat opposite Cain in a conference room. A huge wooden table with a pitcher of water and four cups on top divided them. Cain didn't even look her way. Devastated, she gazed at him, wondering how they'd ended up this way. All she'd ever wanted was some kind of love and understanding, and although she knew that what they had was dead, her heart still yearned for him. Day by day, she held on to the memories of what they used to be, but Cain acted as if she were invisible, or better yet, a stranger.

With his side facing her, he talked non-stop on his cell phone with Becky. Cain was making it known loud and clear that any feelings he once had for Billie were long gone and buried six feet deep. Billie despised the fact that every time she came in contact with him, the ache inside her heart intensified to its highest extreme. It didn't matter that she wore her most expensive suit or that her hair was perfectly styled and her makeup was flawless the divorce was happening whether she liked it or not.

"You ready to start?" Her lawyer, Chad Bergman, asked.

"Yeah." She nodded without hesitation.

"Let's begin, shall we?" Chad announced.

"Baby, let me call you back," Cain said sweetly into the phone. "We about to get this shit started. A'ight, love you too."

Billie couldn't help but roll her eyes.

"To start things off, my client is asking that she keep the apartment in the city, the beach home in L.A., the Rolls-Royce Phantom, Mercedes Benz GLK, and the Jaguar XJ. Although agreed upon in the prenuptial agreement that my client would receive two thousand five hundred dollars a month per child, my client is asking that amount be raised to ten thousand dollars per child, and the alimony amount of five thousand dollars be raised to forty thousand dollars a month."

"I don't think so," Cain's lawyer objected. "Mrs. Townsend can keep the apartment and the vehicles, but my client is not willing to give up the beach house, and will most definitely not be giving your client ten thousand dollars a month per child. And by the way, we will be contesting the forty thousand dollars a month in alimony seeing that Mrs. Townsend has a fourteen million dollar trust fund."

"That has nothing to do with anything," Billie shot, heated.

"Calm down, Billie." Chad patted her hand.

"I will not!"

"I'm sorry to upset you, Mrs. Townsend, but your trust fund has everything to do with this. You're financially stable, so why should my client be obligated to support you?"

"And your client shouldn't have cheated with every whore that paid his insecure ass a little bit of attention, so why should I be punished for that? It's not like I'm gettin' a settlement. All I want is what's owed to me and my children. Now, would you rather give me the seventy Gs, or go to court and let a judge decide a fair amount?"

Cain finally spoke up.

"Just give her what she wants."

"But what about what we discussed?" his lawyer whispered.

"I don't feel like going back and forth. Just give her the seventy grand and anything else she wants. I just want this over with as soon as possible. Look, Billie." He sat up and placed his elbows on the table. "I figure it's best you find out now rather than later. I've asked Becky to marry me, and she said yes."

All Billie could hear was the sound of her heart beating. The sound was so loud it echoed like a bass drum. For months, all she'd done was think about him, so how could he be proposing to another woman? Billie loved him unconditionally. She put her trust, and most importantly, her heart into him, so how could he treat her like gum stuck on the bottom of his shoe? How could he not recognize all the unnecessary pain he was causing? How could he not think about how this would affect their kids? Did he not know that he was making the biggest mistake of his life?

Billie sat back in her chair. She swore the blood in her veins had stopped circulating. She didn't know whether she wanted to faint or die. Everything that made sense in her life was being taken away. She wanted to scream. She wished that time would stand still and she'd have a minute to calm the raging waters flooding her life.

Billie didn't know how long she'd been there, but at least a half an hour had gone by since she pulled up into her garage at her and Cain's eleven thousand square foot Mediterranean-style estate in O'Fallon, Missouri. It was the first home they'd purchased together, the house they brought the children home to after they were born. She couldn't move. Her hands gripped the steering wheel so tightly that her knuckles had turned white. Billie's mouth was dry and tears dropped from her eyes like hail.

Yeah, she'd gotten what she wanted in the divorce, but at the end of the day, money didn't mean a thing when she'd lost the one she loved. Cain had to have seen the anguish in her eyes when he told her his news. It was as evident as the air he breathed. All Billie could think of was how the man she'd shared vows with, bore kids with, built a home with had turned into the Negro version of Jon Gosselin.

With each breath she took, Billie grew weary of the pain. She was sick of facing it alone. And yeah, the kids had adjusted to their separation just fine, but she hadn't, and the news that Becky would be a permanent fixture in their lives caused Billie to crack. She had nothing more to give. All she knew was that the pain in her chest could no longer be a part of her existence, so she turned the key and started the engine.

In a trance, Billie rolled down the windows, allowing the fumes to flow up her nose. After a few inhales, it would be all over. Billie took in a deep breath and coughed. The smell was drowning her, but all she had to do was sit for a little while longer.

Then memories of how Kyrese used to suck his thumb and watch *Spider-Man* over and over again as a toddler came to mind, and Kenzie and Kaylee's first time saying "Mama." Yes, Billie was tired, fed up, and broken down, but one thing she wasn't was a quitter, especially not when it came to her kids. They were the best thing that came of her marriage. They were the ones who kept her motivated and at peace. Cain could take his love away, but he could never take the love of her kids away.

Realizing that she was making the biggest mistake of her life, she covered her nose with her hand and opened the garage door. After pulling her car out into the cool, crisp air, Billie leaned her head against the headrest.

She was tired of fighting a battle she couldn't win. She could no longer be afraid to hear the sound of just her heartbeat at night. It was a new dawn, a new day, and a new life for her, and Billie was determined to feel good.

"Ay yo', babe?" Angel called out to Dylan from downstairs in the living room.

Two months had passed and they hadn't spent a day apart. Gossip sites like Young Black and Fabulous, Concreteloop, and MediaTakeOut all talked about their budding relationship. Dylan loved every second of it. They'd done everything from creating home movies to going horseback riding and wine tasting. They took long walks with each other, debated on who the better rapper was—Tupac or Biggie—and cooked soul food meals at home. When in public, he held her hand, and at night, he held her tight. Dylan couldn't get enough of Angel.

She wanted all of him and more. When he whispered in her ear, she came alive. She ached for the touch of his hand. She often found herself wanting to bury her nose in the enthralling smell of his skin. The feelings she harbored for him were like every emotion she had ever felt before. It was bigger than hip-hop. It was more satisfying then a seventy-five percent off sale at Nordstrom's. It was like a spoonful of homemade soup on a cold winter's afternoon.

Dylan even loved saying his name. The way it rolled off her tongue and floated into the air reminded her of heaven each and every time. But the feelings also scared her. Dylan never thought she would feel this way about someone so soon, but like the sun in the morning and the moon at night, she couldn't escape him. His affection and attentiveness outweighed everything. He made her feel sweet, special, and good. He'd become her biggest supporter and fan. It was almost as if she were a spider caught in Angel's web. She prayed to God that she'd stay entrapped there forever.

"Yes, Angel darling?" She leisurely walked down the stairs.

"Wassup wit' all the boxes?"

"I bought a few things online." She batted her eyes, hoping he'd fall for it.

"Yo', that shit don't faze me. On the real, ma, you need to slow down. Yo' accountant already told you what the deal was on your finances, and the shit ain't lookin' too good. Remember you only had fifteen Gs left."

"I know. I just wanted to look nice for you." She pouted.

"That's cool and all, but what, you'd rather be fly and homeless? And I ain't stupid, Dylan. The last time I checked, Apple didn't sell clothes." He picked up the box.

"Umm . . ." She placed her finger up to her mouth. "See, what had happened was . . ."

"Yeah, save it."

"I'm sorry, Daddy." She kissed him on his cheek, neck, then mouth.

"Kissing me ain't gon' save yo' ass."

"I know what will." She eased her way down.

"See, you think yo' ass slick. I'll tell you what; you better get all you can now, 'cause when I leave in two weeks for camp, we can't be gettin' down like we have been."

"How about we scratch that no sex rule off the list?" Dylan unzipped his jeans.

"You know my trainer ain't having that." Angel inhaled deeply as she took him into her mouth.

After giving him the best blow job known to man, Dylan zipped his pants and got up.

"Where that come from?" Angel asked, feeling drained.

"Me." She giggled.

"I know it came from you, smart ass, but damn." He pretended to wipe sweat from his forehead. "That right there was on point. I needed that. Thank you." He planted a kiss on her lips.

"You're welcome." She went into the bathroom to brush her teeth and gargle.

"Oh yeah, whateva you got in those boxes better be something you can wear, 'cause I was just booked to present at the MTV Music Awards next week."

"Shut up!" Dylan wiped her mouth with a paper towel after gargling.

She was almost sure Ashton and State would be there. This would be the perfect chance for her to redeem herself and look perfectly striking. Modeling her entire wardrobe in her head, Dylan immediately vetoed everything. She was determined not look like a charity case. She had to get something new. There was no way Ashton was going to one up her in the style department this time.

"Don't go gettin' yo' G-string in a bunch, shawty. It's just an awards show," Angel teased.

"What-and-ever," Dylan said, doing an impression of a Valley girl.

"I'm serious, though. Don't go spend no more money on shit you don't need," Angel ordered.

"I won't."

"Swear."

"I swear." Dylan crossed her fingers behind her back.

"She rejects what I give while
she nurse the wounds by them."
—Wale, "Diary"

Chapter 16

Backstage at the MTV Awards was on and poppin'. It was mixture of intense energy and pure, uncontrolled pandemonium. Dylan loved every second of it. Every which way she turned, there was a stagehand, agent, publicist, artist, or journalist.

Angel wasn't at all intrigued by any of it. To him, this was just another day at the office. All he wanted was to present his category and go back to his seat and enjoy the rest of the show.

Dylan, on the other hand, was on cloud nine. She cherished being catered to and fawned over. She couldn't get enough of people oohing and ahhing over her outfit. Opting for a sexier ensemble than she normally wore, Dylan rocked a black Kaufman Franco lace bustier, a leather mini skirt, fingerless gloves, and a pair of Swarovski crystal pumps with spikes lining the heel. The outfit cost her an entire month's rent, but it screamed that she didn't care that Ashton was only twenty-one and had married her ex.

"Excuse me, Mr. Carter," the stage director said.

"Yes."

"There's been a slight change in programming. Instead of you presenting an award with Lady Gaga, we would like you to introduce R&B singer Ashton's performance of her hit single 'Sex Me Tender.'"

"I don't know about that," Angel protested in Dylan's defense.

"It's cool, baby. I don't care." She tried to play it off like it didn't matter when it did.

"You sure?"

"Yeah," she assured.

"A'ight, I'll do it," Angel said reluctantly.

"Great. You'll be going on in ten minutes," the stage director said before walking away.

"You know that you don't have to put on a front with me." Angel turned to her. "If you don't feel comfortable with me introducing ol' girl, I won't."

"Angel, it's fine. Don't worry about me. I'm stronger than you think I am."

"Keep it up and a niggah gon' fuck around and make you his wife." He took her by the hand and held her close.

"Yeah, right. You don't mean that." Dylan looked down at her feet.

"What I tell you about that?" He lifted her head up. "I'm right here. Now, tell me why I shouldn't speak the truth."

"'Cause I'm unlovable. My mother never gave a damn about me, and well, you know what happened with State. Besides that, love makes fools out of women . . . especially me. Why are we talkin' about love anyway?" She tried to change the subject. "We're at the freakin' MTV Music Awards. Taylor Swift is right over there."

"I swear you are the most emotionally unstable woman I have ever met," Angle joked.

"Look at Britney and Lindsay. Crazy is the new sexy." She giggled.

"Straight up, all jokes aside. I care about you a lot, and I can't even front no more. I love the fuck outta you."

"Really?"

"Yeah."

"I love you too," she said truthfully.

But before the moment could be relished, the annoying sound of someone yelling, "Move out the way! Clear a path! Ashton is leaving her dressing room and heading toward the stage!" It was Lisa, Ashton's personal assistant.

"Showtime," Dylan said to herself, turning around.

And there she was, Mrs. State, all five feet three inches of her. Even off screen Ashton seemed to be larger than life. She walked as if she had her own theme music. There wasn't a fan within miles, but somehow her hair blew in the wind. Her makeup resembled a work of art painted by Picasso, and her body was nauseatingly sick. The chick had a body like a video vixen. Everything from her shiny hair to her perky breasts, petite hips, and round butt screamed *Boom, Boom, Pow!* The leather leotard, leather thigh-high boots, and whip enhanced her come hither look even more.

Bitch, Dylan thought.

But all of that went out the window when she spotted the man she'd dreamed about and cried about kissing Ashton lovingly on the hand. Dylan had pictured the moment she would run into State over and over again in her mind. Unlike her reality, she saw herself standing tall and confident, but the moment her eyes met State's, she felt small. Despite her to-die-for outfit, she felt naked. She couldn't mask the fact that she still wondered if he missed her or thought about her at night.

Pretending that she hadn't noticed him, she gave them both her back.

"Baby, I'll be back. I gotta go over my lines," Angel said.

"Okay, go ahead. I'll be right here." Dylan let go of his hand.

Dylan pulled out her cell phone and acted as if she'd received a text message. From across the room, State watched Dylan in awe. She'd always been a pretty girl, but there was always a li'l hint of tomboy in her style. But in the months they'd been apart, something had changed. She was sexier, edgier, and more confident. Her hips had spread and her ass . . . shit, State wanted to take a bite out of it.

"Ay, yo', Dylan?" he said, approaching her.

A sly grin tried to appear on her face, but Dylan would never let him see. Instead, she acted like she hadn't heard him.

"Dylan?" He placed his hand on her shoulder.

The fact that the simple touch of his hand caused a stir in the pit of her stomach disturbed her.

"Yes." She looked over her shoulder.

"It's me, State."

"Oh, hi." She turned and finally gave him full eye contact.

"It's been a while." His eyes traveled the dips and curves of her physique.

"Two and half months to be exact. How's your wife?" she stated bluntly.

State stood quiet for a minute then he said, "No matter how many times I say it, I know you'll never believe me, but I never meant to hurt you, Dylan. I wanted to tell you—"

"It's cool. You have nothing to explain," she said, trying to avoid his eyes.

"Yes, I do."

"Nooooo you don't," she stressed.

"So, what you doing here? Who you here with?" He gazed around the room at the sea of people.

"My boyfriend."

"Your boyfriend?" he repeated in disbelief.

"Yeah, I think you know him. Baby?" Dylan shot State a sinister grin as she called out for Angel.

"Wassup?" Angel came in behind her.

"I wanted to introduce to you someone. Angel, this is State. State, this is my boyfriend, Angel."

"What up?" State said, in utter shock, pissed. Sure, he was the one who left Dylan alone, but that didn't mean he wanted another man to have her.

"Honey, what are you doing?"Ashton whined.

"Uh, just catching up with an old friend. You remember Dylan, don't you?"

"Mm-hmm." Ashton shot Dylan a snide look. "How could I forget? C'mon, baby." She tugged on his arm. "It's time for me to take my place."

"A'ight . . . Dylan." He gave her a once-over glance.

"State."

"I have to go too," Angel said. "Be right here when I get back."

"Where else would I be?" she said as he walked off.

Just as the lights were cued and the host announced Angel, Dylan took a quick glance to her right and caught State watching her every move. Mission accomplished.

Dylan had dreaded this day for weeks. Over the past two months, Angel had became her compass, her moral anchor, the one she leaned on. He'd brought her out of the dark and showed her what a good love was all about. She never wanted him to leave, but work overruled everything, including love. Broken down, Dylan sat on the edge of the bed with a box of tissues next to her.

She'd been crying since the night before. It was like someone was taking her favorite Chanel bag away, or Henri Bendel was going out of business. Dylan honestly didn't think she could handle it.

It wasn't helping either that each time she looked at him her pussy tingled. *It should be illegal for a man to be so fine,* she thought. He was dressed in all black, which she loved. He wore a black leather jacket, black hoodie, black jeans, and high top Lanvin sneakers.

"Baby, you gotta stop cryin'," Angel said.

"But I can't," she wailed. "They won't stop coming out."

"We'll only be apart for the first three weeks of my training. Remember, you're going to fly out."

"I know, but I'm gonna miss you so much."

"I'm gonna miss you too." He sat down beside her and pulled her onto his lap.

Dylan wrapped her arms around his neck. "But we won't be able to sleep together every night anymore."

"When we do, though, it'll be even more special." He kissed her.

"You're right."

"Now, help me finish packing." Angel slapped her on the thigh.

An hour later, he and Dylan stood at the door saying their final good-byes before he went downstairs and got into his black Lincoln Town Car and headed to the airport.

"You know I love you like cooked food."

Dylan covered her mouth and giggled. "You stupid. I love you too." She brightened up and smiled.

"I'ma call you as soon as I land, okay?" He tried to set her mind at ease.

"Okay." She nodded.

"Bye." He caressed her cheek with his thumb.

"Bye."

Dylan watched with sadness in her eyes as Angel boarded the elevator. Once the doors closed, she closed her eyes, wishing that the three weeks would go by fast. With nothing to do and no place in mind to go, she sat on the couch and flicked on the television. HSN always made her happy, but then she remembered that Angel would tear her a new one if she bought something else, so she turned it off. She thought about waking Fuck 'em Gurl up to play with her, but nixed the idea. Dylan didn't feel like her licking and following her around everywhere. She even thought about telling Consuela to come into work on her day off, but knew she didn't have the extra cash to pay her.

Fuck it, I'll just go back to sleep, she thought, getting up.

Halfway up the steps, the phone started to ring. Dylan never ran so fast in her life.

"Hey, baby. Miss me already?" she said sweetly.

"I been missin' the hell outta you."

"Who is this?" she shot, not recognizing the voice.

"State."

"What the hell you want?" she spat aggravated by the sound of his voice.

"Come outside."

"What?" She looked around the living room as if she could see him. "Please do not tell me you're here."

"I'm gettin' ready to come up." He opened the driver's side door to his car.

"No, you're not!"

"Why?" He stopped.

"'Cause I don't want you here, and plus, Angel is here," she lied.

"No, he's not. I just saw him leave."

Fuck, she thought.

"Okay, psycho. What are you, some kinda stalker now? You better get yo' retarded ass on somewhere," she warned.

"Why you talkin' to me like that?" State said, shocked by her reaction to him calling.

"'Cause I don't want anything to do with you; that's why."

"But what if I told you I missed you and that I can't stop thinking about you?"

"What if I told you to kiss my ass?"

"That's fucked up," State replied, actually hurt.

"Look, I'm in a really good relationship and I finally have someone in my life who wants to be with me, so I suggest you crawl back to the dungeon you came out of and feed your wife that load of crap you just tried throwin' at me. Now, I would advise you to go home before I call security on yo' ass!" she spat before hanging up.

"Now, you know damn well if Angel was here you wouldn't be buying all of this shit." Tee-Tee gave Dylan a disapproving look with his hand on his hip.

He and Dylan were at Saks Fifth Avenue, having a private showing of the latest and hottest fashions. Racks and shelves of clothing and shoes were there, all at their disposal. Dylan was like a kid in a candy store. She had Alexander Wang, Current/Elliot, and more to pick and choose from. They'd only been there twenty minutes, and Dylan had already racked up a bill of five thousand dollars on her credit card.

"What Angel doesn't know won't hurt him, and secondly, I'm not gonna keep any of this stuff," she whispered. "I'ma keep the tags on it, wear it, and bring it back." She grinned.

"You are such a hood rat." Tee-Tee looked at her with disgust.

"Whateva. Like, don't you get tired of hating? Like, do haters ever take a day off? There got to be a holiday or vacation time for y'all muthafuckas," she teased, taking a sip of champagne.

"I'm not gon' even entertain your nonsense with a response. 'Cause see, I've been practicing Buddhism, and Gandhi says that peace begins within, so the new calm me is going to continue to focus on peace, whereas the old me woulda bust yo' ass for tryin' to play me."

"You know I love you. Give me love." She wrapped her arms around him, squeezing him tight.

"Yeah . . . whateva. So, have you talked to my auntie?"

"No." Dylan looked at him. "What, have you?"

"Yeah. She called me a couple of days ago." Tee-Tee picked up a sheer blouse.

"To say what, that she got my money?"

"No. She actually asked if she could borrow a thousand dollars."

"You have got to be kidding me," Dylan said, stunned.

"Nope."

"What the hell she do with the fifty grand she stole from me? Smoke it?"

"She said that once she gave the man her half of the investment for what's it called?" Tee-Tee twisted his lips to the side. "Suck a dick, eat it good—I don't know . . . that he got ghost and she never heard from him again."

"Well, isn't that surprising. That's what her ass gets."

"She also wanted me to tell you that the only reason she took the money is because she really thought that this time she would be able to pay you back. To me, it seems like she just wanted you to be proud of her for once," he reasoned.

"She can't make me proud of her by stealing from me, and frankly, you stupid for even listening to her ass. As soon as she called you should've hung up," Dylan said coldly.

"See, now I'ma have to cut ya, 'cause you done fucked around and let the new peaceful me fool ya. Just 'cause you fuckin' a boxer don't mean that I won't jab yo' frail ass in the throat. Now, try me, bitch. Try me," he warned with his fist in the air, ready to strike.

"Why you gotta be so violent?" Dylan ducked.

As Tee-Tee fingered through a stack of shirts, Dylan quietly debated on whether or not to tell him about State. Dylan trusted her cousin, but she knew that there was some things you just can't tell people without it coming back to haunt you.

"Seriously, though, I got something I want to tell you, and it cannot get back to Billie."

"Cross my heart, swear to God," Tee-Tee pledged.

"State called me the other day."

"Shut the—" He inhaled deeply. "What the fuck he say?"

"That he misses me and he can't stop thinkin' about me."

"Now, like you told me, I hope you gave that niggah yo' ass to kiss and hung up on him," Tee-Tee shot.

"Of course."

"Okay, but please don't feed into the bullshit."

"I'm not," she protested.

"I'm just sayin', every time he do something wrong, he always finds a way back in. Don't let it happen this time, Dylan."

"Tee," she said as she stared him square in the eyes, "I am not thinkin' about State. Angel has my heart, and ain't nothing gon' change that."

"A'ight now, we'll see."

"I still really, really love you."
—Sade, "Love Is Stronger than Pride"

Chapter 17

"And if I can't have yo' body . . . I don't want to have nobody."
Dylan sang along with Trey Songz while lathering soap onto
her arm. The scene for a romantic rendezvous for two was
set, except she was all alone. Vanilla candles lit the room.
Thousands of big, fluffy white bubbles popped against her
skin. Steam rose from the water, and a glass of champagne
was in reach. All Dylan needed was Angel to complete the
fantasy, but it was cool. The next day, she would be hopping
on a plane to see him.

Dylan couldn't wait. Every time she saw him was like Val-
entine's Day, Christmas, and New Year's Eve wrapped in one.
Plus, it had been three weeks since she last saw him. She needed his companionship, being that the only form of attention
besides kissing and hugging was all she could get from him.
The no sex rule while training was killing her. To be around
Angel while he sparred did nothing but make her want to
jump on his dick and ride it until the roosters crowed and
the sun came up. *Ummmmmm,* she thought. And the primal
noises he made when hitting the bag caused juices of all different flavors to run down her thigh.

Turned on by just the thought of him, Dylan leaned back
and massaged her already hardened nipples. Using her index
finger and thumb, she playfully toyed with them.

"Would you please take your clothes off . . . or would you rather

me do that part?" She sang softly as her hand traveled down her stomach and landed on the face of her pussy. Slowly, she turned her fingers clockwise. Just as she was about to reach her highest peak and climax, her cell phone rang.

"Goddamnit!" Dylan slapped her hand against her thigh.

After drying her hands off on a towel, she picked up the phone and said, "Hello?"

"What you doing?" Angel asked, noticing she was out of breath.

"You wouldn't want to know. It might make your dick hard," she teased.

"Oh, word? You doing it like that?"

"Hey, a girl's gotta do what a girl's gotta do."

"Well, go 'head and do yo' thing. I ain't mean to interrupt." He pretended to try to get off the phone.

"You ready to see me tomorrow?" She ignored him.

"About that . . ."

"What?" She panicked.

"You gon' have to cancel your flight and come out next week," Angel said, hating to disappoint her.

"Why?"

"'Cause I gotta fly to Miami tonight to do a fuckin' Pepsi commercial."

"You didn't tell me about that. Congratulations, babe. I'm so happy for you," Dylan said, excited.

"Thanks."

"Okay, well . . ." She contemplated. "What I'll do is just change my flight and come down there instead."

"Nah, it's a one day thing. I'ma be in and out. Like I said, just come down next week."

"I guess I have no choice then," she shot with an attitude.

"You mad?" He spoke deep into the phone.

"What you think?"

"Don't be that way. You know I want you here, but business comes first."

"Obviously," she answered, upset.

"What you gettin' ready to get into?" Angel changed the subject.

"I guess nothing." She sighed.

"Well, look, give me a minute and let me call you right back."

"A'ight," Dylan said, not really wanting to get off the phone.

Two hours passed by and Angel hadn't called back or answered his phone when she called. It was so obvious by his actions that he was on some other shit. Angel had gotten back to L.A. and wasn't even beat for her anymore. *That no sex rule probably wasn't even true,* she thought. *His ass probably been fuckin' his ass off this whole time, while my dumb ass been over here playin' with my pussy so much it got tire marks. As a matter of fact, I think I may have carpal tunnel.* Dylan massaged her wrist.

"Fuck this." She got up from the bed. "He ain't gon' play me like a goddamn dummy."

By eleven that night, Dylan was dressed and ready to head out for a night on the town. Angel's cheating ass wasn't going to stop her shine. After getting dropped off at the door by her driver, she headed into the club. HOME nightclub at the Ameristar Casino Resort Spa was one of St. Louis's hippest clubs. It had the latest in everything, from their decadent red furniture to audio visuals, and celebrity guests and performers. That night, N.E.R.D. was hitting the stage. Dylan adored N.E.R.D. She couldn't miss the opportunity to see them live. As soon as she stepped foot inside the building, Dylan was bombarded by people she knew from the club scene. She felt like a fuckin' rock star. The only thing she was missing was a black guitar. Dylan spotted Kema, who was one of Tee-Tee's best friends. Dylan loved kickin' it with Kema. Outside of herself, Kema was the ultimate party girl.

"Hey, gorgeous." Dylan air-kissed both of her cheeks.

"Hey. Cute face," Kema said, complimenting her makeup.

"Cute bag." Dylan appreciated her Valentino hobo purse.

"So, tell me . . ." Kema poked out her chest. "Too much lady lumps, or just enough?" she said, referring to her breasts.

"Just enough."

"Cool." Kema brought her chest back in.

"What you doing here?" Dylan asked.

"Girl . . ." Kema smacked her lips. "Like you don't know. I'm tryin' to make Pharrell fine ass my husband." Kema was referring to the lead singer of N.E.R.D.

"Well, before you do that, let's go get a drink first," Dylan suggested.

"You ain't said nothing but a word. Where the Patrón at?"

After having bottles of Cristal and Ace of Spade sent to them in the V.I.P section, Dylan and Kema toasted to the good life as they listened to N.E.R.D. perform their set. After, rockin' her hips, Dylan zoned out to the beat of "Love Come Down" by Dirty Money. It was her song, and although she couldn't sing worth a damn, Dylan sang every lyric like she was Kalenna and Dawn. Then the DJ began to spin Latoya Luckett's fuck-his-ass anthem, "Regret."

"You must regret the day that you left me," Dylan sang, clapping her hands, thinking of State. Bobbing her head, she grooved to the beat. Being the one in control of her and State's relationship never felt so good. She couldn't get him off her phone. Every five seconds, he was calling or texting

her. Dylan wanted to act like she couldn't care less and that he was a lame, but her ego fed off his constant attention, whining, and begging.

Dylan was having so much fun that she had almost forgotten about her troubles with Angel; that was, until Kema opened her mouth and said, "Girl, ain't that yo' man?"

"What?" Dylan immediately stopped dancing.

She knew damn well Angel wasn't in St. Louis, let alone up in the club.

"Where?" She searched the crowd.

"Right there." Kema pointed toward the door.

"Oh, hell naw." Dylan's lips curled.

Her instincts were right. Angel wasn't there, but State's coon ass was.

"Honey, that niggah right there is so five minutes ago." Dylan waved her hand.

"You ain't got to tell me twice." Kema kept on drinking and dancing.

Deciding it was time for her to leave, Dylan gulped down the last of her drink. "I'm about to go."

"Why?" Kema said, disappointed. "I was just about to order another bottle."

"'Cause I cannot be around him. If he even look at me the wrong way, I might fuck around and hit him in the head with one of these bottles."

"Well, all right. I do not need you going to jail, Sheila," Kema joked, comparing Dylan to the character in the movie *Why Did I Get Married?*

"I'll call you, though," Dylan promised.

"Okay."

With the crowd being as packed as it was, Dylan assumed that she would be able to sneak out without State noticing her, but one of the bouncers just had to go and shout, "Where you going, sexy?"

The word sexy was like a moth to a flame, a wet tongue to a dick for State. There was no way he could hear the word and not a put a face to the comment. Once he saw Dylan, a bomb exploded inside him. She looked even more succulent than she did at the VMAs. She had on a sleeveless light blue denim crop jacket, a cutoff tank top exposing her flat stomach, dark skinny leg jeans, and a pair of bright yellow Givenchy heels. He had to have her.

"Dylan!"

"Why, God? Why?" She stared up at the sky. "I should've stayed my ass home."

Dylan didn't want to admit it, not even to herself, but secretly she was overjoyed to see State. Quietly, he'd become the persistent hunger pain in her stomach that wouldn't go away.

"What?" She faked an attitude.

"Quit frontin'. You know you happy to see me." He pulled her into him by the belt loop on her jeans.

"What makes you think I'm happy to see a cheater?"

"That big-ass Kool-Aid smile on your face."

"Whateva." Dylan waved him off, trying not to observe his sly grin.

"I took a chance on runnin' into you here."

"How you figure I would even be here?" she wondered.

"'Cause you never miss an opportunity to be in the midst of celebrities," State answered. He knew her well.

"Whateva. Where is Ashton?"

"Back at the crib, decorating. Everything in my house is now beige." He scowled.

"I thought you wanted beige."

"I did, but it doesn't quite . . . fit." He stared deep into her eyes.

"I just bet." She grinned and looked the other way.

"You look hot."

"I know I do. Anything else you want? 'Cause I was on my way out."

"I don't know why you keep actin' like the past few months ain't been as hard on you as they have been for me. What we had was special and you know that." He pinned her up against the wall, her full breasts pressed against his chest.

"So special that you were married the whole time and couldn't be bothered to tell me? Yeah . . . okay, that makes a lot of sense. You know what? I'm starting to feel sick." Dylan sucked her teeth.

"Why?"

"'Cause this conversation is making me nauseous," she spat.

"Listen, baby, I know that what I did was fucked up, but I miss you."

"And you're tellin' me this because . . . ?"

Unsure of what to say, State stood silent.

"That's what I thought. Now, if you'll excuse me." She by-passed him.

"Wait a minute." He pulled her back into him.

"What?"

"I got a secret to tell you." He whispered into her ear. "My marriage is over. It's not workin'."

Dylan gasped for air. *Why is he doing this to me?* Those were the last words she needed to hear from him, but somehow, a piece of her self-esteem came back.

"You got a pen?"

"Yeah, why?" She gathered her composure.

"Give it to me."

Dylan reached into her purse and retrieved the pen. "Here." She handed it to him.

State pulled a white envelope out of his pocket and wrote a note on it and passed it to Dylan.

"Hopefully, I'll see you soon." He lightly brushed his lips against hers, causing a flame to ignite in the pit of her soul.

With the look of desire in her eyes, Dylan watched him leave. Once he was out of sight, she examined the envelope and recognized that on it was a room number for a hotel room there in the casino. She knew that if she played into her forbidden desires, remorse would eat away at her in the morning. But Dylan's body needed to be touched, teased, penetrated, fucked. There was no reason for her to feel sorry about her erotic thoughts. Angel couldn't care less about her wants and needs. He was probably fucking someone at that very second. And no, Dylan wasn't good at forgiving, but she couldn't hate State if she tried. She still really, really loved him, and at the end of the day, love was stronger than pride.

Fed up with depriving herself, Dylan left the club and boarded the elevator. Fear gripped her lungs as she stood at the door. What she was doing was insane. State was by far her guiltiest pleasure, but she couldn't control herself. Her heart longed to know, was it all real, or had every smile, wink of the eye, or stroke been a lie? Praying she was making the right decision, Dylan lifted her hand and knocked.

State didn't make her wait long before he opened the door. Face to face, she stared into his eyes with fear in her own. This was the hardest part, facing her choice.

With her hand in his, State locked the door behind them. Before Dylan could change her mind, her jacket and tank top were off and State was massaging the curves of her waist with his fingertips. Moans of gratification slipped through Dylan's lips as he unveiled her breasts and flicked his tongue across her blackberry nipples.

Fully naked, she lay on her stomach, State lying on top of her. As she removed his wedding ring and their hands intertwined, he eased himself into her wet slit slowly. Each mind-numbing, gut-wrenching grind of his hips caused images of Angel's face to appear in her mind. For a second, she toyed with the notion of telling State to stop, but the surges of toe-curling currents rising in her pussy wouldn't allow the word to escape.

State had found her spot, the one that caused her eyes to roll in the back of her head and made her speak in tongues. Swiftly, he turned her over onto her back. Her hands rubbed his head while their tongues did the merengue.

Hungry for more, State gripped her thighs and placed her pussy into the perfect alignment of his dick, which was covered in sticky white cream. With her left leg draped across his shoulder, Dylan closed her eyes. Every time she gazed into State's eyes, she saw visions of Angel's staring back at her.

The next morning, Dylan woke up at the foot of the bed with State's big-ass size twelve feet in her face. *This can't be happening.* She looked around the room, scratching her forehead. In Dylan's mind, she'd made it all up to be a dream.

Easing out of the bed slowly so she wouldn't wake him, she grabbed her things. State lay on his side, snoring loudly. It was one of the things she didn't miss about him.

Once she was dressed, Dylan slipped out the door. The morning sun hit her face, bringing light to her betrayal. She was almost sure that mascara was smeared all over her face, but that was the least of her problems. Not ready to deal with the cruel facts which faced her, she got into a cab and headed home so she could sleep her mistake away. Unbeknownst to Dylan, things were only about to get worse.

As she unlocked the door to her place and turned the knob, she heard the distinct sound of the television playing. *Oh my God! I'm being robbed,* she thought. Afraid for her life, Dylan dug inside her purse for her cell phone so she could call the police. Then she remembered the Tiffany bracelet Angel had given her.

"Fuck that," Dylan mumbled, pulling a nail file out of her purse.

Somebody was about to get fucked up. Dylan pushed the door open with the nail file clutched tightly in her hand, ready to strike. She wondered where Fuck 'em Gurl was. She didn't even hear her barking or growling. *Maybe they've killed her;* she pondered, even more upset as she tiptoed inside. Her heart raced a million beats per second as she glanced around the living room frantically. Abruptly, Dylan stopped dead in her tracks and inhaled deeply.

To her surprise, instead of finding an intruder, she found Angel lying on the couch on his back, fully dressed, with Fuck 'em Gurl snuggled close next to him. His suitcases sat at Dylan's feet as her heart crumbled into pieces, fading into dust. Angel wasn't cheating or banging some other chick's back out like she'd conjured up in her head. No, he was making his way to her. He'd missed her as much as she did him.

What the hell have I done? She stood frozen stiff. Angel's eyes fluttered open.

"Hey," she said softly, hoping he wouldn't notice the sound of her voice cracking.

"Good morning. What time is it?" He stretched his arms wide.

"Uh." She looked at her watch. "Almost eight."

"Where you been?" Angel gazed into her eyes, searching for answers.

"I went out wit' Tee-Tee and ended up spending the night at his place." The lie caused a sharp pang to sting her chest. Dylan sat down next to him. *Please, Lord, don't let him see that I'm lying.*

"As you can see, I was tryin' to surprise you." Angel pulled her on top of him. "You was mad at me, wasn't you?" He brushed her hair back, thrilled to see her face again.

"Yeah, I was."

Oh, God. What if I smell like State?

"For a minute there I thought you were seein' someone else." She ran her finger across his chest.

"Why, 'cause I ain't seen you in a minute?"

"Yeah."

"Never that." He kissed the palm of her hand. "Only thing that's been on my mind besides this fight is you. And my bad for being kinda rude on the phone. I just had to make sure you ain't know what was going on."

"Trust me; you had me fooled." Dylan lay quietly for a second. "So, how long will you be in town?"

"For a week. I'ma train here just so I can spend some time wit' you."

Why the fuck he gotta be so perfect?

"Angel," she said barely above a whisper as tears stung her eyes.

"Huh?" He answered, halfway asleep.

Dylan pondered telling him the truth about where she'd really been. The words were heavy on her tongue. If she was ever going to tell him, now would be the perfect time. Perhaps he'd identify with what was going through her mind and forgive her; but something in her told her to wait. She wouldn't be able bear the look on his face when she gave him the news. She already felt lower then zero. Exposing her dirty secret would only make things worse.

"Wassup?"

"Nothing." She closed her eyes and allowed the tears in her eyes to fall. "I just . . . love you so much." She held him tight.

"I love you too." He rubbed her back. "Now, enough talkin'. Let's go to sleep."

"Can't read my, can't read my,
no he can't read my poker face."
—Lady Gaga, "Poker Face"

Chapter 18

Four days had passed and Dylan and Angel had spent every waking moment together. She even went with him to watch him train. In place of going out clubbing or to parties, they spent quiet nights at home.

One particular evening, he cooked dinner and she baked his favorite dessert, apple pie. They'd curled up on the couch, drank Moscato wine, and watched her favorite film of all time, *How to Marry a Millionaire*. After the movie they began to kiss passionately. His fingers roamed through her hair, while hers tugged gently on the tip of his hard dick.

Words couldn't describe just how badly Dylan wanted the dick, but like a kid on punishment, she was denied all access. Angel wouldn't give her the thick twelve inches of bliss she longed for; instead, he tortured and teased her. By the refrigerator, they sat on the floor face to face. Angel fed her strawberries covered in whipped cream.

Dylan was in absolute hell. Angel wouldn't fuck her within an inch of her life, and she honestly couldn't blame him. She was a filthy, rotten whore who didn't even deserve him. She could barely look him in the eye without flashbacks of her and State's tryst filling her mind. At night, she lay awake, unable to sleep because of the guilt. Whenever Angel held her close, unworthiness swept over her.

That day, they gathered for breakfast at Billie's. Billie had the table decorated beautifully. It looked like a botanical wonderland. Sferra white linens covered the table. Centerpieces of orange princess tulips, duchess peonies, sandersonia, white sweet pea, and white hyacinths lined the middle.

Everything was so bright and sunny, and the food was mmm-mmm good. For the beginning course, they drank mimosas and ate a quail egg tart with bacon. The rest consisted of traditional breakfast foods.

Dylan sat back silently while everyone else chit-chatted and laughed. She was afraid that if she spoke, her secret would spill out. And although the last couple of days they'd spent together had been great, Dylan couldn't deny that anything Angel said or did got underneath her skin. She'd been snapping on him left and right. In her mind, no human being could be so perfect and polite all the time, but somehow Angel managed to pull it off well. This made Dylan hate herself even more, because a part of her wanted him to fuck up just so she'd have an excuse for what she did.

While everyone's drinks were being refreshed, Dylan's cell phone started to vibrate. She'd gotten a text message from State that read: *When Can I See U?*

"Uh, Earth to Dylan." Tee-Tee snapped his fingers to get her attention.

"Huh?" She jumped, wondering if she had been caught.

"What the hell? Is you over there in la-la land?"

"No, I'm just a li'l tired, that's all." Dylan faked a yawn.

"Well, stop fuckin' and suckin' until the wee hours of the morning and you wouldn't be so damn tired. Oops." He placed his hand up to his mouth. "I forgot you ain't gettin' none."

"Angel got you over there feenin' for the dick!" Billie cracked up laughing.

"You two are so funny I forgot to laugh," Dylan shot with an attitude, not amused.

"That's a'ight. They just hatin', baby." Angel draped his arm around her shoulder and kissed her on the cheek.

"Sure," she responded dryly.

"What's wrong wit' you?" he asked in a low tone while Billie and Tee-Tee continued to talk. "You been quiet all morning, and plus, you haven't eaten none of your food."

"I'm not hungry."

"Just eat a li'l bit." He scooped up a mouthful of shrimp and grits.

"I'm good." She turned her face.

"C'mon, grits are your favorite," he pushed.

"I said no," she snapped. "Damn, give me room to breathe."

"A'ight." Angel took his arm from around her. "I won't say shit else to you."

Dylan closed her eyes and inhaled then exhaled. She was trippin' hard, and if she didn't catch herself quick, Angel was sure to drop her ass like a bad habit.

"I'm sorry. I'm not tryin' to be a bitch," she whispered so Billie and Tee-Tee wouldn't hear.

"You sure been actin' like one," Angel shot back.

"Normally I would've gave it to you raw and uncut for that—"

"You wouldn't give me shit." He cut her off. "I don't know what the fuck yo' problem is, but you need to pull it together."

"I can't even argue wit' you, 'cause you're right. I guess I'm just premenstrual or something." She tried to downplay things.

"Well, you need to hurry up and tell yo' period to come on before I have to fuck you up. Straight up, man, I want the ol' Dylan back and fast."

"I do too, and I promise I'll work on it. For the rest of the day, I will be on my best behavior." She rubbed his back.

Angel just looked at her. Lifting his glass, he took a sip and tried to calm himself down. There was only so much more of Dylan's pissy attitude he was willing to take. Shorty had been wildin' for no reason. Angel chalked her sudden change in demeanor up to hormones. It was a known fact that women were the most emotional creatures on the planet.

Dylan tried to fight it, but being caught between what was right and what was wrong was a muthafucka. To her left sat the love of her life. She would never find anyone better, but for the man texting her, she'd risk it all. She sent him a reply: *Soon.*

"We don't have much time," Dylan said, stepping inside the hotel room. "Angel thinks I'm at the grocery store gettin' organic whipping cream and unsweetened chocolate."

"Cool, 'cause I got a meeting to go to after this, so I don't have much time either." State closed the door then grabbed her by the back of her neck and kissed her roughly.

Two hours later, Dylan searched the room on her hands and knees for her bra and cell phone.

"Fuck," she huffed, frustrated.

"Calm down," State said, pulling up his boxer briefs.

"Ain't no damn calm down! Tony's been downstairs waiting on me for the past ten minutes! And what the fuck am I going to tell Angel when I get home, that the grocery store didn't have cream? This is some bullshit. Where the fuck is my bra?" She stood up straight, perturbed.

"Dylan." State placed his hands on her shoulders. "Chill out. Panicking is only going to make things worse."

Dylan breathed through her nose and tried calming herself down.

"You cannot start trippin'. Just pull yourself together. Your phone is on the nightstand and your bra is over there underneath the chair." He pointed.

"Why the hell didn't you say that ten minutes ago?" She jerked away, upset.

"'Cause you looked so damn cute. Like a li'l bunny rabbit."

"Whateva." She quickly put on her bra and grabbed her cell phone and purse. "I gotta go."

Dylan rushed out the door, not even caring that her shirt was open or that when she walked through the lobby, the guy at the front desk whistled at her. The entire ride back to her crib she ran over and over in her mind what her excuse would be. Angel had called her over twenty times. She just prayed that whatever she came up with, he'd believe her.

Deciding that she needed an alibi, Dylan called Tee-Tee.

"Hey, doll. What it do, boo?" he answered cheerfully.

"I need your help," she said quickly.

"What?" he said, nervous.

"And please when I tell you this, either help me or don't, 'cause I do not have time for a bunch of slick talk."

"Bitch, get to the point," Tee-Tee snapped.

"If asked, I need you to tell Angel that I just left your house."

"Why?"

"'Cause."

"'Cause what, Dylan?"

She finally fessed up. "I was with State the last couple of hours."

"You's a dumb bitch!" he shot angrily into the phone. "That niggah treated you like shit and you steady going back for more. Ain't you full by now?"

Dylan tried to explain. "It's not what you think. It's complicated."

"Complicated my ass. You ain't got no business messing with that man. He's married! Or have you tricked yourself into believing otherwise?"

"I'm fully aware that he's married. That's why I'm gonna end it." She tried to convince herself.

"No, you're not, but you know what, Dylan? That's all on you. When the shit hit the fan, don't come runnin' to me. I told you not to fuck wit' him, but like always, you gon' do what you want to do, despite everybody else's feelings. You finally got somebody that treat you halfway decent, and you don't even know how to act.

"I'ma cover for you this time, but don't involve me in this mess no more, 'cause Billie is my friend too, and I don't want to have no parts in this when she finds out."

The next thing Dylan knew, Tee-Tee had hung up on her. Minutes later, she was home. Her whole body shook as she opened the door.

"Man, why the hell haven't you been answering yo' phone?" Angel barked, coming down the steps with the cordless phone in his hand.

"'Cause my phone was off. Duh." She tried to lighten the uncomfortable situation.

"Duh, my ass. How was your phone off and it rang every time I called? If your phone was off, it would've went straight to voice mail," he disputed, knowing better.

"I don't know, Angel. I'm a professional shopper, not a cell phone technician." She took off her jacket, avoiding eye contact.

"What the fuck took you so long then? I'm up here thinkin' something happened to you."

"Huhhhhhh." Dylan groaned. "I went to Whole Foods 'cause I like to use a specific brand of cream and unsweetened chocolate when I bake, but they were out, so I had Tony drive me all the way out to the one in Chesterfield. Once I got there, I got the stuff that I needed, and then Tee-Tee called me and asked me to come through."

"Hold up." Angel screwed up his face. "I thought you said your phone was off; and Tee-Tee just called here lookin' for you about a half an hour ago."

"Damn." Dylan laughed. "What are you, the police?" She went into the kitchen and grabbed a Mystic drink. "My phone *waaaas* off, then I turned it on and saw that you and Tee-Tee called. Tee-Tee called last, so I called him back first. Do you mind?"

"Yeah, a'ight, Dylan." He nodded his head. "You must take me for a sucka or something."

"What are you talkin' about?" She narrowed her eyes. "You act like somebody lyin' to you."

"Where the shit at you got from the store then?" He eyed her, pissed. "'Cause I don't see a muthafuckin' bag nowhere, unless you got it hid up yo' ass."

Okay, Dylan, think.

"Ahhhhh, fuck!" She waved her hand for an added effect. "When I went over Tee-Tee's house, I had the bag in my hand. I must've left it over there on the counter."

"You know what?" Angel gave her a menacing stare. "I'ma take two steps to the right and modulate. Hopefully by the time I get back, you done thought of a better lie than that."

"Modulate?" She screwed up her face, confused. "Angel, just 'cause you call yo''self being upset don't mean you gotta go around using big words."

He gave her a severe look of disgust and said, "Big word? Eight lousy letters. Dylan, are you serious?"

"What?" She shrugged.

"*Modulate* is not a big word, Dylan. Would you like for me to explain the meaning?"

"And spoil the pleasure of me lookin' it up in the dictionary? I think not." she shot back sarcastically, knowing he was trying to play her.

"Yo', I'm out," Angel said, fed up.

"You're seriously gettin' ready to leave?" Dylan was stunned.

"What I'ma stay here and continue to let you lie to me for?" His nostrils flared.

"I'm not lyin' to you!"

"Just be straight up wit' me. You seein' somebody else?"

Dylan swallowed hard. Tears filled every crevice of her face. All Angel wanted was her time and her love, and she was too selfish to give it to him. She hated letting him down, but the damage had already been done.

Angel stood waiting patiently for her answer. There had to be a reason she was acting this way. Nothing had changed about him. He still treated her like a queen, but every time he turned around, she had a frown on her face. When she wasn't home, she didn't answer his calls. It was either off, or his calls went ignored. They never talked, and when they did, she appeared distant. Angel couldn't take it anymore. He was at his breaking point.

"Why would you say something like that?" Dylan came from out of the kitchen and got in his face. Right then and there, she realized that if she ever lost Angel, she would die.

"You know I love you." She reached up and stroked his cheek with her hand.

"Do you? 'Cause lately you ain't been actin' like it."

"Of course I do. Angel, I love you." She tried her best to make him see, despite her inability to look into his eyes when she said it.

"I wish I could believe you, but until you can say it without lookin' everywhere but at me, I think it's best we spend some time apart." He stepped back.

"But—" Dylan tried to object, but Angel wouldn't let her.

As she parted her lips to speak, he placed his finger up to her mouth. There was nothing else to be said. It hurt like hell, but he had to walk away from her. He'd given all of himself and more to Dylan ,but it was like it wasn't enough. She didn't even seem to care that she was the first women he'd ever given his heart to. This whole thing hadn't been easy for him to accept, but Angel didn't fight it. His biggest fear was like anyone else's in love: he didn't want to get hurt. But with each call that went unanswered, empty kisses, and distant presence, Dylan shattered his heart.

Clouds of cigarette smoke danced in front of Dylan's face as she gazed absently at the paisley print comforter resting on her legs. State lay next to her, puffing on a Newport. The smell of the cigarette, stale Thai food, and sex made Dylan want to vomit. She felt dirty, sticky, and tainted. How she'd ended up in this predicament of lies, secrecy, and betrayal she didn't know. All she knew was it had become too much for her to stomach. Angels and devils weren't supposed to look alike, but somehow, she'd blurred the lines with her choices. This was not her destiny. Somehow she'd forgotten State's ID and mistaken him for a man of comfort, when all he'd really done is cause her more pain.

After the first time they had sex, she vowed to herself that it would be over. But the urgency of intimacy outweighed her better judgment. Angel's demanding schedule and constant vacancy in her life became too much for her to handle. Loneliness consumed her constantly, and only being able to see him every other weekend wasn't cutting it. With Angel she felt whole, loved, relevant, and pure. Without him, her insecurities shone brighter than the sun.

Every fiber of her being wanted to believe that his actions and his words were real, but she'd felt the same way with State in the beginning, and he'd hurt her in the worst way imaginable. Maybe her fucking State was her way of hurting Angel before he hurt her.

Dylan glanced over at State, who'd been talking the whole time about God knows what. All she saw was a silly grin plastered on his face. It was as if he didn't have a care in the world. Homeboy was on cloud nine. He'd been fed, fucked, and sucked. It fucked Dylan up to know that once he went home, he'd get the same treatment all over again from his wife, when she'd go home alone and fade into black.

His wife, she thought. *Girl, you are a fuckin' mistress. But hell, you ain't even that no more. He treatin' you like a fuckin' whore. Got you up in a goddamn Super 8. You ain't even worth the cost of the Four Seasons anymore.*

But you can't be mad at him, Dylan, she told herself. *You met his ass here like a fool, so what does that make you? A goddamn dummy. At least Angel respects you enough to treat you well. State don't give a damn about you, Ashton, or anybody else. Angel ain't did nothing but try to love you, and this is how you repay him, by breaking his heart?*

Dylan looked over at State again. She wanted to hurl. He was never going to change, and Dylan didn't want or expect him to. He was always going to be a self-absorbed, cold-hearted snake who couldn't care less about anyone else's feelings. He was the same guy who led her to believe she was the one, while he was married to another. And that wasn't what she wanted, so she decided to walk away, because she knew he never would.

Dylan pulled the horrible, cheap covers off of her and got up.

"Where you going?" he asked. "You about to get in the shower? 'Cause if so, I'ma get in there wit' you, 'cause I want to hit it again before we burn out."

"No." Dylan slipped on her jeans. "I'm going home."

"Why?"

"'Cause I have no business being here, and neither do you."

"Here we go with this shit again." State sighed, rolling his eyes. "Dylan, you know damn well you wanna be here."

"Not anymore." She pulled her T-shirt on over her head.

"Why, 'cause of ol' boy?"

"Yeah."

"Now all of a sudden you wanna act like you got a heart. You don't give a fuck about that man. Face it, Dylan, the shit between you and him ain't workin'. If the man was holding it down like he should, you wouldn't even be here right now."

Dylan stopped and stared at him. "And the sad part is you believe every word that is coming out of your mouth. Let me explain something to you." She got into his face and pointed her finger. "Angel holds it down in ways yo' simple-minded ass would never be able to understand. That man is the best thing that has ever happened to me. And trust and believe that any problems we have is not because of him; it's because of me. And you wanna know why? 'Cause I let men like you fuck it up for a man like him to come into my life."

"Okay." State yawned, unimpressed. "Blame everything on me. Dylan, if you love him so much, then why are you here with me? Huh? Answer that."

"You're exactly right." She smiled.

"I know I am." State pulled the covers back so she could get in. "Now, come lie down with me."

"I'll pass, but thank you. For the first time since I've known you, you've said something that was true. Why am I here with you? Hmm." She smirked before walking out.

"I told ya I was trouble."
—Amy Winehouse, "You Know I'm No Good"

Chapter 19

The scene was set. Mos Def's underground smash "The Panties" floated throughout the room. Chamomile- and honey-scented candles were lit. The table was set. White chicken lasagna with spinach baked in the oven. With all of that taken care of, Dylan put the finishing touches on a freshly made romaine salad. The French chocolate strawberry torte she baked was on the counter, ready to be devoured.

Dylan knew she only had minutes to spare before Angel walked through the door. He had no idea she was even in L.A. They hadn't spoken since the day he left her house upset, which had been two weeks before. She couldn't wait to see the reaction on his face when he saw her. It was now or never for them, and if Dylan didn't make things right, their relationship would be over for good. Dylan had a lot of making up to do. A romantic dinner for two was just the start of her showing Angel just how dedicated to him she was.

And yes, it would take time for him to believe in her again, but she was willing to do anything to gain back his love and trust. She wasn't trying to be without him at the right moments. He was everything she'd been missing and more. She just hoped that she hadn't waited too long to get her shit together.

Suddenly, Dylan heard the sound of him entering the house. Wiping her hand on a towel nearby, she headed out of the kitchen to greet him.

"Hey." She smiled nervously.

"How you get in here?" He eyed her suspiciously.

"I had the doorman let me in, but don't be mad at him. I bribed him with a hundred dollar bill." She laughed to ease the tension.

"Oh." He set his keys down on the table.

"Surprise!" Dylan tap danced then raised her arms in the air.

"You should've called before you came," Angel replied, not impressed.

"I know, but I hoped that you would be happy to see me."

"I mean, I don't know what you want me to say. Things between us ain't good."

"I know." She spoke in a soft tone.

Dylan stood before Angel and gazed into his warm brown eyes. "And it's my fault that we're in the mess we're in. I know that things between us have been a li'l fuzzy, and I'm to blame for that. I just didn't want to believe that this was real, that we were really a couple, and that you loved me as much as you said you did. I mean, look at you. You're beautiful. You can have any woman in the world, but you chose to be wit' me. Me." Dylan pointed at her chest with skepticism. "Broke-ass, uneducated, ditzy Dylan Monroe."

"It's not good for you to talk about yourself like that." Angel took off his coat.

"Hell, its true."

"A'ight, if that's how you feel." He walked past her.

"Look, I ain't even mean to get off into all that. Angel, I love you." She reached out for his hand and pulled him back. "And I don't wanna lose you. You're all I know, and I ain't tryin' to get to know nobody else and their weird-ass quirks and the shit that make them tick. I wanna be wit' you," she cried.

"I ain't never tryin' not to wake up to your face, have you sing to me at night even though you can't sing, have you hold my hand when we cross the street, or at night remind you to pick your cup off the floor 'cause after a while you're sure to knock it over with your big-ass feet—"

"Look, Dylan," Angel said, cutting her off. "What you said was nice and all, but the last few weeks for me been hell, and I ain't tryin' to go through that again. You gotta understand that I'm scared too. I ain't never gave my heart to a woman, and I'll be damn if I let you or anybody else play wit' my heart."

"But I'm not playin'. I love you, Angel, and I promise I won't hurt you again, straight up. And I know that things between us are fucked up right now, but I'm willing to do anything I gotta do to get you back. Just please"—her bottom lip trembled—"don't leave me," she begged as tears streamed down her face. "I couldn't take it if you did."

Angel wished to God that his heart was made of stone as Dylan stood before him on the verge of having a nervous breakdown, but he loved her too much not to feel a thing for her. He'd given too much of himself to let go of her now. She was his first true love, the yellow to his blue. And yeah, there was more to her erratic behavior than she let on, but Angel would rather not know the truth and be with her, then be hit with something that might cause his heart to bleed.

"Come here, man." He pulled her into him. "Stop cryin'." He kissed her tear-stained face. "You ain't never gotta worry about me leaving you. As long as you act right, everything gon' be cool."

"I promise things between us gon' be better than ever," Dylan declared. "I promise on everything I love, including my bracelet and my grandmother Dahl's vintage Chanel necklace, that I will make everything right. My main concern from this point on is making you happy."

"That's wassup, but what you mean about being broke?" He held her at arm's length. "The last of your money is gone?"

"You might as well say it is. I don't even have enough money to pay my rent this month."

"I got you," Angel said, hoping he was making the right decision.

"No, I'll handle it myself. You've done enough for me."

"Fuck that. I want to. Plus, if I don't, then what you gon' do? Move to L.A. wit' me?" he replied.

"The offer sounds tempting, but St. Louis is my home. You know that."

"I feel the same way too." He kissed her softly. "But fuck all that right now. My stomach growling like a muthafucka. What you got in there to eat?"

Ashton sat alone on the couch with her legs crossed. The heel of her Stella McCartney two-tone pump touched the marble floor. All the lights in the house were out. The only thing that lit the room was the light from the television screen. Pent-up anger filled her veins to the point she couldn't think straight. She wanted to throw plates, rip up State's clothes, spit in his face, and scratch his eyes out. The good part was she would be able to do all of it in a matter of minutes.

At any minute, State would be walking through the door. He had no idea that he was in for the surprise of his life. Ashton reached over onto the coffee table and grabbed her lighter and a cigarette. Placing the cigarette in her mouth, she lit the end of it and inhaled the potent yet calming nicotine. Ashton took the cigarette from her mouth, tilted her head, and exhaled the smoke up toward the ceiling. She couldn't wait for State to get home, 'cause as soon as he did, she was gon' . . . get . . . in . . . that . . . ass!

"Yeah, a'ight," she heard him say from the other side of the door. Ready to strike, Ashton flicked the ashes, which dangled from her cigarette, into the ashtray sitting beside her, then picked up her glass of Merlot.

"I'ma get at you, though." State talked on his cell phone as he walked inside the house. "Just hit me on the jack tomorrow. Bet, one." State was so consumed with his conversation that he didn't even notice what was going on around him.

"Wassup, baby?" he said to Ashton while taking off his coat.

"You muthafucka!"

"What?" State turned around, alarmed.

His concerns were answered once his eyes landed on the TV screen. A sick and twisted smile formed on Ashton's face as a look of shock and horror spread across his once he saw a recording of him and Dylan fucking. Photos of them going out to restaurants, concerts, and shopping while she was on tour were sprawled all over the coffee table and floor. Ashton even had voice recordings of their phone conversations.

The biggest surprise was not only did she have evidence of his dalliance with Dylan, Ashton even had evidence of State and another woman. State couldn't believe his eyes. He hadn't suspected a thing. He thought that Ashton was young and naïve and that she was none the wiser of his infidelities, but Ashton was by no means a fool. She understood from the moment she said "I do" what she was getting herself into. State had an infamous reputation that preceded him. He was a liar, a manipulator, and a cheat. Ashton didn't expect that just because she wore his ring he'd be faithful; so, before she left to go on tour, she had surveillance cameras placed strategically around the house.

She also hired a private investigator to follow his every move. When she first saw the footage while on tour of him on his knees, hitting Dylan from the back and slapping her hard on the ass while shouting, "Whose pussy is this? You wanna have my baby? What you want, a girl or a boy?" tears the size of lemon drops tumbled down her rosy cheeks; but after she cried herself to sleep, she vowed to never let another tear fall. No, she'd gather all the ammunition she needed to not only get his ho ass back, but to trap him in his own deceit.

"Listen, baby. Let me explain," he began.

"No, you listen to me." Ashton raised her voice, shocking State. "Is she worth one hundred fifty million dollars?" Ashton cocked her head to the side and took a sip from her glass, her hand shaking nervously.

"Yo', Ash—" He tried to explain once more.

"Is she worth a hundred fifty million dollars, niggah?"

Fuck! State placed his head down. Ashton straight had him by his nut sack. If they divorced, she'd take everything, including the kitchen sink. State was backed into the corner with no way out. He couldn't lie or bullshit his way out of this one. He couldn't pretend that Dylan was just a friend anymore.

State sucked his teeth and held his head up high. Now was not the time to buck. Ashton had a peculiar look in her eye, one that reminded him of Rebecca De Mornay in the thriller, *The Hand that Rocks the Cradle*.

"No."

"All right, then." Ashton stood up, pleased. "I'm really glad that we could have this conversation. I feel a lot better. Now that that's settled, what should we have for dinner? I was thinking about ordering Chinese."

Stunned by her sudden change in attitude, State stood puzzled. He didn't know what type of emotion to feel. Should he be scared or relieved? Should he try to talk to her, or give her time to cool off? It was all too complex, especially when he couldn't get a good read on Ashton. She was behaving like a lunatic. Most women would've cussed him out, cried hysterically, or at least tried to fight him, but not her. Ashton held all the cards in her hands, so she didn't have to wild out to prove her point that she was hurt.

"Oh, and by the way," she said, peeking her head out of the kitchen. "I fired Lisa today. How long did you actually think you'd get away with fuckin' my assistant? That's the problem; you never think. But that's all water under the bridge now." She smiled with delight. "But I do want my new ring by tomorrow. As a matter of fact,"—she took off her wedding ring—"give this piece of shit-ass ring back to that bitch the next time you see her." She threw it at him, hitting him directly in the center of his forehead.

A stream of warm water ran through Billie's hair. The shampoo girl at Mina's Joint Salon and Spa was doing a fantastic job shampooing and massaging her scalp. The soothing sensation felt so good, she damn near fell asleep. The chitter chatter around her and the music playing didn't even bother her.

Billie loved coming to the salon. Mina's Joint had become known for its work with models and celebrities. It sprawled over 1300 square feet and was one of the largest hair salons in St. Louis city. The chic salon sported a palette of various brown shades and silver, issuing an air of elegance. Luxurious cushioned panels were suspended from the ceiling, and silver blinds formed several gateways for clients to cross before they finally reached the heart of the salon, which was the styling area.

Billie was high off life. Cain and Becky were planning their wedding, but she couldn't care less. She'd finally moved on. She had no time to fret over a man that didn't want her, because she knew eventually another one would.

Plus, it felt good to make all the rules. Cain no longer controlled every aspect of her life. She didn't have to cook. The French chef she'd hired now did that for her. She didn't have to clean the house from top to bottom anymore either. That was now Zoila, her maid's job. The best part of it all was that she didn't have to keep her hair the way Cain wanted her to. She was now free to do whatever she pleased with it, and on that cold November day, she was getting her hair cut and styled they way she desired it to be.

Delicious, stylist to the stars extraordinaire and the queen of all queens, was going to cut the sixteen inches of hair she'd taken eleven years to grow into a short pixie cut inspired by Nia Long. After getting her hair washed, razor cut, and set, Billie sat underneath the hair dryer. Author TuShonda L. Whitaker's bestselling novel *Millionaire Wives' Club* was her book of choice while waiting. Once she got to chapter five, she was ready to get into the chair, so Delicious could work his magic.

"You ready, B?" He looked at her through the mirror.

"As ready as I'll ever be," she replied anxiously. A haircut wasn't a life-changing experience for some women, but for Billie, cutting her hair was a declaration of her independence.

"All right." He popped his lips. "Well, let's go get 'em."

Thirty minutes later, Delicious spun her chair around so she could view herself. Billie could hardly recognize the woman staring back at her. She looked like an entirely different person. Her brown eyes sparkled, and her cheekbones seemed higher and more defined. She even noticed that she sat up straighter.

"Delicious, you have outdone yourself," Billie said in awe.

"Well, it didn't take much. You're gorgeous, girl."

"Thank you. Let me get my wallet so I can pay you."

Billie was so overwhelmed with excitement that she didn't even look up when the salon door opened. If she did, she would've noticed Ashton swoop in with her new personal assistant, Hadley, and bodyguard, Crusher. As always, Ashton was the epitome of a diva. Everybody in the salon wanted her fitted Balmain leather jacket, black V-neck tee, black leather skinny-leg pants, suede calf gold-studded boots, and water-snake satchel.

"Oh my God, it's Ashton!" One of the ladies in the waiting area shrieked. "Can I please have your autograph?" The lady rushed over. "My daughter loves you."

"Umm . . ." Ashton shielded the left side of her face with her left hand and gave her assistant a stern look. "Handle this, please."

"Yes, ma'am. Excuse me, everyone!" Hadley clapped her hands. "Ashton is not here to sign autographs, take pictures, or socialize. As a matter of fact, don't even look her way. If any of you even so much as breathe her way, Crusher will have no choice but to step in and take care of the situation. Hopefully, I've made myself clear."

"So, I take that as a no on the autograph," the lady said, outdone.

"Oh my God, get her away," Ashton shrilled. "I think I'm starting to get hives."

Crusher growled, scaring the living daylights out of the woman.

"This bitch." Delicious curled his upper lip.

"You can't stand her ass either?" Billie handed him his payment.

"Hell naw, I don't like that ho. The bitch tone deaf and got two left feet. I swear to God I can't stand her ass. I been tellin' Mina to cuss her stuck-up ass out for the longest, but she won't 'cause the lip-syncing ho brings publicity to the shop. But you know what I say. Fuck all that, 'cause that bitch got one time to come at me crazy, and I'ma stick one of these Marcels up her ass."

Billie laughed as Ashton walked toward the back and their eyes met. At first Ashton didn't know where she knew Billie from. Her face looked familiar, but she couldn't pinpoint how she knew her. *Is she a fan, or one of State's sideline hoes?* Ashton wondered.

Then she remembered that night in Vegas when State ran into Dylan. Billie was Dylan's homegirl. This was perfect. Ashton hadn't planned on letting State's indiscretion go past the four walls of their home, but there was absolutely no way she could pass up the opportunity to send Dylan's ass a message.

"Belinda, isn't it?" She pushed her sunglasses down to the tip of her nose.

"No, sweetie, it's Billie." Billie rolled her neck.

"Whateva." Ashton waved her hand. "You and Dylan are friends, right?"

"We sure are. She's my best friend, to be exact. Why?"

"Okay then, best friend, do me a favor and tell that skank whore to stay the fuck away from my husband."

"Oh, shit." Delicious placed his hand on his heart, appalled.

Every woman in the salon stopped talking and focused in on the conversation.

"Excuse me?" Billie stood up, ready to attack.

"Don't even think about puttin' your hands on me, trashy. Crusher." Ashton snapped her fingers.

Like a lap dog, Crusher immediately stepped up, fully prepared to hem Billie up if need be.

"You better fall yo' monkey ass back!" Billie shot him a look that could kill. "Now, back to you, fire crotch. I don't need to tell Dylan shit. What you need to do is check yo' so-called husband. Dylan don't want him. When she was seein' him, she didn't even know he was married to you. And when she found out, she left his ass alone. Now, if you'll excuse me, pardon my back." Billie picked up her purse, ready to leave.

"I'll let you go, but before you do, you might wanna ask your girl what she was doing at the Super 8 motel three weeks ago."

Billie wished it was all a lie and that Ashton was just talkin' out of her ass, but it all made sense. Dylan was never quiet, subdued, and moody, but in the past month, that was all she'd been. Angel had confided in her that things between him and Dylan had been rocky. On top of that, every time Billie called her, she never answered the phone, or when she wanted to go to lunch, Dylan was always sick or busy. Totally embarrassed and pissed, Billie walked out of the salon without saying another word. It made no sense to continue to defend Dylan to Ashton when she had her best friend to confront.

"If you've ever kept a secret from the one you love, this is what it feels like."
—Keri Hilson, "Tell Him the Truth"

Chapter 20

Things between Dylan and Angel had been better than ever since they returned from L.A. Dylan couldn't think of a thing she didn't like about him. She loved the way he said good morning, he called her baby, but most of all the fact that he loved her even though she was a train wreck.

That afternoon, she stood in front of her walk-in closet. She was trying to figure out just what she would take to Vegas with her for Angel's fight.

Angel and his team of people had been training non-stop. Now it was a week before the bout, and they were going to fly to Vegas that night for the last stretch of training. Dylan was so proud of him. It hadn't been easy preparing for the biggest fight of his career while being in a new relationship with a woman who had been giving him grief, and traveling back and forth between two states while training, but Angel's love for her never waivered. He stuck with her despite her many flaws, and she loved him even more for it. Dylan had so much to do in so little time.

Their flight was scheduled to leave at seven that night, and it was already 4:30 and she was nowhere near ready. Purses, six-inch heels, and hundreds of designer duds were thrown about the room. Angel was going to kill her if he got back from the barber shop and she wasn't packed and ready to go. He would be happy that she hadn't spent a dime on anything new, which had been extremely hard for her. It wasn't like she had the means to anyway, but at least she was trying. While debating on taking her Bottega Veneta Marco Polo luggage collection or her Louis Vuitton monogram set, she heard a loud knock on the door.

"His ass done forgot his keys again." She shook her head as she went to open it.

But it wasn't Angel who was knocking; it was Billie.

"Now, that is cute." She admired her hair. "Turn around," Dylan beamed, not noticing the menacing scowl on Billie's face.

"So, how long did you think you could keep it a secret?" Billie seethed with anger.

"Keep what a secret?" Dylan turned around.

"That you've been fuckin' State behind my brother's back."

Dylan stopped dead in her tracks. The first thing to do in her mind was to lie, but it was useless trying to get anything past Billie. She was like a K-9 dog. She sensed bullshit from a mile away.

"Answer me, bitch!" Billie screamed.

"Billie, I'm sorry. I didn't mean for any of it to happen."

"I knew it." Billie stomped her foot and swung her arm. "I fuckin' knew it. You been actin' hella funny here lately. Now it all makes sense."

"You have to understand; it just happened," Dylan reasoned.

"What, you slipped and his dick landed in you?"

"No!"

"Well, what then?"

"I don't know. I got upset one night—"

"Don't even waste your breath." Billie waved her hand. "I don't even wanna hear it. Like, don't you feel stupid?"

"Yes!" Dylan began to cry.

"Oh, bitch, don't cry now!" Billie eyed her with disgust. "I can't believe you! Oh, but wait; yes, I can! This ain't nothing but typical Dylan! You don't care about anybody but yourself!"

"That's not true."

"Oh my God, you're so stupid. I swear you're just like your mother," Billie shot, not giving a fuck.

"What?" Dylan , visibly hurt.

"Yeah, I said it." Billie stood back on one leg and rolled her neck. "You and Candy are just alike! Two whore-ass peas in a pod! Y'all put your feelings before anybody else's, no matter if it hurts them or not! You couldn't even be there for me when my husband served me with divorce papers 'cause you was so busy tryin' to make a niggah that don't give two shits about you see how much he'd hurt you! Nobody comes before State, not even yourself!" She pointed at Dylan. "You will play a muthafucka left and right for his ass, and for what? That niggah don't even like you. All you good for is giving some head, but shit, you probably ain't even good at that!"

"A'ight, Billie, I understand that you're mad at me, but you going a li'l too far." Dylan gave her a sharp look.

"Oh, naw, I ain't took it far enough. Did you even think about how much this is going to hurt my brother? Nooooo, you didn't." Billie threw her hands up in the air. "That's not in your makeup. I feel sorry for you, though, Dylan 'cause you had a real good thing going wit' my brother. He really cared about you, but once he finds out, he's not going to want to have anything to do with you. I tell you one thing, though: you're not going to go another day without tellin' him what you did."

"Billie, I can't," Dylan pleaded with tears in her eyes. "Please don't make me tell him. I love him so much. I can't lose him, Billie. I can't. Just—" Her chest heaved up and down. "Give me some time. I can't do this to him now. His fight is in a week."

"You should've thought about that when yo' ratchet ass spread your legs for that dirty-dick muthafucka. Now, you gon' tell my brother tonight or else I will," Billie threatened before slamming the door behind her.

Dylan clutched a wad of tissue in her hand while rocking back and forth. Her right leg wouldn't stop trembling, and the hundreds of tears that poured from her eyes wouldn't stop falling. This feeling was far worse than the one she felt when she learned State was married, mainly because she wasn't the one being hurt; she was the one doing the hurting. All of her life, she'd searched for a man like Angel, and in a matter of minutes, she was going to lose him. No amount of "I'm sorry" or "Will you forgive me?" would do the trick.

Once she told him the truth, he'd never look at her the same again. He'd probably hate her. If she were him, she would. What she'd done was despicable and unforgiveable. Dylan was so nervous that her stomach ached. She wanted to pee, but gripping fear held her in place. She wondered if she should start out by saying "I didn't see it coming" or "it wasn't on purpose."

Then the sound of Angel's keys entering the lock pierced the silence. She wanted to run and hide or dream it all away, but Dylan couldn't sweep this under the rug like she did everything else in her life. She was finally forced to deal with herself and the poor choices she'd continued to make.

"What you doing sittin' there?" Angel asked, placing his keys in his pants pocket. "Why you ain't packing?"

Dylan tried to speak, but the huge lump in her throat wouldn't let her. He was so handsome. The black Yankees cap, heather gray crew neck sweatshirt, gray jeans, and Christian Lacroix sneakers enhanced his sex appeal.

"Are you cryin'?" He eyed her, alarmed. "What's wrong wit' you?"

Dylan hung her head low and wailed.

"Did somebody die or something? Talk to me," Angel demanded, sitting beside her.

"I love you so much." She looked up. Her eyes were swollen with tears.

"I love you too, so what's wrong?" Angel wiped her face.

"I fucked up."

"How?"

"I did something so wrong."

"What?"

Dylan blew her nose and continued to cry.

"Yo', tell me what the deal is, 'cause you trippin' right now," Angel demanded to know.

Dylan rubbed her face then looked off to the side. "I . . . I cheated on you."

Once she said the words, an earsplitting silence filled the room.

"What?" Angel's nostrils flared.

"I'm so sorry. I was just so fucked up in the head, and that night you told me you didn't want me to come to L.A., I thought you were cheating on me—"

He stopped her mid-sentence. "So, instead of coming to me like a woman, you fuck some other niggah? Who was it?"

There was so much to say, but so little time, despite Dylan's empty mouth. What she needed to say would destroy everything they'd built.

"Oh my God," she groaned, ready to vomit.

"Who was it, Dylan?"

"State," she finally confessed. "But I ended it weeks ago."

Angel laughed. Now everything made sense. Prior to Dylan's confession of everlasting love, she hadn't been hugging, kissing, or holding hands with him like she used to. Anything he said or did resulted in her having an attitude, and it was all because she was fucking State.

"Aw, man." He stood up, seething with anger. "This shit is wild."

"I never wanted to hurt you, Angel. I swear to God. You're my life."

Angel was at a loss for words. The niggah in him wanted to choke the shit out of her and call her every foul name under the sun, but the man in him understood that Dylan wasn't even worth it. Hearing that she'd fucked the man she'd cried on his shoulder about hurt like hell, but he couldn't let that get in the way of what was important, which was his fight. Once he beat the living daylights out of Sanchez, he'd deal with the pounding sensation of throbbing pain in his chest.

"It's all good, ma."

"No, it's not, because you're going to leave me." Dylan's chest heaved up and down.

"That is true," he shot back. "Look, I'm up. I'll send someone to get my things."

"Angel, please don't go. Just let me explain," she pleaded.

"Nah, man." He walked toward the door.

"But I love you."

"Is that right?"

"You know I do."

"I don't know shit!" he yelled, wanting to knock her in her mouth.

"Yes, you do. Everything I said to you was real, babe. You're my heart." She placed her hands on his chest.

"Man, I'm out," Angel said, unable to take anymore.

"No! Angel, please don't go!" She tugged on his arm.

"Dylan, chill out. Let me go."

"But if I do, you're gonna leave me for good." She held on to him as tight as she could.

"Huhhhhhhhhh," he groaned. Angel was trying his best not to feel a thing, but the more Dylan cried and begged, the more he wanted to break down. All he wanted was for her to let him go in peace.

"I can't breathe," he said as a single tear slipped out of the corner of his eye. Angel tried to pry Dylan's hand from around his neck, but her grip was too tight.

"Baby, please just stay." She kissed him hungrily on the neck.

"I can't. You gotta let me go, ma," he said.

"No, I can't," Dylan replied, knowing full well what he meant.

"But you have to," he cried.

"Why? We can make this work."

"I don't wanna make it work." Angel wiped his face.

"You don't mean that." Dylan held his face in the palms of her hands.

"Dylan, let me go, man."

"Nooooo," she whined.

Fed up, Angel pushed her off of him with so much force her entire body jerked back as she slid across the room. He didn't want to put his hands on her, but Dylan just wasn't getting the fact that he was done. He would never fuck with her again. He didn't even want to see her face. The sight made him sick. In a matter of seconds, she'd turned his love for her into hate. He couldn't give a fuck about the tears that spilled from her tranquil eyes. At this point, all Dylan could do was cry him a river, build a bridge, and get over it.

"Get the fuck off me! You fucked up, so deal wit' it!" He screwed up his face, heated.

"You don't mean that." Dylan shook her head. "You still love me like I love you."

"Yo', it's obvious you can't handle the truth, so don't fuck wit' it! I'm through fuckin' wit' you! Don't call me, don't text me, nothing! It's over!"

With that said, Angel left Dylan behind to wallow in her own misery.

For weeks, Dylan drove herself insane wishing she could touch Angel's face, but the truth remained that he was gone and there was nothing she could do to get him back. The only piece of him that she had left was what she saw of him on television. She'd ordered the fight and watched it a million times. But even seeing his face on TV didn't take away the fact that life was so cold without him. Everything was falling apart at the seams. She was behind on her rent; the phone was disconnected, and the gas and electric was next. Dylan would give her heart, soul, anything to have Angel back in her life again.

The hold he had on her was too strong to let go. Every second of the day, thoughts of him and how things used to be ran through her mind. On top of that, she couldn't stop wondering what he was doing or who he was with. All she knew was that she couldn't take another day waking up alone. She was sick of crying.

The champagne diet she was on didn't help much either. It only intensified the ache in her chest. Dylan was bitter and miserable. She needed her man back in the worst way. They should've been together, but now all she had was photographic proof that he ever existed in her life.

Over in her master bath, Consuela wiped sweat from her forehead as she scrubbed the toilet. All day long she'd been sweeping, mopping, and dusting while Dylan lay in bed, weeping and barking orders. All day long it had been "Consuela, get me more champagne! Consuela, turn up the heat! Consuela, turn down the heat! Consuela, come rub my feet!" Beyond fed up, Consuela slammed down the toilet scrubber and took off her gloves. She cared for Dylan, but she wasn't about to continue to work for her for free anymore.

"I not doing thees! I'm outta here!" Consuela announced, coming out of the bathroom. "Ju no pay me in weeks!"

"What?" Dylan peeked her face from under the cover.

"Ju heard me." Consuela wagged her finger. "I done!"

"No no no no no!" Dylan yelled, hopping out of bed. With the speed of lightning, she raced across the room, stood in the doorway, and blocked Consuela's path. "You can't leave me now. I need you. You're all I have left!"

"Ju can't pay me! Broke ass!" Consuela snapped like an around the way girl.

Dylan narrowed her eyes and said, "And since when did you become so money hungry? You once wrestled a pit bull for twenty-five cents!"

"*Cash rules everything around me. Cream get the money. Dolla dolla bills, y'all.*" Consuela sang Wu Tang Clan's "Cream" while waving a wad of dough.

"Where did you get that from?" Dylan's eyes grew wide. "I haven't given you a raise in years!" She tried to snatch the money from Consuela's hands, but she was too slow.

"I save." Consuela placed her hand behind her back. "Something ju know nothing about."

"Save? I don't even know what that means," Dylan said.

"I have to go." Consuela tried her best to get past.

"Nooooo." Dylan pushed her back. "Look, I can pay you." She ran across the room to her closet.

"Now we can talk." Consuela nodded her head.

"See." Dylan pulled out a tweed jacket. "This is vintage Chanel. This should cover a whole month's pay."

Consuela took the jacket from Dylan's hand and checked the label. "It's a size ten. I'm a size twenty." She threw it back at her.

"Okay . . . well . . . that will only motivate you to lose those few extra pounds you've been complaining about."

"Forget it." Consuela rolled her eyes. "I have to catch my bus."

"Consuela, please," Dylan whined with tears in her eyes. "I need you."

Consuela saw the sincerity in her eyes and sighed. In a weird way, Dylan did need her. Over the past couple of years, they'd become somewhat of a dysfunctional family. Consuela saw firsthand what a lonely life Dylan led. Yeah, she had Billie and Tee-Tee, but at night, all she had was herself. She didn't have a mother she could count on, and her father was dead. All Dylan had was a bunch of materialistic shit to keep her satisfied. It was sad, but it was her reality.

"Dylan," Consuela said genuinely, taking her hands, "ju don't need me. All ju need is jurself. Ju stronger than ju think ju are. If ju need to talk, call me." She smiled then turned and walked out the door.

"What I gotta say? What I gotta do?"
—Jazmine Sullivan, "Need U Bad" Remix

Chapter 21

Dylan's life had crumbled into pieces. She'd lost her best friend, her man, her maid, and her apartment. With Angel being gone, she no longer had someone to help her out on rent. The building manager had done all he could to help Dylan out, but after waiting two months on her promise to pay and getting no payment, he had to put her out. Dylan wanted desperately to keep her place, but she had no one she could borrow the money from.

Billie was absolutely out of the question, and Tee-Tee wouldn't give it to her if he had it, due to his theory on dishing out tough love. She thought about asking State, but quickly nixed the idea. Dealing with him was part of the reason why she was in the position she was in. This time Dylan was stuck, so with the little bit of money she had left, she packed up her things and put it all in storage—except her clothes, shoes, and accessories, of course. Dylan had lost enough. She wasn't about to lose the one thing she had left in her life that made her happy.

With her things in tow, Dylan sadly rang Tee-Tee's doorbell. Seconds later, he opened the door dressed in a pink bathrobe with hot curlers in his head.

"Oh, hell to the naw," he said, eyeing all of her suitcases.

"I love you." She poked out her bottom lip.

"I love you too, but not enough to let you in here."

"But why?" Dylan stomped her foot.

"'Cause you lazy. You don't like to clean up behind yo"self. Uh-uh, honey, no-no. You and that mutt ain't gettin' up in here fuckin' up my nice stuff, and plus, you ain't gon' be boo-ty-blockin' me."

"Please, Tee-Tee, we have no other place to go," Dylan pleaded, holding Fuck 'em Gurl in her arms.

"And whose fault is that, material girl? We all told you to stop spending so much goddamn money, but nooooo, Dylan wanna be the flyest chick in the club wit' no money in her pocket. You better take some of them shoeboxes you got and go build you a house. It's time for you to suffer. Toodaloo, bitch!" He slammed the door in her face dramatically.

Dylan was stunned. She didn't know what to do or where to go. *Am I going to have to stay in a public restroom tonight like Will Smith did in the* Pursuit of Happyness? she thought. Just as Dylan had come to the conclusion that she was homeless, Tee-Tee reopened the door.

"Get yo' ass in here, coon, but if I have to remind you one time to clean up behind yourself, yo' ass is out!"

Billie, Angel, and the kids looked on with other St. Louis natives as the Christmas tree in Keiner Plaza went up. It was a yearly tradition for the family, and even though this year the kids' father was M.I.A., Billie was dead set on making sure that not too much in their lives changed. Kenzie and Kaylee were already having a difficult enough time dealing with the fact that their father had run off and married a woman who had a lower I.Q. than they did.

Cain was so caught up in his new lifestyle that he didn't even bother inviting the kids to the wedding, which was filmed for

VH1. Billie herself didn't learn of the nuptials until she saw a news update on the E! channel. She simply chalked Cain's erratic, idiotic behavior up to a midlife crisis. He would be the one that had to answer to the kids for leaving them behind for a chick he'd known five minutes. And he would be the one to learn that his and Becky's relationship was destined to fail because it was built on a lie.

Angel stood beside his sister with his hands inside his pockets. He couldn't take his eyes off the mesmerizing lights. They were magical. The only thing missing was Dylan. They were supposed to experience the holidays together, but Thanksgiving had come and gone, and they hadn't spoken once. She'd called him repeatedly, but he couldn't stand to hear the sound of her voice. What hurt the most was when he looked over his shoulder the night of the fight. The space where she should've been sitting was empty.

After his victory, she was supposed to hold him close and kiss away any pain he felt, but life had other plans for them. She'd done the one thing any man would fail to forgive. Angel still couldn't wrap his head around how blatantly disrespectful she was to their relationship. He'd put it all on the line for her. He'd even gone as far as to cut his playa card up and throw it in the trash. No other chick would've been able to come in between them. All he saw was her, but she'd made her bed, and now she would have to lie in it.

"Niggah, is you cryin'?" Billie joked, interrupting his thoughts.

"What?" He snapped back into reality.

"I said are you cryin'?"

"Really, Billie?" He looked at her like she was retarded.

"I'm just sayin'. You eyes all watery and shit." She laughed.

"That's 'cause it's cold, niggah." He laughed too.

"Well, what's on yo' mind then?"

"None of yo' business, li'l nosey-ass girl."

"Oh, so you gon' try and play me. Angel, I know you like I know the back of my hand. You over there thinkin' about Dylan, aren't you?"

"If I am?" He looked at her out of the corner of his eye.

"You miss her, don't you?" Billie said sympathetically.

"Yeah, but me and shorty is a wrap. What she did was foul, man."

"I still can't believe that she would be dumb enough to fuck back wit' State after how bad he dogged her. Like, what the fuck was she thinkin'?"

"Evidently not too much," Angel joked.

"You got that right." Billie laughed. "I just hate that it all had to play out like this. Like, once I found out y'all was seeing each other, something told me it wasn't a good idea, but I kept it to myself. You two looked good together, and believe me, I wanted y'all to work, but on paper, y'all asses got an F."

"Damn, well, tell me how you really feel."

"I'm just sayin'." She giggled. "One of y'all were bound to hurt the other sooner or later."

"If she wouldn't have fucked ol' boy, I coulda seen us workin'," Angel confessed.

"If you say so." Billie shrugged.

A million and one thoughts ran through Dylan's mind while she lay curled up on the couch. She wondered how her life had become so fucked up, how she was going to get it back on track, and what Angel was doing at that very moment. Was he thinking about her? Did he miss her? Would he ever forgive her?

For more than a month, she'd waited for him to return her calls, but each day passed and the phone never rang. Dylan was resilient, though. She refused to give up or believe that he didn't long for her the way she longed for him. And yeah, she hadn't appreciated him when she had him, but Angel was the best thing that ever happened to her. He was better than Fashion Week in Paris, Versace in the '90s, and the perfect little black dress wrapped in one. Angel was the man other men strived to be. He was strong and thoughtful—just like his sister.

Dylan missed Billie terribly. She'd tried calling her, too, but like her brother, she wanted nothing to do with Dylan. The notion that their friendship was over tore Dylan up inside. Normally they spoke at least once a day. To go from that to not speaking at all was like outlawing red lipstick: preposterous. Dylan just wanted her life back, but really, what kind of life did she have?

There were no boundaries, consequences, morals, or truth in her world. Everything around her was a facade. The designer clothes and shoes masked how insecure she felt on the inside. It covered up not having a mother who cared, a deceased father she never really got to know, the loneliness of being an only child, and the fact that she felt she had no place in the world. Going from one man to the next wasn't because she liked the single life; it was because it was all she knew. Unknowingly, she'd become an updated version of her mother.

Morty was right. Dylan did live in a make-believe world, and now that she was forced to stop viewing the world through rose-colored glasses, she was afraid, very afraid. Dylan didn't know if she could survive the jungle we called civilization without falling into life's traps. She didn't have the strength to fail again, so day after day she lay curled up inside the house, hiding from the scary world that lay on the other side of Tee-Tee's door.

"Look, honey!" He entered the house and flicked on the light. "I rented us a video." Tee-Tee held up a bottle of champagne.

Once he saw Dylan and Fuck 'em Gurl lying in the same spot she was in when he left for work that morning, he flipped.

"Uh-uh!" He placed down the bottle of champagne, having had enough.

"Come on, Tee-Tee. Turn that light off." She shielded her eyes with a pillow.

"Bitch, it's almost nine o'clock! And why are you still moping around? You've been here almost a month."

"Leave me alone, Tee-Tee," she warned.

"And what you gon' do if I don't? Whoop me? I thinks not! Especially not when you living underneath my roof. Now, get ya bitch ass up!" He snatched the comforter from her. "Got my damn house smelling like pig feet and pork rinds! Have you even eaten anything?"

"No."

"That's a damn shame." He pursed his lips. "Bitch, you need to eat something. Anorexia is so 1998."

"I'm not hungry." She took the pillow from off her face and looked at Tee-Tee for the first time. If she had the energy to laugh, she probably would have, but she didn't. Tee-Tee had on the worst outfit she had ever seen. He wore a white cowl neck sweater, fur drawstring pants, and leopard print Christian Louboutin platform booties.

"Well, it's time for you to stop trippin' off shit you can't change and pull what's left of ya li'l sad life together!"

"How?"

"Shit, I don't know." He popped open the bottle. "Think

of something you're good at and make a career out of it—and
I don't mean shoppin'. That's my job."

"Maybe some of us aren't good at anything." Dylan continued to stew in her pity party.

"Save it, adulterer. Everybody's good at something. Look
at Superhead."

"I may have cheated on my man, but I'm not a whore, Tee-
Tee." Dylan rolled her eyes.

"Chile, please. Everybody got a li'l freak in 'em." He whined
his hips. "And stop taking everything I say so literally. I'm not
sayin' go perfect suckin' dick and write a book about it. I'm
sayin' think about what you do best, something you love, and
make that the thing you do for a living."

"All I'm qualified to be is a trophy wife, and you see how I
fucked that up," she sulked.

"It got to be something else."

"The only thing I'm naturally good at is baking."

"Okay." Tee-Tee snapped his fingers then pointed. "There
you go. Start a baking company."

"Nobody's gonna buy my stuff." Dylan dismissed the idea.

"Girl, please. You better stop short-changing yourself. Your
pastries are just as good as Paula Deen and the rest of them
Food Network bitches."

"You did not just call Paula Deen a bitch." Dylan chuckled.

"Heffa, please. You act like she Jesus. Now, c'mon and get
yo' stank ass up. You finna go put some warm water on that
pussy." He pointed her in the direction of the bathroom.

"Shut up. I don't stink that bad." Dylan got up.

"Shiiiiiiiit, you need to stick a hole up yo' ass and let it
come through yo' mouth. You smell like Jerrod musty balls."

"I know you ain't talkin' with them country-ass fur pants
you got on," she joked.

"Girl, I'm so goddamn hot I don't know what to do wit' myself. My nuts been on fire all day. It's like chestnuts roasting over an open flame." He fanned his crotch.

"I am officially done."

Since her divorce, Billie had decided to not only change her appearance and the way she ran her household, but herself. There were a list of things that she'd never done before, and with all the free time she had on her hands, now was the time to start doing it. Billie had no room for the fear of the loneliness in her life anymore. She would no longer allow it to knock on her door. Every day that went by, she kicked loneliness in the ass.

So far, she'd gone to the movies by herself, had dinner alone at a crowded restaurant, and taken a tropical getaway. Her next goal was to hit a nightclub by herself, and that Friday night she was going to do just that. Billie even decided to step out of her comfort zone and dress a little sexier. She was wearing the hell out of a hot pink strapless Michael Kors dress that stopped just above her knees. A Fallon multi-strand necklace with crystal, pearl, metallic chain, braided leather, and faux barbed wire and cross charm details highlighted her angelic face and toned shoulders. Billie also rocked a mean pair of aqua-colored python heels. She felt better than she had in over a year, but on her way to Red Kitchen and Bar, a new swanky hideout, she started to second guess herself.

"Maybe I shouldn't have worn so much makeup." She looked at herself in the rearview mirror. "I look like a Russian whore, and these damn Spanx are way too tight." She tugged on the top of them. "Shit, if I breathe in too deep, I'ma bust my spleen. I should just turn around and go home. Bravo is showing reruns of *The Rachel Zoe Project*."

But then Billie's inner voice kicked in. *You are not takin' yo' scary ass home. You are going to go into this club and have a good time.* Billie didn't want to admit it, but she wished that she could call Dylan for a much-needed pep talk. Dylan was always good at being a social butterfly. Billie, on the other hand, often kept to herself, and didn't bother to socialize with people she didn't know. She didn't like to dance, hated crowds, despised cigarette smoke, and most of the men who tried to hit on her she felt weren't educated enough to even approach her in the first place.

But Billie vowed that tonight would be different. She wouldn't prejudge, and she'd let loose.

After valet parking her car, she paid the ten-dollar entrance fee and walked inside the club. Soft gold lights lit the open space. The color palette was a mixture of brown, tan, gray, and red. Mahogany wood floors and tables filled the bar area.

Billie felt weird being around a room full of people she didn't know. Plus, some song called "Stanky Legg" was on. Hell, she didn't even know what the Stanky Legg was. Billie didn't know whether to drop it like it was hot, or bob her head to the beat. Unsure of what to do, she decided to head to the bar. Thankfully, the line wasn't too long, but once Billie realized who the bartender was, she couldn't decide whether to drink whatever she ordered or throw it in his face.

Recognizing her, too, he smiled and said, "You know, I've been hoping to run into you."

"You know what? I have too, so I could cuss your ass out. What, did Cain hire you to follow me or something? 'Cause every time I go somewhere, I swear you in my shadow," she shot.

"I don't even know who Cain is." He eyed her with a puzzled expression on his face.

"Yeah, right. You served me my divorce papers, remember?"

"I'm just a process server. I don't know what's inside those envelopes," he answered honestly.

"Mm-hmm, tell me anything." She rolled her eyes.

"What, like you're beautiful, or that the dress you're wearing got every man in the spot, including me, going insane?" He licked his bottom lip in a suggestive manner.

Billie placed her elbows on the bar and leaned closer. "Flattery will get you nowhere with me, understand? I don't like you."

"Yes, you do." He leaned forward and flashed a winning smile.

"How you figure that?"

"'Cause of every time you say something to me, your lips tremble, which means you're nervous, and why would you be nervous unless you liked me?"

"I swear I thought black men were cocky, but you white boys are just as over confident," she replied, trying not to notice the liquid lava building in her panties.

"That was rude."

"That was the truth."

"You seein' anybody?" he asked, cutting to the chase. "You got a man?"

"No."

"Why not?"

"'Cause I don't want one," Billie lied through her teeth.

"That's a bunch of bullshit. I don't believe that and neither do you. Ain't no woman out here that don't want a man," he shot.

"Well, I can't speak for other women; all I can do is speak for myself, and right now, I don't feel comfortable being anyone's girlfriend. Honestly, I don't feel comfortable being anyone's anything. Too much responsibility that comes along with it, and frankly, after eleven years of marriage, I'm tired of being someone's everything and gettin' nothing in return."

"Look, Billie." He placed his lips inches away from hers. "I'm diggin' you. I think you're fly, and if you'd stop tryin' to be so goddamn hard, you'd see that I got my heart on my sleeve. It's been there for days on end, waiting for you to open up yours too. But it's up to you, Miss Lady, to let me in."

Billie's entire body blushed. She couldn't front; homeboy was cute. No, scratch that. He was fine with a capital F. Everything from his boyish charm, Carey Grant haircut, ocean blue eyes, megawatt smile, and cocky persona reminded her of Robin Thicke. And yeah, he was a bartender by night and a process server by day, but that didn't define who he was. Billie was fully prepared to take a leap.

"How can I let you in when I don't even know your name?" She finally gave in.

"It's Knox."

"Well, Knox, I'll let you take me out, but know that I'm a newly divorced woman with three bad-ass kids, and I don't have no patience or tolerance for bullshit, so if you can't handle it, then let me know now."

"Are you done?" He spoke while admiring the curves of her waist.

"Yes." She placed her shoulders back and stood up straight.

"A'ight. Now that you're done spittin' a bunch of unnecessary shit, sit down so I can get you something to drink."

"I had to set you free, away from me, to see clearly the way that love can be when you are not with me."
—Maxwell, "Pretty Wings"

Chapter 22

"Ahhhh, I look like a fat pig," Billie complained while trying on clothes in the mirror. Her stomach, hips, and thighs all seemed to be ten times bigger all of a sudden. It was all mind-boggling, since she'd worked out five times that week. She hadn't even had any sweets, which was her favorite meal of the day.

Knox would be there to pick her up in fifteen minutes, and she was nowhere near ready. Her makeup wasn't even done. All she had was concealer under her eyes, which made her look like a linebacker. She was disgusted with her clothes and herself.

Nothing seemed to be going as she planned. She was supposed to be dressed and waiting to make her grand entrance. She'd come down the steps slowly and Knox would smile. He'd take her hand then softly kiss her cheek and tell her she looked beautiful, but because every outfit she tried on was too tight, too big, too casual, or too old lady-ish, none of her fantasy would come true. On top of that, Billie was nervous as hell. She hadn't been on a date since Iceberg shirts were in style. What was she supposed to talk about? Since she obviously made more money than he did, was she responsible for paying the bill? It was all too much for her to handle.

"Fuck it." She pulled the Jason Wu top over her head and threw it down. "I'm not going."

Just as Billie came to that conclusion, her doorbell rang.

"I'll get it!" Kyrese ran to the door. "Who is it?" he yelled before opening it.

"Knox. Is your mom home?" he said through the door.

"What's the magic word?"

"Can I come in?" Knox chuckled.

"Wrong!" Kyrese swung the door open. "It's open sesame."

"Um, is your mom here?" Knox looked down at him.

"Yeah, why?"

"'Cause I'm here to pick her up." Knox laughed.

"She's upstairs waxing her upper lip, or whateva old ladies do."

"You a funny li'l dude. What's your name, man?"

"Kyrese. Do you know my dad? He's Cain Townsend. You know, the greatest football player in the world." His eyes lit up.

"Nah, but that's wassup. Can I come in?"

"Yeah, yeah, sure, but wipe ya feet off before you do," Kyrese warned. "If my ol' bird see a hint of dirt on her floor, er'body in here gon' get a whoopin', ya dig?"

"I dig." Knox grinned, stepping inside. "Thanks for giving me the heads up."

"No problem."

Knox knew Billie had dough, but damn! Her foyer was bigger than his entire apartment. A Swarovski crystal chandelier hung from the ceiling. Two long spiral staircases cascaded down from the second floor, and the floor was made of heated marble.

"Ay! You like to play NBA Live?" Kyrese asked, interrupting his thoughts.

"Yeah. What, you got it?" Knox replied.

"Do I look like a stunna to you? I get all the new video

games before they come out. Shorties at my school call me Mr. Never Rock the Same Thing Twice. That's just how fly I am." He popped his collar.

"I feel you."

"Now, where you plan on taking my moms out to eat?" Kyrese posed in a B-boy stance as Knox took a seat. "McDonald's or Burger King? I suggest McDonald's, 'cause she love they Filet-O-Fish and fries."

"Nah, man." Knox laughed. "I'ma take her some place a little nicer than that. We going to this spot called Phi."

"A'ight, a'ight, I can swing with that. You on some ol' playa ish, but check it, home slice: if you even think about hurtin' my moms, me and my Transformers gon' be seein' you. You feel me?" Kyrese warned, giving his best impersonation of a tough guy.

"No worries. I got you," Knox assured.

"Now that that's squared up, let me get this broad for you. Ay yo', Ma!" He placed his hands up to his mouth and yelled, "Yo' boyfriend here!"

"Boy, hush. He is not my boyfriend," she said, coming down the steps. *At least not yet.*

"You look . . ." Knox stared her up and down.

Billie was dressed in a pair of plaid pajamas.

"Under dressed," he said, dressed handsomely in a black sweater with a white button-down and black tie underneath, black pants, and black-and-white shell toe Adidas. "Am I missing something?"

"Kyrese, go in the play room with your sisters, please," Billie said.

"Do I have to?" Kyrese groaned. "They tryin' to make me dress up like Michelle Obama again."

"Just go in there, please." She giggled.

"A'ight, but if they even think about puttin' some lipstick on me, it's on."

"Bye, boy."

Once Kyrese was out of the room, Billie focused her attention on Knox. "Look, I'm sorry for having you drive all the way over here, but I'm not going."

"Why?" He looked at her, disappointed. "It's obvious that you're not sick, and your son just gave me my warning speech, so we good to go."

"It's just too soon for me. I've only been divorced a couple of months, and here I am dating. Like, that's crazy."

"It's not like we're gettin' married, Billie. All I'm tryin' to do is show you a good time and make you smile."

"And I appreciate that, but I'm just not ready; plus, I have nothing to wear." She halfway told the truth.

"I can understand the not being ready part, but you not having anything to wear is a load of crap and you know it. Every time I see you, you be fly as hell, so how about this: instead of going out, why don't I cook us dinner?"

"Are you serious? You would do that?" She tried her best to remain cool and hide her excitement.

"I'd do anything to spend a little time wit' you, ma." He stepped closer and lightly kissed her lips.

"Well, all right." She smiled. "We can have dinner here."

"What are your girls' names?"

"Kenzie and Kaylee."

"You mind if I ask them to come help? Maybe we could all do it together," he suggested.

"I'd like that."

***

Some of the wealthiest women in St. Louis gathered at Ivey-Selkirk for Dylan's furniture, fine art, and fine jewelry auction. After her talk with Tee-Tee, Dylan realized that she needed to get off her butt and do something to change the state of her life. Plus, she needed to make a buck and quick. Creditors were on her ass. Without any job skills, the only way she could make money was to auction off her most prized possessions. It was the only way to get herself out of the pitch black financial hole she was in.

Dylan was proud of herself, though. It was her idea to do the auction. Tee-Tee's pep talk really helped her realize that things needed to change. Sure, she didn't have Billie or Angel in her life anymore, and she didn't have a pot to piss in, but with the faith of a mustard seed, she knew that all of that would change in due time—but she had to get off her ass and do something about it first.

Nothing besides losing Angel and Billie hurt more than to give up the things she'd acquired over the years. At times throughout the auction, she wanted to scream out "Stop!" but Dylan knew it had to be done. She'd burned a lot of bridges, but the fighter in her wasn't going to give up on the ones she loved, even though they'd given up on her.

"Where in the hell are you taking me?" Billie asked, surveying her surroundings. She and Knox were driving farther and farther into the hood, and she didn't like it one bit.

"You are so hard-headed. Didn't I tell you to sit back and relax?" He looked over at her, amused by her behavior.

"It really fucks me up that yo' white ass is so laid back about going to the hood, but I'm sittin' here afraid for my life."

"And it fucks me up that I fell in love with a racist." He laughed.

"You need to stop." Billie wrapped her arm around his neck. "You know I love yo' white ass." She lovingly kissed his cheek.

Billie was totally enthralled with Knox. He'd come into her life and turned her into a bumbling fool. Butterflies filled her stomach each time she heard his voice. To see his face was like eating cotton candy on a warm summer's day, and after months of dating, her knees still trembled whenever she kissed his lips. Knox was a perfect ten. The kids loved him, which only made Billie love him more.

And yes, they were different like day and night. Knox threw caution to the wind, while Billie was overly cautious. Where he was provocative, she was conservative. He liked hip-hop; she preferred R&B. Billie couldn't live without a morning cup of tea; Knox, on the other hand, couldn't tolerate the taste. Yet and still, what she saw in him was more than likes, dislikes, habits, or race.

When she made it hard to enter her heart, he never gave up his quest. Knox calmed her down when she was too uptight, and made her smile when she wanted nothing more than to be sad. Every day with him was like no other. He gave his love so freely and abundantly, and Billie wanted nothing more than to give every emotion he gave to her back to him.

"But seriously," Billie said. "All jokes aside. Where are you taking me?"

"Does it matter? We're here now." He parked the car.

Billie looked to her right at the building. It was a hole in the wall club called Cougars.

"Are you tryin' to be funny?" She turned back to Knox.

"Man, if you don't get yo' ass out this car and come on . . ." He opened his door and got out.

Billie sat still. For a second she thought about calling her driver to come get her, but then she looked up at Knox's face as he waited for her by the club's door. There was no way she could break his heart and leave. He'd been talking about bringing her there all week. Billie quickly said a silent prayer to God that he would keep her safe and that her Tory Burch bag wouldn't get stolen, then she got out as well.

Excited, Knox escorted Billie inside the small nightclub. The place was packed like sardines. Everybody in the spot knew who Knox was. They couldn't get through the crowd without someone giving him a hug or pound. Once they made it to the bar, Knox asked what she wanted to drink, but Billie refused to drink anything. She was absolutely petrified.

She hadn't seen so many thugs in her life. All the men were dressed in white tees and baggy jeans. Billie swore that in a matter of minutes a fight would break out or someone would start shooting. And the women were a whole 'nother conversation within itself. One lady had finger waves, a freeze, and a two-tone black and blonde crinkle ponytail in her head, with two golds in her mouth. Billie stuck out like a sore thumb in her Donna Karan collection cobalt blue twist blouse, stirrup leggings, and black Balenciaga pumps.

"Baby, why did you bring me here?" she asked, ready to go home.

"'Cause it's fun. I enjoy myself here more than I do any other place I've been. What you need to do is loosen up. For real, ma. Allow yourself to have some fun. Quit lookin' at what everybody got on and chill."

Billie wanted to, but she just didn't think she could.

"Come dance wit' me." Knox held out his hand.

"You've got to be kiddin' me, right?" Billie crossed her arms, staring at him.

"No, I'm not, and trust me, I'm doing you a favor by even askin'. 'Cause in a minute, you ain't gon' have no choice."

Billie loved when Knox got forceful. It turned her on.

"Huuuuuuuuh! Come on!" She stomped toward the dance floor.

Not into the notion of dancing in public, Billie stepped from side to side; that was, until the DJ began spinning M. C. Breed's "Ain't No Future in Yo' Frontin'." Billie was instantly reminded of her childhood, and she started grooving to the beat. Then MC Hammer's '90s classic, "Pumps and a Bump" started playing, and Billie really lost her mind. Any inhibitions she had went out the window. Billie started doing the Roger Rabbit, followed by The Cabbage Patch, and then The Snake. What really got her going was when Oaktown 357's "Juicy Gotcha Krazy" came through the speakers.

Knox stood back in amazement as she popped her torso hard to the beat. If he had known that all he had to do was bring her to Throwback Thursdays to get her to open up, he would have done it a long time ago.

Things slowed down a bit when Bone Thugs-n-Harmony's "Thuggish Ruggish Bone" came on. Billie waved her hand in the air and sang, "*We got Laaaaaaaaaaaayzie and Kraaaaaaayzie . . . Biiiiiiiiiiiiiiiiiiiiiiiiiiiiiiiiizzy . . . Wiiiiiiiiiiiii iiiiiiiiiiiiiiiish . . . and Flesh . . .*"

She'd totally transported back to the age of thirteen, when Dickies and Karl Kani pants were in. Dudes donned cornrows, and chicks rocked dookie braids. Nobody even thought about diamonds. What made you hot was if you had an add-a-bead or herringbone chain.

After working up a sweat on the dance floor, Billie and Knox ordered two drinks, with an order of chicken wings and cheese fries. Billie enjoyed the food so much she ordered seconds.

The karaoke portion of the night had begun to take place.

Billie cracked up laughing as one by one, people went up on stage and made absolute fools of themselves. After an older gentleman in a plaid Steve Harvey–like suit finished singing Rick James's "Superfreak" a stool, a mic, and an acoustic guitar were brought on stage. Billie had no idea what was about to happen next.

"I'll be right back," Knox said, getting up.

Confused, Billie followed him with her eyes across the room.

Oh, no, he isn't, she thought, wiping her mouth and hands.

Knox hadn't said a damn thing about participating, nor had he ever mentioned that he could sing. Afraid of what type of sound was about to come out of his mouth, Billie said a silent prayer to God that he wouldn't embarrass the hell out of both of them.

Knox took a seat on the stool and grabbed the acoustic guitar. "Wassup, everyone?" he said into the microphone.

"Heeeey!" The ladies in the crowd meowed. The women at Cougars loved when Knox performed.

"Tonight I wanna do things a li'l different and sing a song called 'Wonderful' by Timothy Bloom. Billie, this is for you."

Knox tapped his foot and began strumming the guitar, releasing beautiful sounds of joys into the air.

"Uh . . . Since we hooked up . . . things been going really fast and crazy enough. . . ." Knox bobbed his head and rocked to the beat. "*I can love you over and over and over and over again. I can loooooove you.*"

Never before in her thirty years on earth had Billie heard words filled with so many emotions behind them. Tears of complete and utter bliss fell from her eyes. Her heart never felt so full. The look on Knox's face and the euphonic sound of his voice said it all. What he and Billie shared was rare and special. Yeah, things were moving at lightning speed, but with the connection they shared, it only seemed right. Nothing between them was forced or fake.

Once the song was over, she was the first person on her feet, clapping and cheering. Hearing him sing to her was better than sweet potato pie on Christmas Day. Once he walked back over to their table, Billie lovingly took him into her arms and kissed him until both of them had to come up for air.

Dylan couldn't have been happier. After her auction and getting herself out of debt, she started selling her baked goods as Tee-Tee had suggested. She first started selling them to his coworkers at Neiman's, then at Mina's Joint. Soon after that, orders started pouring in left and right. Before she knew it, Dylan had private parties, birthday parties, weddings, baby showers and more to sell her stuff. She was so busy that she had to hire employees and rent a space.

People seemed to love her couture-inspired cakes, cookies, and pies, so she named her pastry shop Edible Couture. Dylan never knew that something she did as a hobby when bored or sad could translate into a career and a reliable source of income. She didn't have the money she used to, but that was okay. At the end of the day, she was doing something she loved and pulling her life together.

The next step on her road to redemption was to get her own place. She would forever be grateful to her cousin for blessing her with a place to stay, but after six months, it was time for her to leave the nest. She'd been looking for weeks and finally found a nice tri-level, two-bedroom townhouse in the historic Soulard area of St. Louis. The place was ten times smaller than her old place and far less expensive, but it was hers, and she absolutely adored it. Dylan didn't have any furniture but a bed, but with hard work, everything else she needed would come.

She'd only been in her new place two weeks, and it was her first time going to the laundromat to wash. Tee-Tee was there with her to teach her how.

"Bitch, have you been eating?" he asked, looking at her sideways.

"Yes, I've just been working out. Nicole Richie's my new *thin*spiration." Dylan posed.

"Well, you need to stop. It look like ya damn chest is on backwards." Tee-Tee tooted up his nose.

"Whateva, hater. Oh, did I tell you that I served food to the homeless at the parish next door to my house the other day?"

"Okay, Mother Teresa. You baking shit, got yo' own place, feeding the homeless, shoppin' at Old Navy, and clearly doing your own weave." He flicked her hair.

"So?" Dylan jerked her head back.

"So you're boring."

"I'm being responsible," she shot back.

"Same thing."

"Whateva. So, what is this place?" she asked, looking inside a washing machine. "It's pretty, but where are all the fish?"

"Help her, Jesus." Tee-Tee looked up at the ceiling. "Sweetie." He took Dylan by the hands. "That's not an aquarium. That's a washing machine."

"Oh, well, they need to put a sign up that says that, 'cause I bet a lot of people get confused."

"Did Candy drink when she was pregnant with you?" He eyed her, confused. "'Cause I swear there's something wrong."

"Knowing her, probably she did."

"So, you still haven't talked to her?" Tee-Tee questioned.

"No, and I'm not until she apologizes and pays me back my money," Dylan said adamantly.

"I can't be mad at you for that. Fifty thousand dollars is a lot of money. Every time I see her I'd be whoppin' her ass," Tee-Tee said jokingly.

"You stupid."

"Oh, guess who's gettin' married?"

"Who?" Her heart raced. She prayed he wouldn't say it was Angel.

"Billie, girl."

"What?" Her jaw dropped.

"Yep. Knox proposed to her last night."

"Wow, and she said yes. That's so unlike Billie," Dylan said, amazed.

"Billie is a hot girl. She still doesn't dress like we do, but she is showing a li'l skin now. Knox has really been good for her, and the kids love him. Every time I talk to her they doing something together, either by their self or with the kids."

"I'm happy for her. If anybody deserves to be happy, it's her. So. when is the wedding?" Dylan asked.

"In September. Can you believe it?"

"Really?" Dylan said, even more stunned.

"Girl, Billie love that white boy. You remember how he look, don't you? Shit, I would be at the court house next week pledging my allegiance to his sexy ass." Tee-Tee popped his lips.

"Well, the next time you see her, tell her I said congratulations." Dylan looked down at her feet.

"Why don't you try callin' her yo''self? Enough time has passed." Tee-Tee rubbed her back.

"Boy, you tryna get me cussed out again?" Dylan looked up at him. "Billie ain't fuckin' wit' me, and I don't blame her. I just wish . . ." She got misty-eyed.

"It's okay, cousin." Tee-Tee consoled her. "Wounds take time to heal, and eventually Billie will come around."

"I hope so."

"Everybody says we're through.
I hope you haven't said it too."
—Chris Brown, "Crawl"

Chapter 23

"Honey, you look fierce!" Tee-Tee snapped his fingers in a Z formation.

He and Billie had been searching for gowns for months, and they hadn't been able to find anything that matched her style until now. Billie walked out of the dressing room at Vera Wang's flagship store in New York. She was dressed in a sample size A-line gown with an asymmetric portrait neck and softly swirling skirt, but Billie wasn't satisfied.

"What's wrong?" Tee-Tee hugged her as she cried.

"This dress is the one, but I can't fit it," she sobbed. "I'ma have to have it altered, and the wedding is three weeks away."

Tee-Tee knew that what he was about to do was over the top, but desperate times called for desperate measures. In his heart he knew that it had to be done.

"Bitch, snap out of it." He slapped Billie in the face. "I know you're stressed, but, bitch, are you high? You know the rules. Now, say it with me."

Billie held her cheek and said, "You don't alter your dress to fit you. You alter yourself to fit Vera."

"That's better." Tee-Tee blew out a sigh of relief.

"I know the rules. I just . . . wish Dylan was here. But I have to keep reminding myself that I don't like her." Billie continued to sob.

"Girl, y'all need to stop. Both of y'all are miserable, missing the hell out of the other, but don't wanna make the first move."

"I love her, I do, but I just can't be friends with her after what she did." Billie wiped her eyes.

"Look, just go back in the dressing room and take off the gown, 'cause we gettin' it. Yo' big ass just gon' have to go on a diet and that's the end of it. Now, go!" He shooed her back inside the room and closed the door.

Tee-Tee was tired of seeing the two people he loved most, outside of Bernard, hurt for nothing. Billie and Dylan's feud was about to end, and Tee-Tee was going to make sure of it.

Moxy Bistro, a contemporary restaurant with affordable upscale cuisine was bombarded with their daily lunch crowd. Dylan sat alone, sipping on a glass of lemon water. She and Tee-Tee were scheduled to have lunch, but he was running late. Dylan was starving, and if Tee-Tee didn't arrive soon, she was going to order without him.

Billie took off her shades and followed the hostess to her table, where she was supposed to meet Tee-Tee. To her dismay, in his place was Dylan.

"Is this some kind of joke?" She gave Dylan a nasty look. "What are you doing here?"

"I should be askin' you the same thing," Dylan replied. "I'm supposed to be meeting Tee-Tee here for lunch, but he's running late."

"He's not coming," Billie spat. "It's obvious that he asked us both out for lunch and had no intentions of showing up. I guess this was his way of making us talk."

"Oh . . . well, you don't have to stay if you don't want to," Dylan replied, although she was hoping she would.

"I know I don't, but I'm here and I'm hungry, so . . ." Billie sat down.

She and Dylan placed their orders and waited in silence. Both of them had so much to say, but neither wanted to be the one to say it first.

"How are the kids?" Dylan spoke up hesitantly. "I bet they've gotten big."

"They're fine. I heard you opened up a pastry shop." Billie draped her napkin across her lap.

"Yeah, it's doing good. I just got asked to do a cake for the anniversary of Meesa's clothing line."

"Really?" Billie perked up then checked herself. "That's cool," she said in an even tone.

"Look, Billie," Dylan said, tired of beating around the bush. "It's apparent that you're still upset with me, and you have every right to be."

"You damn right I do. You cheated on my brother with the scum of the earth."

"And God knows I'm sorry for that. If I could go back and redo it all, I would, but I can't. I just wish that somehow you could find it in your heart to forgive me." Dylan pleaded with her eyes. "You're my best friend, Billie, and I miss you. I wanna be able to come to your wedding and watch you get married. I wanna see the kids. I wanna be able to talk to you and tell you what's going on in my life. I want my friend back."

"I don't know, Dylan." Billie shook her head, unsure if she could trust her.

"I wanted to tell you, too, that you were right." Dylan looked down.

"Right about what?"

"About me being like my mother."

"Dylan, I didn't mean that—"

"No, it's okay." Dylan stopped her. "It's true. I was like my mother. All my life I've treated the right people wrong and the wrong people right. I was so caught up in my own so-called happiness that I neglected everyone else's feelings. I let keeping up with the Joneses and a man ruin everything in my life. And for what? When the rent needed to be paid and I didn't have any money, my Zac Posen blouse or Prada bag didn't help with a damn thing.

"And like you said, State never gave a damn about me. I always knew it, though, deep down inside. I guess a part of me just wanted to believe that he did."

"I know how that feels." Billie played with her fork. "I was going through the same thing with Cain toward the end of our marriage. You just find yourself wanting desperately to hold on to the feeling of love, 'cause you know that once it's gone, all you're left with is a big-ass hole in your chest. You feel numb. Every part of you hurts. You can't eat and sleep." Billie chuckled. "Hell, you don't even know what that is anymore."

"Don't I know the feeling? Girl, when me and yo' brother broke up, I had the blues something terrible."

Uncertain of how to respond, Billie sat quietly.

"I know that Angel is a touchy subject, but I want you to know that I did love him a lot . . . shit, I still love him. There is not a day that goes by that I don't regret my decisions." Unwilling to cry, Dylan swallowed the tears that were creeping up her throat.

"Mm-mm-mmm" Billie wiped her eyes with her napkin. "What am I going to do with you? You make me so sick, but I love you just the same." She giggled.

"I love you too, girl, no homo." Dylan laughed too. "So, how has the wedding planning been going?"

"Well, I found my dress," Billie began to explain.

For the next three hours, she and Dylan ate and drank while catching up on each other's lives.

Billie's wedding day had arrived. She hadn't stopped smiling since she rose from bed that sunny September morning. There wasn't a trace of rain in the sky. Billie and Knox were to be married at one of her favorite places in the world, the Japanese garden at the Missouri Botanical Gardens. The ceremony site was breathtaking.

Billie and Knox would be married under a giant oak tree with hundreds of orchids hanging from the limbs. R&B crooner Chrisette Michele sang "Love is You," setting the mood for a romantic sunset wedding. Seventy-five guests sat patiently awaiting Billie's arrival.

Dressed and ready to go, she stood back with her father and watched as her girls walked across the bridge, lightly tossing white rose petals along the way.

Tee-Tee and Dylan went next. He wore a long strapless chiffon dress. Dylan rocked a mind-blowing oyster-colored Valentino ruffle halter gown. Their bouquets were made of amnesia roses, dahlias, antique pink roses, and cream-colored hydrangea.

At the altar, Dylan watched with tears in her eyes as Billie and her father made their way across the bridge. No one could deny how beautiful she looked that day. Every ounce of her glowed. Billie was a vision in ivory. A long cathedral veil hung from her hair. Being the non-traditional bride she was, she carried a single café au lait spray rose.

During the ceremony, Dylan tried to listen to the pastor, but she couldn't keep her eyes off of Angel. He stood on the groom's side in a black three-button tuxedo and satin bow tie. During the rehearsal and rehearsal dinner, he had played it so cool. Angel acted as if she didn't even exist, but she didn't care. His presence alone meant the world to her. Seeing his face again in person was the greatest gift in life she could receive, and she'd gladly swim the ocean's floor or crawl over broken glass to experience it all over again.

After they said their vows and committed their lives to one another before God, Knox took his wife into his arms and gave her a long, sensual kiss. Everyone clapped and cheered.

Billie couldn't say "I love you" or "thank you" enough. Knox would never know how much he meant to her. In a single day, he'd taken away years of pain from another man. From that day on, he would be her king, her Prince Charming, and her friend.

The reception was even grander. It was held at the legendary Boathouse in Forest Park. Purple hues of light lit the walls. Centerpieces of pink, white, and green flowers in square vases were accentuated with candles on each reception table. Fifty paper lanterns in assorted sizes hung above the dance floor in soft shades of green and purple. Billie and Knox sat alone at a sweetheart table, while the rest of the wedding party sat at a table together.

Dylan could hardly eat her food. Angel sat across from her, laughing and talking to Knox's brother as if she weren't even there. She wanted to ask him whether he enjoyed his steak, or how long he would be in town, but she didn't want to risk him playin' her in front of everybody, so she stayed quiet.

An hour later, dinner was over, and Billie and Knox had cut the cake. Everyone was on the dance floor, partying and having a good time. Dylan wanted to join in and pretend that everything was all good, but being around Angel and not being able to even say hello was proving to be too difficult. With a glass of Dom in her French-manicured hand, she sat alone at the table on the verge of tears. It if hadn't been for Billie, she would've left a long time ago, but this was Billie's day, and she wanted to see it through to the end.

As Dylan wiped away the tears that were begging to fall, the song "You Don't Know Me" began to play. The words to the song captured Dylan's heart, and for the first time in two days, she and Angel locked eyes. He stood across the room on the wall with his arms crossed over his chest. Dylan expected him to look the other way, but to her surprise, he didn't.

Angel was done with hiding his true feelings. He'd made a pact with himself that he wouldn't allow his heart to feel a thing for Dylan when he saw her, but the task was damn near impossible. She was gorgeous, and the same naïve innocence that drew him to her in the beginning drew him to her now. Through his sister, he'd learned of her many accomplishments and her new humble lifestyle.

Angel was proud of her, but that didn't take away the sorrow she'd caused him. What she did to him still stung tremendously, but he couldn't deny that underneath the surface of anguish—and yes, sometimes hate—was love. Ready to give in to how he felt, Angel unfolded his arms and made his way across the room to her.

"Would you care to dance?" He placed out his hand.

Dylan could hardly speak; her heart was beating so fast. "I would love to." She inhaled deeply and smiled.

Cheek to cheek, they danced slowly. It was irrefutable how well they fit together. Anybody with eyes could tell they belonged with one another—except Billie, who looked on from her husband's arms. Concern filled her heart for them, but it wasn't the time or the place to bring it up. Besides, her brother and best friend seemed so at peace. It was as if this moment were pre-destined in time to take place.

Then Anthony Hamilton took the stage and sang, "*Wish I could see through . . . see deep into you . . . and know what you're thinkin' now.*" It was everything Dylan felt and more. Was he thinking that he wished this moment would never end? Would this dance lead him to giving her another chance? But she wouldn't dare ask. Since the day he walked out of her life, she'd dreamed of this, the day she'd get to hold him in her arms and squeeze him tight.

Caught up in the moment, Angel sensuously kissed the side of her neck. The feel of his lips upon her skin made Dylan weak in the knees.

Before either of them knew it, the wedding was over and they were back at her place. Their clothes found a resting place on the floor. In her bedroom, their lips met. Dylan found herself lying naked before him. His eyes never left hers as his mouth placed warm kisses upon her skin. Screams of joy threatened to fill the air, but Dylan was so caught up in the rapture of his love that she couldn't find the sound.

After kissing her body from head to toe, Angel found the place he'd longed to explore. The pink lips of her pussy tasted like sugar against his hungry tongue as he ran his fingers along her quivering thighs. Each thrust of his tongue told a story of how much he pined for her, needed her, breathed her.

Overcome with emotion, Dylan closed her eyes tightly and relished the sensation of him licking, sucking, and biting her pussy. After a flood of creamy lava flowed from her valley, Angel found his way back up top. Dylan gripped his back tight while he placed wet kisses all over her neck.

Seconds later, the twelve inches of thickness that she'd long for entered right where it belonged. A fine line between pleasure and pain transcended through her body.

Gripping her wrists, Angel gazed into her eyes and whispered the words she'd yearned to hear: "I love you."

"I love you too," she whimpered, submersed in the enthralling taste of his skin.

Grinding his hips slow, Angel traced her jaw line with his lips. With each stroke, their desires turned to greed. Jolts of unexplainable currents rippled through Dylan's body. An explosive orgasm was edging near. Angel felt the exact same way. Neither one of them could speak. Breathing was even difficult as their bodies succumbed to the sexual pot of gold.

Then time slipped away. The moon had dissolved and the sun showed its face. Dylan hadn't slept a wink. She'd found complete and utter bliss in his embrace. She couldn't sleep if she tried anyway. She'd gone without Angel for so long that she didn't want to miss a minute of having him around. Lullabies of the night before sang softly in her ear, keeping her company while he slept.

Around eight, he awoke to find Dylan lying with her head on his chest.

"Good morning." She gazed up at him anxiously.

"Wassup?" Angel sat up, not even bothering to ask Dylan to move her head. "What time is it?" He rubbed his neck.

"Um, around eight," she said, caught off guard by his actions. "You hungry? 'Cause I can go fix us something to eat. I finally learned how to make eggs." she laughed.

"Oh, word?" Angel replied, unable to look in her eyes. "That's wassup, but nah, I'm good." He pulled the covers off and got up. "I'ma head on out."

Dylan closed her eyes and willed herself not to cry. Crying

wouldn't make him see that she'd changed, that she was more mature, that she could be all he needed and more.

"So, that's it?" She opened her eyes and found him almost dressed. "What about last night?"

"What about it? I mean, it still don't change nothin'," he said, wishing it would.

"So, what about you tellin' me you loved me? You tryin' to tell me that ain't mean shit either?"

"I do love you, and honestly, I don't think that I'll ever stop . . . but I just can't be wit' you." Angel looked her directly in the eyes. "And I'm not tryin' to hurt you. I thought last night that maybe I was ready to put the past in the past, but I can't . . . I just can't. 'Cause every time I look at you, I think of him."

Dylan hung her head low and swallowed. She'd hoped that maybe this could be their chance to get past the drama and crawl toward reconciliation, but the stars in the sky hadn't aligned for them yet. Angel knew how she felt for him. Dylan would love him till the day she died. It was sad and unfortunate that this would be their fate, but Dylan could see through to his heart. One day, Angel would be hers again.

"I understand," she said regrettably.

Unable to find the right words to say due to the awkward circumstances, Angel gave her a look that said his heart was breaking just as much as hers. Turning his back on her once again was hard, but it had to be done.

Epilogue

"Smile, baby." Ashton smirked, posing for the camera, decked from head to toe in designer duds courtesy of her husband.

Mustering up all the strength he had, State did as he was told and smiled, despite the fact that the blinding light from the flash bulbs burned his eyes. Over the last year, he and Ashton had perfected the image of the perfect couple. No one knew that behind closed doors they didn't even sleep in the same room.

Life for State had been hell on earth. He couldn't blow his nose without Ashton being all up in his ass. Whenever he went out, the constant thought of being followed tormented him. At all times, he had to be on his best behavior. There would be no more fucking around. Ashton's was the last piece of pussy he'd ever get to have. And yeah, he could divorce her, but as the old saying goes, it was cheaper to keep her.

After seeing how much Billie and Knox were in love, Tee-Tee and Bernard decided to put all the games aside and get married. They'd had a small wedding in Massachusetts that consisted of Billie, Knox, and Dylan. Tee-Tee couldn't ask for more. He had the thug of his dreams and was making plans to adopt his first child.

***

Married life for Billie had been nothing but bliss. Two months had gone by since her nuptials, and with each day, life got better and better. Knox continued to show her different ways of love that she'd never experienced before. All the walls she'd built had completely tumbled down. Everywhere she turned, she was surrounded by his embrace, and on a cold November afternoon, she, along with Knox and the kids, danced giddily around the living room to Michael Jackson's "Remember the Time" until they were out of breath.

Bobby "Blue" Bland's "Cry, Cry, Cry" played from the jukebox, filling the empty space of the dive bar Candy was in. She sat at the bar with her favorite drink in hand, puffing on a Black and Mild, wondering what her next move would be. She had only two hundred dollars in her pocket, and a suitcase filled with dreams. Often she'd thought about turning her life around, but running was the only thing she knew. It was how she survived.

And yeah, she needed to apologize to Dylan for all the wrong she'd caused, but Candy had never apologized to anyone in her life. She figured if she laid low and gave it time, things would mend themselves on their own. Till then, she had to figure out where she would lay her head next.

Inhaling the sweet smoke from the cigar, Candy swayed from side to side while surveying the bar. *Bingo,* she thought, landing her eyes on a distinguished gentleman sitting at the opposite end of the bar. Ready to pounce on her prey, Candy took one last swig of her drink, put out the cigar, and popped a piece of gum in her mouth. The guy never even saw her coming.

"Hi, I'm Candy." She smiled wickedly with her breasts in his face. "Let Mama buy you another round, sugar."

No matter how hard he tried, Angel couldn't get the visual of the night he and Dylan shared out of his head. It followed him wherever he went. The trace of her lips still lingered on his skin. Angel wasn't afraid of much in life, but the thought of loving Dylan without caution or care scared the shit out of him. There was no way he was going to allow himself to be hurt by her for a second time, but the fact still remained that he needed her as badly as he needed air to breathe. He loved everything about her, from her sexy lips to her pretty eyes. No other woman could satisfy him. They just didn't qualify.

Walking on Rodeo Drive, Angel pulled out his cell phone and started dialing Dylan's number. It was time for him to put aside his pride. Six digits in, he was interrupted by the sweet sound of a woman's voice.

"Angel," Miliania called out, shocked to see him.

Angel spun around. "Damn, wassup?" He greeted her with a hug, just as shocked.

"Nothing. Just doing a li'l shopping." She held up the bags.

"Word? Let me get that for you." Angel hung up his phone and placed it back inside his pocket.

"So, how have you been?" she asked.

"That's a long story."

"Well, I got plenty of time."

Most days of the year are unremarkable. They begin and they end, with no lasting memories made in between. Most days have no impact, but on that cold afternoon, Dylan Monroe's life changed forever. One thousand, five hundred ninety-three miles away from Angel, she took Fuck 'em Gurl for a walk around the neighborhood. She would've never thought a year before that she'd grow to love the dog so much. Her mother leaving her behind was the best thing she'd ever done for Dylan.

Dylan glanced around at the fallen leaves and dark sky. She marveled at how much in her life had changed since the year before. That time last year, she and Angel had just broken up, Billie had cussed her out, and she was evicted from her place.

Now she was back on her feet. She had a nice home, a thriving business, a loving friend, and a cousin she'd give her life for. Were her nights filled with emptiness and regret? Yes. Did it hurt like hell to know that she couldn't have the man she loved? Yes. But Dylan had faith that eventually her wounds would heal. Besides, it didn't matter whether or not she and Angel were together. She'd always have a piece of him in her life. Dylan placed her hand on her stomach and thanked God. In seven months, she would be a mommy.

Notes